MW00736687

A Matter of Courage

Joann Hakala

a matter of courage

The story of one man's determination
and one family's commitment.

Joann Hakala

Beaver's Pond Press, Inc.

ISBN 1-59298-044-9

Library of Congress Catalog Number: 2003114539

Cover Photos: Joann Hakala
Cover Design by Joann Hakala and Linda Walters
Typesetting by Linda Walters, Optima Graphics, Appleton, WI

Printed in the United States of America

First Printing: January 2004

06 05 04 03 02 6 5 4 3 2 1

Published by Beaver's Pond Press, Inc.
7104 Ohms Lane, Suite 216
Edina, MN 55439-2140
(952) 829-8818
www.beaverspondpress.com

Beaver's Pond Press, Inc.

A Matter of Courage is dedicated to my grandchildren,
Katelyn and Andrew, born on July 9, 2000.

They have given me the inspiration to write this book and
continue to be a special blessing to our family.

You have to accept whatever comes and the only important thing is that you meet it with courage and with the best you have to give.

Eleanor Roosevelt

Contents

Acknowledgements

Many thanks to my family and friends who offered encouragement as I took on this emotional project; my son, Gerry, who helped me remember some of the specific details; his wife, Laurie, for her proof-reading skills; my husband, Ed, for his total support in this endeavor; Jim, Mike, Joellyn and Roberta for their continued faith; my mom for her praises; my sisters and brothers for cheering me on; and my friend, Judy Farrell, who always believed in me.

To Dan Prusi - hunter, author, friend - I am most grateful for all the help and guidance he so willingly offered.

To Linda Walters, for her patience and understanding while creating the cover for my book; she was an inspiration.

To Cindy Rogers, for sharing her professional knowledge of the written word; it was a gainful experience.

Chapter One

January 1983 was, as always, a wild and crazy month in the Hakala household. If I had known that that winter would be the last "normal" season for many to come, I might have appreciated all the minor ups and downs we experienced.

I sat at the dinner table with my husband and three of our five children, all of us rushing through dinner, so we could get to the high school boys' basketball game on time. As I chewed my food, I thought about spring break. In the school district where I worked as a librarian, our break was scheduled for the first week of March. But it was already January, and if we were going on vacation we had to begin making some plans soon. A trip to Florida might be fun. It had been several years since our whole family went on vacation together, and I was feeling a bit sentimental thinking about the "empty nest" people talk about. I knew that our three youngest, Joellyn, Gerry, and Roberta, would enjoy the trip, but I wasn't sure I could talk Jim and Mike into coming along. They hadn't traveled with us since high school. Jim had his own apartment, and I was pretty sure he'd look at me and chuckle if I suggested a family vacation together. Mike still lived at home, but I also had my doubts that he'd be interested in coming. I was so deep in thought that I hadn't heard Ed say my name, until he said it again. When I looked across the table he was smiling at me. "Where have you you been?" he asked.

"I'm sorry. What did you say?"

"Nothing important. Just wondering if you're still planning on going to the basketball game tonight."

"Of course. What time do we have to leave?"

"Soon. Does anyone need a ride?"

"I do," said Bertie.

Gerry shook his head, "Not me, I'm going with some friends."

"I'm going with friends, too," mumbled Joellyn still chewing her food as we were clearing our plates from the table.

Despite the rush, I decided it was a good time to ask the big question. "How about a family vacation in Florida during spring break?" There was a clanging of dishes and, suddenly, on the floor next to my feet lay a broken dish.

"Are you serious, Mom?" Joellyn yelled.

"I'm sorry about dropping the dish," said Bertie, as she bent over to pick it up. "Are we really going to Florida?"

"I've been thinking about it. What do you think, Dad?"

Ed just glanced at me and smiled. "It sounds as if you've already made up your mind."

With a big grin Gerry asked, "When do we leave, Mom?"

"Well, let me see," I pondered, "Our spring break is scheduled for the first week of March." Joellyn and Gerry were students at Northern Michigan University and had the same spring break. Bertie was a freshman in high school. "We'll have to get permission to take Bertie out of school that week, and if her grades aren't up to par we'll have to leave her home with a babysitter," I joked.

With a smirk on her face Bertie declared, "You guys wouldn't have any fun without me, Mom." She was right, too.

Ed broke into the discussion, "What about me? I'm not sure when my spring break is, or if I even get one." We all laughed because Ed was a workaholic. He operated a small well-drilling business along with Jim and Mike.

"Check with the boss," I said smiling, and then we scurried off to the game.

After we got home that night, I lay in bed thinking about our vacation and hoping that Jim or Mike might want to come along. Even though March wasn't a busy month, one of the boys should probably stay home to take care of the business. That problem was solved the next day when Jim stopped by for coffee. When I asked him if he would like to go on vacation with us to Florida, he said someone should be available in case of an emergency. Since he was the elder son, he offered to stay home. I could tell by his face that he really wasn't interested in coming with us.

"What about Mike?" he said, "I bet he'd like to go."

"I'm planning to ask Mike, but I doubt he'll be interested."

When Mike stopped by later that afternoon, I put the question to him. He said he would think about it, but I knew he was just trying to make me feel good. "I need to make reservations, Mike, so let me know soon if you plan to come. I know you'll have a good time," I said smiling.

I was surprised later that day when Mike came by and told me he definitely wanted to go on vacation with us.

I put my arms around him and gave him a big hug. "Thanks, Mike. I know you'll have a good time, and Gerry will be happy that his big brother is coming along."

I was flying high! I couldn't wait to tell Ed and the kids. I didn't know why, but for some reason that trip was very important to me. It was approximately four months before I learned why.

There's a good reason why God doesn't let us know what our future holds, and for that I am very thankful. However, I do believe He gives us an inner sense to do something with our loved ones that we wouldn't otherwise have done. If I had known beforehand what was ahead for our family I am certain I wouldn't have had the energy, or the enthusiasm to plan a family vacation . . . which is exactly what I did.

At the beginning of March we left Marquette for Sarasota, Florida, where we had reservations at a beautiful motel on Lido Beach. We couldn't have asked for a more splendid spot to spend a week with our children. What a week it was. The weather was perfect and the kids had a great time swimming, sunbathing, eating, shopping and hanging out together. Gerry and Mike even got to spend time together without the girls, which I'm sure they enjoyed. Gerry referred to it as "man things" so I had a pretty good idea what he meant. We knew it as "girl-watching." We will all remember and cherish that trip for many reasons, but most of all because our world fell apart a few months later. Nothing, and I mean nothing, could have prepared me for what happened on May 22nd, early Sunday morning.

It was a usual busy weekend with everyone pitching in, doing chores and making plans. Being a working mom meant Saturday was my day to get the house organized, do the wash, and make sure everyone else was taking care of their obligations. Ed also worked on Saturdays. We were all accustomed to this hectic lifestyle as were many families in our area, and we enjoyed it.

Gerry came by that Saturday afternoon to say he was going on an overnight venture. "Hey, Mom, I'm going out to Hank's family camp with some of the guys, and his parents said we could spend the night. What do you think?"

"That sounds like fun, Ger."

"I can't wait to see everyone. We've got a lot to catch up on."

Most of these boys had been on the high school football team together and were very respected in our community. Some of them had just finished their first year of college and were getting together for a reunion to talk about their experiences. I wasn't at all concerned about Gerry going.

"Have fun!" I yelled, as he hurried out the door to a blowing horn in the driveway. I didn't give it another thought.

That night, around 3:00 A.M. we were awakened by a ringing phone. At first I thought I was dreaming, and then I heard it again. I reached over and nudged Ed because he was close to the hallway phone. Suddenly I heard Mike's voice. His bedroom was just across the hall and he had already answered it. I was hoping it was a wrong number, but within minutes Mike opened our bedroom door and told us that Gerry had been hurt.

Ed jumped out of bed and grabbed the phone from Mike's hands. I heard him ask, "What's wrong with Gerry?" I quickly sat up in bed, my body shaking so much that I had to hold my knees with my hands. Silence, and then, "We'll be right there."

My husband looked at me and with his voice quivering said, "That was Hank. Gerry was hurt while wrestling with one of the guys at camp and they've called for an ambulance. We have to meet them at the hospital."

Ed was very concerned about what he had just heard on the phone. He usually kept his emotions hidden, but this time his face said it all. As I tried to get out of bed, my legs caved and I landed with both knees on the floor. I had to get myself dressed quickly, so I grabbed the same clothes I had worn the night before and threw them on my shivering frame. My head ached and my stomach churned as if I had swallowed a live fish. I slipped on my shoes and hurried downstairs. Ed was already in the car waiting for me. Mike wanted to come with us but we asked him to stay home with Joellyn and Bertie who were sound asleep.

It was dark and very quiet outside as we raced to the hospital, only a few miles from where we lived. Being on the highway at that early morning hour was spooky; most people were home in bed. We passed only two cars on the way.

I thought about Gerry as we drove. He was our fourth child, third son, born on November 27th, which happened to be Thanksgiving Day that year. I was especially thankful because it was ten days before my due date. The birth was normal and we were both released from the hospital within a few days. However, on the day we were to go home, the nurse brought Gerry to my room and asked the doctor to take a look at some blisters on his tummy. The doctor didn't seem overly concerned with what he saw, but he did give us some medication to put on the blisters at home. At that time, he hadn't told us how serious the rash was, and Gerry ended up back in the hospital with a staph infection. We later learned that he contracted the infection while in the hospital and, if untreated, it could have caused his death. We were relieved that they got the problem under control in a matter of days and we were able to take Gerry home.

Ed hadn't said much of anything as we headed to the hospital, but that was his way of handling his emotions. Even though I was afraid to hear the truth, I finally got the courage to ask if he knew how badly Gerry was hurt.

He had a difficult time getting the words out of his mouth. "He can't move his legs," he whispered.

I sat frozen in my seat, wrapping my arms around my body to keep from shaking. I didn't speak another word until we got to the hospital.

We pulled into the parking lot and the car stopped moving. Ed took the keys out of the ignition and opened the door to get out. I tried to get out, but my legs wouldn't move. What was happening to me? Ed shut his door and came around to my side of the car. He opened the door and put his hand out to help me. I reached for his hand twice before I got hold of it, and then he put both arms around me to make sure I was able to stand up. I wondered if I could even walk to the door. I don't remember actually going into the hospital, but suddenly we were inside walking down a hallway.

Hank was already there along with some of the other guys who had been at the camp. He moved toward me looking pretty scared. I grabbed his arm. "Hank, what happened to Gerry?"

With his voice shaking, he said, "It was an accident, Mrs. Hakala. Gerry and Rob were just playing around."

"What do you mean by playing around?" I continued.

"I'm not sure," answered Hank. "I think they were wrestling. Rob said it was an accident, that he didn't mean to hurt him."

"Well, Gerry may be seriously hurt," I said fighting back tears, "and all because of horseplay."

"I'm sorry," he murmured.

"So am I, Hank." I walked away holding Ed's arm to try and stop myself from shaking.

Down the hallway, some men were pushing a stretcher toward the emergency room. I hurried over and found Gerry lying on the bed trying to swing his fist. He was using language I had never heard him use before. I put my hand on his and tried to calm and comfort him, but he pushed it away. I desperately needed to be close to him at that moment, but he wasn't allowing me to do so. My feet felt frozen to the floor and I just stood there staring at him.

He became very feisty; it was evident that he realized something was terribly wrong. Seeing Gerry in that state made me even more frightened, but I didn't want him to see how scared I was. More than anything he needed Ed and me by his side and we had to try to be strong for him. They wheeled him into the emergency room. I tried to follow them in, but was told to wait outside.

I can't remember how long Gerry was in the emergency room, but it seemed like forever. Ed and I sat in a small room holding on to each other, and waiting for someone to tell us how badly he was hurt. Finally, the doctor came out and said they were transferring him to a larger hospital about fifteen miles away. They said I could ride with Gerry in the ambulance and Ed could follow us in the car.

It was the longest ride of my life. I tried to talk to Gerry telling him not to worry and that we would take care of him. He wasn't interested in anything I had to say. Something was seriously wrong because he complained of neck pain all the way to the hospital. I wanted to take him in my arms and assure him that everything was going to be all right, but I knew it wasn't a promise I could make.

When we arrived at the hospital, a neurologist met us at the emergency entrance. He studied Gerry on the stretcher and then touched his legs asking, "Do you feel anything?"

Gerry, with a quiver in his voice, answered, "No, but I will!" The look on his face said it all. He was scared to death, and like many young people who have had similar accidents, probably wondered if this was just a temporary condition, or would he ever be able to feel his legs again. He was quickly moved him into the emergency room where he was examined more thoroughly by the neurologist.

We hardly said a word to each other as Ed and I sat waiting for the doctor to come out and tell us about Gerry's injury. I was afraid to say what I was thinking, and Ed just kept shaking his head. He was as nervous as I was, wondering what the doctor was going to tell us. After what seemed like several hours, the doctor came by. He told us that Gerry had a broken neck and there was damage to his spinal cord. We sat there staring at the doctor waiting for him to tell us that Gerry would recover from his injury, but he didn't. Instead, he said he wanted to talk to us privately. At that moment, I wanted to run out the hospital and never return, but we stood and followed the doctor into another room. I felt sick to my stomach.

After we sat down, he sternly stated, "There's a ninety percent chance that your son will never walk again." Ed and I looked at the doctor without saying a word. I thought I must have heard wrong. A doctor was standing in front of us saying that our son would never walk again and neither one of us could respond. Finally, he said very emphatically, "Do you understand what I'm saying to you?"

We both nodded our heads. He went on to tell us that most spinal cord injuries end up this way. I felt numb from my head to my feet. I wanted to pinch myself to see if I was truly awake. I couldn't wait to get out of there and far away from this man. Surely, he didn't realize what he was saying.

As soon as the doctor left, Ed and I entered the emergency room to see Gerry. Some kind of a metal contraption was attached to Gerry's head and he was pale as a ghost. If I could have changed places with him at that moment, I would have. My insides were hurting so much that I wanted to scream, but I had to remain calm for his sake.

My watch showed that it was 6:00 A.M. We had been away from home for almost three hours. One of the nurses reported to us that Gerry was going to be moved to a room on the surgical floor. As we walked out of the ER, I thought about going home to tell the rest of the family about the accident. I didn't know how I was going to tell his brothers and sisters that Gerry might never walk again. My first thoughts were not to say anything about him being paralyzed, but I soon realized that wasn't such a good idea. When they got to the hospital they would find out immediately that he couldn't move his legs. I had to figure out how to break it to them gently.

As we got on the elevator to go up to the surgical floor, I asked Ed, "Is this actually happening, or am I dreaming?"

He nodded his head and put his arm around me whispering, "We have to be strong for Gerry and the other children. I know it's going to be difficult, but we need to help each other by being positive in front of Gerry and the rest of the family. Otherwise, we're not going to make it." Ed always had a way of keeping things in perspective. As we got off the elevator he took my hand and said, "We're going to make it through this." I thanked God that he was by my side.

Gerry was sitting up in bed looking very uncomfortable. That contraption he was wearing was called a "halo" and was screwed into both sides of his head. I stared at him, unable to speak. Ed walked over and asked Gerry how he was doing. He mumbled, "I don't know." I reached for his hand, but there were splints on both and he was unable to move them. My eyes were welling up with tears, so I took some deep swallows. Both arms were hanging numb at my sides. I didn't want him to see how frightened I was so I quickly asked a question.

"Did the doctor explain to you why they put the halo on your head?"

"It's to keep my neck from any further damage. I have to wear it for three months, or until my neck is stable."

My throat grew thicker and thicker and I could hardly breathe. How on earth was he going to lie down with these pieces of metal screwed into his head? "Oh," I stammered. "Is it uncomfortable?"

"Yes," he said. "I'll probably have to sleep sitting up."

Ed tried to make conversation with Gerry, but I could tell by the tone of his voice that he was just as fearful as I. Suddenly, we were both at a loss for words. In fact, all three of us were speechless. I wanted to punch someone - or something - but I couldn't. I wanted to take that halo off his head and those splints off his hands, but I couldn't. I just stood there staring at him.

One of the nurses came into the room to tell us that we would have to leave for awhile because they wanted to take care of some things for Gerry. We decided to go home and tell the rest of the family about the accident. We both gave Gerry a hug and told him we'd be back shortly. We walked out of the room and down the hall to the elevator without speaking to each other. I couldn't wait to get out of there.

By now the parking lot was quite full, and people were walking from their cars to their jobs within the hospital. I couldn't imagine what it must be like to go to work every day and see hundreds of sick and injured people. Some said, "Good morning." I managed to respond, but said to myself, "If they only knew why we were here so early this morning." As our car got closer and closer to home, I tried to think of what we were going to say to Gerry's brothers and sisters. There was no easy way to put it. We had to tell them the truth. They were going to be devastated.

It was 6:30 A.M. when we got home. Ed and I went upstairs to Mike's bedroom. As soon as he heard our footsteps, he got up and opened his door. We told him about his brother as gently as we could, and the prognosis given by the doctor who examined Gerry. He gave us a blank look at first, and said nothing. Then he went back into his room, slamming the door behind him and yelling, "Doctors don't know everything!"

Both the girls were asleep when we opened their bedroom door. I put my hand on Joellyn's head and she opened her eyes. I was a bit surprised when she asked, "Is Gerry all right?" I wasn't aware that after we left for the hospital, Mike had gone to their bedroom and told them that Gerry had been hurt while wrestling at Hank's camp, but that was as much as he knew.

Bertie, looking a little frightened, whispered, "How's Gerry doing, Mom?"

I tried to explain that Gerry had had an accident out at camp and, after being examined at one hospital, was transferred to another hospital fifteen miles away.

"What's wrong with him?" asked Joellyn.

We tried to explain to both girls that Gerry had a broken neck and couldn't move his legs . . . yet. I didn't want them to think he would never be able to walk again.

As we told them about the accident, Joellyn cried and pulled the covers up over her head. "No!" she yelled, "Gerry's going to move his legs."

Bertie turned over in bed and punched her pillow, sobbing uncontrollably. "How could this happen?" she cried.

"Hank said Gerry was wrestling with one of the guys when he got hurt. He said it was an accident."

"How could he break his neck if they were just wrestling?" cried Bertie.

"I don't understand it either," I said softly. We cried and held on to each other for several minutes without saying another word. Finally, I left them alone to talk and I headed downstairs.

There was one more person we had to tell and that was our son, Jim, who lived a few blocks away. Ed realized that I was not up to making the call. He went to the phone and in less than ten minutes, Jim came walking in our kitchen door. He had a frantic look on his face and said he wanted to go to the hospital right away. We explained briefly what had happened to Gerry. Jim was very upset.

I got up from my chair and walked aimlessly around the house. I knew I had to take a shower and get back to the hospital for a meeting with Gerry's rehab doctor, but I couldn't seem to get myself moving. I also had to tell my mom, and I didn't want to give her the news over the phone. I decided to drive to my sister Sue's house first and then we'd go together to tell Mom. I headed for the stairs and a quick shower.

When I came back, Jim was talking with Ed about Gerry. "How the hell could this happen?" Jim wasn't one to mince his words.

"We don't know for sure, Jim," I answered, "But Gerry's friend, Hank, said it was an accident."

"When can I go to the hospital?" asked Jim. "I want to see for myself how Gerry's doing."

"We can go together," I said. "I'm sure Gerry wants to see both you and Mike, but first I have to go and tell Grandma."

I drove to Sue's house and then she and I went to tell Mom about Gerry. Ironically, this wasn't her first grandson to have suffered a spinal cord injury. My sister Fern's son, Steve, had a car accident about two years earlier while driving home one night. He was alone at the time and hit a tree. A farmer found him about 4:00 the next morning; he had a broken back and ended up a paraplegic. My mom had a very difficult time dealing with Steve's accident and I worried how she'd handle another one.

As soon as we walked into her apartment, Mom seemed to sense that something was wrong. She studied us, then said, "What are you two doing here so early?"

I told her about Gerry and she began to cry. Sue and I tried to comfort her by saying that it could turn out differently for Gerry. I thought if we sounded optimistic, it wouldn't be quite so hard for her to handle this time. I gave her a big hug and told her that I would be in touch. Sue stayed with her to make sure she was all right. I'll never forget the sad look on her face as I walked out the door that day.

When I got home, Joellyn suggested that Ed and I go to the hospital with Jim and Mike, saying she and Bertie would follow as soon as they were ready. Ed agreed and said he thought it might be easier on Gerry if everyone didn't arrive at the same time; it could be too overwhelming for him. We left for the hospital with the boys. We didn't say much to each other on the drive, but we didn't have to. I had a feeling we were all contemplating the same question, "Would Gerry ever walk again?"

At the hospital, our anxiety was high. Jim and Mike kept looking at each other and shaking their heads. I had to do some deep breathing as we got on the elevator. What would Gerry's rehab doctor tell us? I had already made up my mind that I wasn't going to believe anything he said. All doctors make mistakes, and I was sure the emergency room doctor made a big one when he told us that Gerry would probably never walk again.

We met in a small conference room with the rehab doctor. He introduced himself and immediately began discussing Gerry's therapy. He wasn't as straight forward about the prognosis as the emergency room doctor had been. However, he did leave us with the impression that Gerry might never walk again. I wouldn't allow myself to believe him. If I were going to get through this ordeal, I had to hold on to my faith that some day Gerry would walk out of that hospital. That hope was my only salvation; it was all I had to hold on to.

As our meeting continued with the doctor, I noticed a familiar person walk by the conference room. It was the friend that Hank told us had wrestled with Gerry at his camp. He kept looking in the room where we were meeting and appeared somewhat confused. I excused myself and went out in the hallway to see him. The young man seemed somewhat puzzled.

"Hi, Mrs. Hakala," he said. "How's Gerry doing?"

I was rather surprised by his question. "Don't you know? I asked. I thought you were the one wrestling with Gerry."

"I was," he answered, "but, I haven't talked with anyone since it happened."

"Gerry's spinal cord is injured and he's paralyzed," I said. "The doctors tell us he may never walk again."

Rob began to cry. "I'm sorry, Mrs. Hakala. We were just fooling around. I didn't mean to hurt him."

"That's what Hank told us when we arrived at the hospital early this morning."

Rob stared at the floor. "Is it okay if I go in and see him?"

"I'm sorry," I said, "but they aren't allowing anyone in to see Gerry except his immediate family. Maybe you should come back later in the week." Rob turned and walked down the hallway. The sadness of his face said that we weren't the only ones headed for some rough days. The meeting was almost over when I went back to the conference room. Ed and I talked with the doctor for a few more minutes and then we left for Gerry's room.

Gerry (right) in his boxing days.

Gerry had been moved to the surgical floor and into an electric bed. He was on his stomach part of the time, and then the bed rotated so he could be on his back. The nurse told us he had just spent an hour on his stomach and an hour on his back. She said it was amazing for someone to be able to do that so soon after an accident. I told her she would see more amazing things from Gerry because he had "*sisu*," a Finnish word meaning "inner strength."

She smiled as if to say, "He's going to need it."

Jim and Mike had a tough time when they first saw their brother with the halo screwed into his head. They tried to make conversation, but it was difficult. They both liked Gerry a lot and always enjoyed joking around with him. Even though Gerry was the youngest of the boys, he usually held his own. He was involved in the boxing club and had won a championship in his weight class, so his brothers didn't attempt to take advantage of him too often. It was hard for me to watch someone throwing punches at my son, so I didn't go to his boxing matches. One Saturday morning after a Friday night boxing match, his face was all puffy and bruised. I screamed, "Oh my gosh, Gerry! What happened to you?"

With a big grin, he declared, "You should see the other guy, Mom." Then he laughed and told me not to worry. I loved his sense of humor.

"Easy for you to say," I countered. "Remember, I'm your mom." After much persuasion he did convince me to go to his last boxing match, but it wasn't an easy thing to watch. There were many times when I put my hands over my face because I didn't want to see him get hurt. When he did win a match I was very proud of him, but I still hated the sport.

Joellyn and Bertie arrived at the hospital about an hour after we got there. They were both on the verge of tears. Joellyn, with her voice quivering, asked Gerry how he was feeling. He gave a one-word response, "Okay."

"Does that thing in your head hurt?" she asked.

"It doesn't feel too good."

"Why is it there?" asked Bertie.

"To keep my neck stable." Gerry was merely answering their questions, not adding anything extra to the discussion. He was uncomfortable with all of us staring at him, so I took a walk to the bathroom. My eyes were filling up with tears, and I didn't want the girls to do the same. Gerry needed his brothers and sisters around him more than anyone else at that moment. They were all very special to him.

The day continued with family members in and out, all of us trying to keep Gerry in good spirits. When visiting hours were over, the kids gave Gerry a hug and left for home. Ed stayed a while longer, and then said good night to both of us. I was able to stay the night in the other bed because Gerry didn't have a roommate. I wanted desperately to be with him in case he woke up and needed something. I was hoping they wouldn't need the bed for another patient.

I stayed awake until Gerry fell asleep, and then I lay in bed thinking about everything that had happened since the phone rang at 3:00 that morning. I dozed a little, but I kept waking up wondering if I had dreamt the whole thing. All I had to do was glance at the other bed and I knew it wasn't a dream. Gerry was lying there unable to move. I was scared to death. He must be, too. I began to pray.

Chapter Two

There was something unfamiliar about my surroundings when I first sensed the light coming through the window. Those aren't my bedroom curtains and my walls have striped wallpaper on them, not yellow paint. I lifted my head off the pillow and looked across the room. Ed was talking to someone in the bed next to mine and, as I was trying to wake up, I noticed something strange. The person he was talking with had several pieces of metal sticking out of his head. Suddenly, it all came back to me! I remembered the horror of our son's accident, and the doctors telling us that Gerry might never walk again.

Ed glanced my way. "How was your night?"

"Not too bad. What time is it?"

"It's six thirty," he said. "I just got here." As I was getting out of bed, one of the nurses walked in and asked us to leave for a few minutes so she could take care of Gerry. I quickly freshened up and Ed and I went to the cafeteria for a cup of coffee. It gave us a chance to sit down and talk. The accident still seemed like a bad dream; I wanted to wake up and find everything the same as it had been two days ago. Ed was good at keeping me calm, and it really helped to have a few moments alone together. We talked mostly about Gerry, but we also talked about our family, and how we could help each other cope during this very difficult time. The road ahead was going to be a long and tough one. Ed went back to be with Gerry, and I headed for home to shower and change clothes.

Everything was quiet at the house. The girls were still sleeping and I didn't wake them. I knew they probably stayed up late talking about Gerry, and I wanted to get back to the hospital. It was hard for me to be at home for any length of time; I had to keep moving in order to protect my sanity. I wanted to spend every minute possible with Gerry, because I wanted to be there when the feeling came back in his legs. I was confident that was going to happen, and I didn't want to miss out on anything. I arrived back at the hospital by 8:30, but didn't see much of Gerry because of all the medical personnel who were in and out of his room. Bertie and Joellyn arrived around 9:30. They were very nervous about seeing their brother because they didn't know what to expect. It had to be difficult for Gerry, too, not knowing if he'd ever walk again. Both girls came into his room with scared looks on their faces.

Joellyn spoke first and asked, " How are you doing, Ger?"

He answered with a blank look on his face, "Okay, I guess."

Then Bertie moved over and put her hand on his. All she said was, "Hi, Ger." She was trying to fight back tears.

Normally, these three were never at a loss for words. Gerry had Ed's dry sense of humor and he could easily get a few chuckles out of the girls. But, they could also come back with remarks of their own that touched Gerry's funny bone. However, this was different. The girls had been in the room for only a few minutes when a nurse came by and asked them to leave while they took care of some things for Gerry. They almost looked relieved; it gave them time to regain their composure before going back in. Gerry also needed a break.

Several of Gerry's friends started arriving at the hospital hoping to see him, but only family was allowed in his room. We explained to everyone who came by that the doctor didn't think Gerry should have other visitors at that time. My school principal, Sam, stopped by to see me and to offer his support. I told him I had no idea when I was coming back to work, and he told me not to worry about it. He said that I had more important things to take care of.

"But, how am I ever going to take care of this?" I asked myself. Whenever the children were little and got hurt, it was easy to make them feel better. I'd just put my arms around them, give them a hug or a kiss on the cheek, and it always worked. But all the hugs and kisses in the world weren't going to make Gerry's pain go away.

Gerry was alone in the room when Bertie went back to see him. He was upside down in the electric bed with the front part of his body facing the floor. I was just outside the door and heard Bertie tell Gerry that she didn't know what to say. He told her it was all right, that she didn't have to say anything. I started to choke up, so I took a walk to the visitors' lounge. It gave me a chance to visit with others who had family or friends in the hospital, and it helped to get my mind on something else for a few minutes. When I came back Bertie was standing outside of Gerry's room, sobbing. She told me that while they were talking, Gerry's tears were falling on the floor in front of her as he lay upside down in the rotating bed. She said she wanted to give him a hug, but she couldn't reach him because his bed was up too high. I put my arms around her, and we cried together as I held her.

Despite the difficult day we'd had so far, we did get one bit of good news from a nurse who was working with Gerry. She said she thought there was more movement in his left arm. We were cautiously excited because of the doctor's prognosis on the morning of Gerry's accident: "There's a ninety percent chance that your son will never walk again." But he hadn't said much about his arms. I felt that each development, no matter how small, was a positive step toward his recovery. "If each day brings some good news," I said to myself, "maybe our son will prove the doctors wrong." I hung on to that thought.

I couldn't believe how busy everyone was. Hardly ten minutes went by without a medical person coming by to take care of Gerry. The neurosurgeon came to tighten the halo pins in his head, but it made me sick to my stomach, so I took a walk down the hall. When I returned the doctor was gone and an occupational therapist was talking to Gerry about hand splints. He said the splints would keep his fingers from curling up. Later on, a physical therapist stopped by and spent about fifteen minutes working with Gerry, explaining the kinds of exercises she would be doing with him in his room. Eventually, she said he would go downstairs for his therapy. Soon after she left, someone brought a pair of special prism glasses for him to wear while watching television, but he could only watch for an hour at a time. He was thrilled because he loved to watch basketball and football.

Before I realized it, it was 10:30 P.M., and Ed was about to head home. Since the other bed was still empty, I was allowed to stay the night again. When I got into bed I prayed they wouldn't get a new patient, because I didn't want the nurse telling me that I couldn't sleep at the hospital anymore. Gerry said he was very tired so we said good night. It didn't take long to fall asleep; I was feeling very tired.

When morning arrived, I actually felt quite rested. I woke up once or twice during the night, but didn't have any problem falling back to sleep. Gerry said he also slept quite well, considering interruptions by the hospital staff who were in checking on him. When Ed came by, we went to the lounge to talk about future plans for Gerry. We didn't know what we should do: keep him at that hospital or transfer him to another facility where they had more experience with spinal cord injury. After discussing it for quite some time, we still didn't have an answer. We were also aware that we'd have to discuss it with our son before any decision was made.

It had been another busy morning for Gerry. The occupational therapist came by for the second time to talk with him about the hand splints. He reiterated the necessity of the splints, and said he'd be back in the afternoon to check the strength in his arms. Another staff member came by to measure Gerry for a brace he would wear on the upper part of his body. I was hoping we'd learn more about the brace, and the reason for it, from his rehab doctor.

Up until that point, Gerry hadn't eaten any solid food. After checking his stomach, the doctor told him he could begin a special ulcer diet for lunch, which consisted of chicken, rice, sherbet, and apple juice. But, the problem was that he had to eat while lying on his stomach in the rotating bed. It was very tough for him to be in that position, let alone try to eat. He had already complained about a sore chin. I couldn't imagine what it must be like having to stay in the same position for hours at a time, not being able to move or scratch an itch. I made myself a promise that day to never again complain about the small things.

When one of the nurses came by to check Gerry, she told us that he seemed to have more movement in his thighs. We were thrilled with the news, but kept in mind what the doctor had told us the morning of the accident. She also removed Gerry's IV, and told him that it was important to drink a lot of liquids.

Physical therapy started that day, and Gerry was excited because he wanted to see what he could do. I knew he'd set goals for himself and work extremely hard to reach those goals; it was that Finnish *sisu*. I learned that about Ed early on in our marriage; he had an inner strength that kept him going, no matter what happened. I saw it day in and day out. If he set out to do something, he eventually accomplished it. Gerry was made from the same mold.

Day three was a very important day for Gerry. He was going to be fitted for a brace at 3:00 that afternoon. According to the doctor, it would help him sit up. Gerry ate a normal breakfast that morning; an

egg, toast and juice, but because of the brace, he was allowed only liquids for lunch. One of the nurses came by at 1:00 and gave Gerry a
Valium, which was supposed to help him relax as they put on the brace.
He seemed somewhat anxious about the whole thing. He wondered just
how much the brace would help. I tried to reassure him, and suggested
that he wait and see how it felt. If there was a problem, he could talk
to the doctor about it. The afternoon dragged on slowly as we waited
for 3:00 to arrive. The occupational therapist came by and spent time
with Gerry discussing the brace, and then about 3:30 he put it on. The
look on Gerry's face indicated that it wasn't the best part of his day. I
felt apprehensive.

Gerry's rehab doctor also came by to talk to Gerry, Ed and myself,
about depression. When he asked how he was doing, Gerry told him he
was doing okay so far, and then the doctor told him that he would get
depressed at some point. He said, "It's only natural after all you've been
through." I agreed with him totally, but I wished he would have talked
with Gerry first, and then us. I think Gerry should have had the option
of discussing this subject in private, if he chose to do so. Of all the children, he was the most private about sharing his feelings. At times that
was difficult but, as a parent, I respected his wishes.

That night, Gerry was transferred to a regular bed which made us
feel a little more optimistic. Each move toward regularity gave us a
boost, no matter how insignificant it seemed to be. I was very pleased
that I was able to spend another night at the hospital with Gerry. I had
no idea when they'd kick me out because they needed my bed. I gave
him a hug, and we said good night around ten o'clock. I lay in my bed
praying that he would have a restful night, and hoping the brace
wouldn't be too uncomfortable. As I looked over at him, I imagined
trying to sleep with all that "stuff" on my body. With a halo screwed
into his head and a brace wrapped around his upper torso, I was terribly worried about him.

Six o'clock arrived, along with Ed. We had a cup of coffee together
and then one of the nurses talked me into going home for a few hours.
At first, I didn't want to leave, but I finally agreed that it might be good
to have a change of scenery. I hugged Gerry and headed for the parking
lot to find my car.

As I drove into our yard, I noticed the beautiful daffodils near the
back entrance. It was the first time I had actually looked at them since
the accident. I walked around the yard to see how many other peren-
nials were popping up. A variety of plants and flowers had come to life,

including some forget-me-nots. I stood staring at the pretty blue flower, thinking how appropriate it was. I picked some and put them in a vase on my kitchen table. I sat there for a few minutes admiring the flowers and thinking about Gerry. A sudden calmness came over me; I wanted to sleep. I headed up the stairs to my bedroom.

Two hours later, I awoke to the sound of a ringing phone. It was my mom asking me to take her to the hospital; she wanted to see Gerry. I was surprised that I had slept that long, but it really felt good to be in my own bed. I quickly showered, and headed a few miles up the road to pick up Mom.

Gerry was in much better spirits than he had been the day before. He said he had had a restless night with the new brace, but that someone had come by that morning to loosen it on the left side, and it really helped a lot. He seemed to be having a pretty good afternoon, and Mom was surprised when he sat up for about twenty minutes. The physical therapist came by to tell us that Gerry was going to be moved to the rehab floor on the weekend, and that he'd be sitting up by 2:30 that next afternoon. Gerry smiled when she made that statement.

She also brought him an electric wheelchair so he could start moving about on the rehab floor. "It will give you a little more freedom, Gerry," the therapist commented.

My stomach jerked when I first saw the wheelchair. "Are you sure rehab is ready for the likes of Gerry speeding down the hallways?"

She faced Gerry, stating firmly, "You will be given a ticket if that happens, young man."

Gerry grinned. He was looking forward to venturing around the rehab floor in his new set of wheels.

That evening turned out to be the best in four days! Some friends came by who were, at one time, in the same situation we were. Their son had broken his neck in a car accident and after several months of rehabilitation, was again able to walk. We visited for over an hour. After they left, I felt like I had been reborn. Now I had much more hope that Gerry would recover. They told us it took two to three months before their son got feeling back in his legs, and it was his big toe that he felt first. I could hardly wait to tell Gerry. I just knew it was going to happen for him, too.

Later that evening, Ed and I had a chance to talk with Gerry about our friends' son. He was very excited, and as I held his hand, he looked at us with the biggest smile I'd seen so far. It was just the kind of news he was hoping to hear; someone had beat the odds. I kissed him on the cheek, and told him how much I loved him. We finished the evening by watching the basketball playoffs and splitting a turkey sandwich. I was definitely looking forward to the next day!

It was Friday morning, and we had been at the hospital since Sunday. I hadn't slept well the night before because there were nurses in and out of Gerry's room, moving him from one position to another. One of the nurses was giving him some ice water and spilled it down his chest, not once, but twice. I could possibly understand that happening once, but twice was too much for me to handle. I lost control of my emotions, and told her just how I felt. I realized immediately that I had done something I shouldn't have, and as soon as Ed came by, I left the hospital and headed for home. When I returned at lunch time, I felt worse about the incident, and apologized to the nurse. She said not to worry about it, saying she understood what I was going through. "How could she?" I thought to myself.

Gerry was in pain. "What's wrong?" I asked.

"I'm so uncomfortable," he said. "The brace is causing a lot of pain to my shoulder blades and back." He must have been hurting badly because he didn't want any lunch. It was the day they were going to have him sit up in his wheelchair. Would he ever have the strength to do it? It didn't take long to get my answer. The rehab doctor came by with two men, who proceeded to lift Gerry into his wheelchair where he sat for over an hour. With tears in my eyes, I whispered, "You're absolutely amazing!"

"It's something I have to do, Mom." He had made up his mind that he was going to sit in that chair no matter what. And he did.

I fed Gerry his supper about 5:30 and soon afterwards he fell asleep. He didn't wake up until almost ten o'clock. He had missed seeing some of his buddies who had stopped by.

We also had a visit from Rob, Gerry's wrestling partner, and his parents. We sat down together and had a good talk, asking them to remain positive about Gerry's recovery. There were some tears shed by both myself and Rob's mother, but I believe it was quite therapeutic for all of us. I tried to put myself in their shoes, and thought about all they were dealing with. I knew we would have had a very difficult time if things were reversed and our son was responsible for such an accident. It was a no win situation for everyone involved.

Saturday: we'd been at the hospital almost a full week. I was hoping for another good day. Gerry, however, was still having problems with his brace. He complained about being very itchy underneath the brace.

He was also itchy around the pins that held the halo on his head. He thought he might get some relief if the dressings around the pins were changed. When the neurologist stopped by, Gerry asked if anything could be done about the itchiness.

"You should try to get used to it," he said. "You have to wear it for a couple of months."

I was very angry with his response. "Easy for him to say," I thought. "He doesn't have to wear it."

After the doctor left, Gerry broke down and cried. That was the first time I had seen him cry since the accident. I put my arms around him, but I didn't know what to say. I felt so helpless!

Later we talked. "It's time to let it all out, Gerry. It might help relieve some of the pressure that's built up inside."

"I'm feeling better now, Mom. But I would like to be alone for a while." I walked down to the lounge and visited with some friends. It was important for him to have private time.

Thirty minutes later, I walked back to Gerry's room and found one of the rehab doctors examining him. "Gerry has some congestion in his lungs which is creating a problem with his breathing," he said. "I will have the respiratory therapist check him and, if needed, I will order something to help him breathe more easily."

"Gerry's been complaining for the past three days about his room being very dry," I said. "He was promised a humidifier four days ago, but so far he hasn't gotten one."

"I will check on the humidifier."

I hoped he wouldn't forget. I was beginning to worry; the staff wasn't following through with some of Gerry's needs. Hopefully, someone would have some answers soon. Gerry and I said good night as I got into my bed. The hospital was starting to feel like a second home.

Gerry was miserable during the night because he just couldn't seem to get comfortable. The brace was causing him a lot of pain. He woke up once, not knowing where he was. He was moving his arms as if he were trying to punch someone. I quickly jumped out of bed. He asked, "Why do I have these 'things' on my hands and this 'thing' on my chest?" He really scared me because he was so visibly upset. I tried to calm him down, but he kept on swinging his arms at me. I rang for the nurse. By the time she got to his room, he seemed to be waking up. She talked to him briefly, trying to calm him down, and told him he had been dreaming. He seemed to relax somewhat. It was less than ten minutes when I realized he had fallen back to sleep.

I got into bed, but I couldn't sleep. I kept thinking about Gerry's dream, and I was feeling afraid. I must have finally dozed off because when Ed arrived in the morning, he had to nudge my shoulder to wake me.

Gerry was still asleep so we went for a quick cup of coffee. I told Ed about the incident during the night and how worried I was about Gerry. I suggested again that we should think about taking him somewhere for a second opinion. But the discussion ended there because the doctor came by and we wanted to talk to him about the brace. "Is there anything that can be done about the brace?" I asked. "It's causing Gerry a lot of pain and discomfort."

"I will have someone take a look at it," he said. I decided I would hold him to his word. If it wasn't taken care of quickly, I was going to make it my business to see that it was. I couldn't watch Gerry suffer like that any longer. Ed went back to Gerry's room and I made my usual trip home.

It had already been one week since the accident. I wondered how long Gerry would have to stay in the hospital. I again thought about moving him to another hospital, one where they had more experience with spinal cord injury. But, where would we go? And, I wasn't sure how Gerry would feel about being moved to a place away from his family and friends. Ed and I could be with him, but his brothers and sisters wouldn't be able to be there as often. I had a lot of unanswered questions to think about.

Suddenly, I heard a horn beeping, and in the rear view mirror saw flashing lights on the car behind me. Why was he blowing the horn and flashing his lights? Then I realized I was driving only twenty miles an hour in the passing lane. I quickly moved into the other lane. When the car passed me, I tried to motion my regrets to the young man. The response I got was not what I had expected. I felt like chasing after him to ask him why he was being so rude. I wanted to tell him about my son, but I didn't want to get in an accident trying to pursue him. I continued on my way.

At home, I sat down at the kitchen table with the forget-me-nots I had picked the day before. I couldn't help thinking about Gerry and all that he had been subjected to: the halo screwed into his head, the brace on his body causing the itchiness, the splints on his hands, the ice cold water down his chest, and the horrible nightmare he had just had during the night. I looked again at the forget-me-nots, and I knew I would never forget what our son had been through that past week. I held my face in my hands, while the tears fell on the table.

Back at the hospital, Gerry seemed in pretty good spirits, despite his not-so-good night. He and Ed were deep in conversation when I walked into the room. I was glad Gerry had his dad to talk to about the things he didn't want to discuss with anyone else. I tried to handle the emotional aspects, but Ed was better with other important matters that needed to be resolved.

I overheard the nurses talking while they bathed Gerry. They told him he was going to be moved to the rehab floor that day. They also said the staff was going to be tough on him, and he would have to work diligently. Gerry just smiled, "They'd better be tough! I like tough!" Hard work was exactly what he hoped for because he wanted desperately to be able to walk again. One of the nurses told Gerry he was doing quite well, considering it was only a week since the accident. Hearing that meant a lot to Gerry, because it came directly from one of the hospital staff. It meant a lot to me as well, because I waited every day for any tiny bit of good news. Besides, it also helped us cope with the many days and weeks we knew were still ahead for us.

I was glad I was in the room with Gerry when his rehab doctor stopped by, because he told us he would have someone take a look at the brace to see if it could be adjusted. He also said he would ask a dermatologist to check the rash on Gerry's neck and shoulders, which he believed was caused from stress. He explained that the adrenal glands were secreting hormones which, in turn, were causing the skin to become oily. He said that Gerry's progress had been good so far and that Gerry would be transferred to rehab the following day instead of that day, as was originally planned. He didn't give any reason for the delay, and we didn't ask. I was pleased about his concern with the brace and the rash it was causing, and I was willing to wait and see what happened next.

The following morning Ed arrived at the hospital at 7:15, and he stayed with Gerry the entire day. They were alike in so many ways and they both enjoyed sports, so it was easy for them to talk about something other than the situation at hand. I took advantage of his being there and went home to take care of a few chores.

As I was walking through the upstairs hallway, I stopped at Gerry's bedroom. I hadn't been in there since before the accident, and at first, I was hesitant. After I got up enough courage to go in, I discovered a note on his pillow. It said "Mom" on the envelope so I opened it. He had written just a few words telling me about the guys getting together for the day to share some of their experiences from college. His last sentence was, "Don't worry about me, Mom. I'll be home in the morning for church. Love, Gerry." The tears rolled down my cheeks. I sat down on his bed and wrapped my arms around his pillow. I was wishing I could go back to the days when I had to break up pillow fights. It was much easier handling pillow fights than what we were up against now. I suddenly realized how hard I was squeezing the pillow and knew I had to do something to change my mood. I grabbed the vacuum and sailed through all four bedrooms before heading back to the hospital.

My plan worked! I felt much better when I walked into Gerry's hospital room. Ed was still there, along with Joellyn and Bertie, who were chatting fast and furious with their brother. I was amazed at how much they had to talk about, and how patient Gerry was being with them. He just listened most of the time, smiling at something they said, or making a brief comment.

Because Gerry didn't have much mobility in his hands yet, I fed him his supper. Afterwards, we watched the Lakers' basketball game together and, shortly thereafter, Ed and the girls left for home. As I crawled into bed, I prayed Gerry would have a good night, and that the hospital wouldn't need my bed for a new patient anytime soon.

Gerry and I both had a pretty good night; at least there were no dreams that I was aware of. Ed came by as I was feeding Gerry his breakfast, and as soon as I finished, I left for home. The girls were still in bed when I arrived, so I relaxed with a cup of coffee before I went upstairs to shower. I sat there for about twenty minutes just thinking. It was very quiet in the house, and for some reason, I felt hesitant about going upstairs. I sat on the couch in the living room staring at the big pine trees outside the large picture window. We lived in the heart of town, but looking through that window made me feel as if I were somewhere far out in the woods. That was one of the things I loved about this one-hundred-year-old Queen Anne Cottage. Of course, the four bedrooms and four bathrooms also played an important part in choosing that particular house, because we needed a lot of space for five children. The kids loved it because no one had to wait for a bathroom in the morning. It was perfect for our large family.

I put my coffee cup down and headed for the shower. As I was turning the corner on the stairway, I met Bertie. She had a very strange look on her face. At first, I thought it was because of her concern for her brother, but then she put her arm around me and whispered something in my ear. All I heard was "Reecy," the name of our little poodle. I sat down on the step with her and she started to cry.

"What's wrong?" I asked.

"I think Reecy is dead."

"Oh no. Where is he?"

"He's lying in the hallway."

Reecy usually slept on the bottom of Bertie's bed. She told me that he had been restless during the night, moving around from one bedroom to another. About a year ago, I had taken him to the vet because he was doing a lot of hacking. The vet diagnosed him with congestive heart failure, and said that he would probably live only a few more years. I quickly ran up the stairs and found him lying very still in the hallway outside Gerry's bedroom. My first thought was, "Why there?" It seemed so strange. His body was still warm, but he didn't move at all. He was gone. I sat there with Bertie for a few minutes, holding her hand and stroking Reecy's little black body. I remembered how much he loved it when someone rubbed his tummy.

Reecy was an adorable, miniature, black poodle who had been with us for thirteen years. I picked him out from a litter of pups because he kept jumping up on me and licking my hand. I brought him home in a shoe box and everyone in our family immediately fell in love with him. Well, maybe not everyone. Ed wasn't very thrilled at first because the dog would have to be home alone most of the day. Since I was working and the kids were in school, Ed knew he was the one who had to stop by and take Reecy out for his daily duty. It wasn't long, though, before Ed and Reecy became real pals. Many times we chuckled behind his back as we listened to him talk "baby talk" with the dog, catering to his every whim. Ed was going to miss him as much as we were. Later that day, our Reecy was buried at Ed's family farm. We then had to decide if we should tell Gerry or wait until he was feeling better.

On my way back to the hospital I thought about Reecy, and how much Gerry loved playing with him. I wondered if hearing the news might set him back, or even cause him to be depressed. I couldn't make up my mind about telling him and when I got on the elevator, I was still very confused. I walked into Gerry's room and heard him telling Ed that he could feel something in his stomach when he rubbed his finger over it. Gerry appeared to be in very good spirits. I put my arms around him and told him how much I loved him. He gave me a big smile; I didn't mention the dog.

It was about 3:30 when one of the staff came by to move Gerry up to the rehab floor. We were told he would be starting a very busy schedule, and we wouldn't be able to spend as much time with him as we had the past week. They said we could only see him during late afternoon and evening visiting hours. I was also told that I couldn't stay overnight anymore; it wasn't permitted for any patient on rehab.

One of the nurses looked directly at me and in a very stern voice said, "It's time for Gerry to go to work, and it's time for you to take a break and get some rest . . . away from the hospital."

"But, I don't want him to be alone at night!"

"That's what we're here for," she insisted. "He won't be alone and, besides, maybe he'll get a roommate soon."

At that moment, Gerry said, "It's time for you to go home to sleep, Mom. Don't worry about me; I'll be in good hands." I choked up and reminded him that I was only a phone call away if he needed me. I guess I wasn't surprised when he agreed with the nurse that I should go home to sleep. He always had more concern for the other person than he had for himself, and I loved him for it. I headed home that night to sleep in my own bed for the first time since the accident. On the way, I told Ed about Reecy. We decided not to tell Gerry until he was feeling better.

Surprisingly, I slept quite well on my first night back home; in fact, it felt good to be in my own bed. I called the hospital before I left that day to see how Gerry was doing, and the nurse told me he had had a pretty good night. I was relieved and couldn't wait to see him.

When I arrived in Gerry's room, the physical therapist was with him and Gerry seemed in good spirits. He, too, told me that he had slept quite well, and that he finally felt comfortable with the brace. Someone from physical therapy had checked it out and made some adjustments, so it wasn't hurting anymore. I was elated, to say the least. I stayed in the room while the therapist worked with Gerry, so I could see what kinds of exercises they were doing with him. He moved his arms in several different positions, explaining to Gerry what he was doing, and why. Gerry was excited about getting some physical therapy, even though it was quite limited for the time being. I also sensed a change in his mood; he seemed more upbeat that day.

The rehab doctor came by to see Gerry. "The next six weeks are going to be tough," he said. "The physical therapists will work you to your fullest potential."

Gerry, showing a bit of excitement said, "I'm anxious to get started."

The doctor also mentioned the possibility of the need for emotional

Gerry fitted with his halo and brace.

assistance. "Gerry, you will have some down times. If you don't, you're just plain weird."

Gerry laughed at the doctor's comment and then glanced at Ed and me. I wasn't sure how to read him, but I knew we'd be discussing that matter with him very soon. "There is a psychologist available if you feel the need to talk with him." Our son didn't appear interested.

"Thanks," said Ed. "We'll discuss the idea with Gerry and get back to you." As the doctor was leaving, he suggested that we take Gerry for a ride around the hospital so he could become familiar with the rehab floor.

Gerry wanted to go, so we headed out. I was surprised how well he handled the wheelchair; actually, he did much better than I had expected. Ed just walked along with us, not saying much as we went down the hallway. I knew it was just as hard for him to see Gerry in a wheelchair, as it was for me. Was that how he was going to look from that day on? Only God knew that answer.

Much to our surprise, when we got back to his room, Gerry had a roommate. He was a young man named Marvin, who told us he had been in a motorcycle accident a year ago on the Fourth of July, and was back for an evaluation.

"How did it happen?" I asked.

"I rolled over on my bike and spent more than three months in the hospital."

"I'm so sorry. How long have you been using a wheelchair?"

"Six months, but now I'm able to walk with a cane," he cheered. As a result of the accident, Marvin received brain injuries and had to learn how to do everything all over again.

After spending some time with Marvin, we realized he had a great sense of humor. He might be just what Gerry needed at that time. Since Jim and Mike took over much of the business duties for their dad, they weren't able to visit with Gerry during the day, but they were with him every night and weekends. They both knew how much it meant to their brother. He needed them now more than ever. Ed and I left the hospital that evening feeling a bit more optimistic about our son's recovery, and Gerry appeared much the same way.

I was planning to go back to work the next day, but I was nervous about seeing everyone.

Chapter Three

On Wednesday, June 1st, I went back to work. I asked Sam, our principal, to talk to the staff before my arrival because I didn't want anyone to question me about Gerry. I knew I wouldn't be able to handle talking about him without breaking down. Sam was very kind, saying that he would let the staff know my feelings, and not to worry about it. When I walked into school that morning the teachers and staff were great, as well as being supportive. I got many hugs and smiles but no one asked me about Gerry. I made it through the day without any problems, and then I left for the hospital as soon as school was out. I couldn't wait to see Gerry and was anxious to see if he had any good news to share.

Gerry was in good spirits. He said the rehab doctor had been by to see him and was very impressed with his progress, especially when he heard that Gerry had fed himself lunch. Gerry wanted to be independent, and it was obvious that he, too, was proud that he was able to eat on his own. He enjoyed sitting in his wheelchair; it felt good to sit up. I thought about all those simple things we take for granted: sitting in a chair or walking up a flight of stairs. We don't realize how important those things are until we can't do them. Gerry had gotten a haircut and I jokingly said, "What happened to your hair, Ger?"

He grinned. "It's a one-of-a-kind rehab zip, and it didn't cost me anything." I glanced at Ed and smiled because Gerry sounded just like him; they both had a dry sense of humor.

Gerry's friend, Rob, came to visit that evening. Ed and I went to the lounge so they could have time to be alone. It must have been difficult for Rob to come to the hospital and see Gerry wearing a halo and a brace. It was a hard lesson for him to learn, but I hoped the accident would make Rob, and others, realize what can happen by horsing around. When Ed and I got back to the room, Rob was gone. Gerry appeared relieved. "How did it go?" I asked.

"We had a good visit." He didn't say what they talked about, but Gerry was a very forgiving person, and I was sure he'd let Rob know that. It was late, and Gerry seemed tired, so Ed and I left. We didn't say much to each other on the way home. I was sure many of the same thoughts that were going through my mind were also going through his. We still didn't know what the future held for Gerry, or if he'd ever walk again, which made it difficult to find the words we wanted to say to each other. Each day was harder than the day before, and there was a pain in the pit of my stomach that wouldn't go away. I wanted God to give us a miracle, and I wanted it soon.

It felt strange that our lives continued to go on; our children were doing the normal things they always did. Jim and Mike were working with their dad; Joellyn was taking classes at the University; Bertie was going to high school; and I was making an attempt to fulfill my duties as an elementary librarian. Yet, I knew our hearts weren't in the things we were doing. I tried to connect with the children on a daily basis, either at home, or at the hospital when they came to visit Gerry. But, we hadn't had the chance to sit down as a family and talk about Gerry's future. I was sure they had many questions they wanted to ask, but were uncomfortable asking, or were afraid of what the answers might be. However, we truly didn't have any answers at that time. Even though the emergency room doctor told us there was a ninety percent chance that Gerry would never walk again, we didn't want to believe it. We had heard of cases where some were given the same prognosis but, in the end, it turned out differently. Therefore, it was important for us to keep a positive attitude, and believe that our son would some day walk again.

Gerry was quiet when I got to the hospital the next day. "Has the doctor come by yet?" I asked.

"Yes," he said sounding very impatient. "And he didn't have much to say other than to ask how I was doing. I was hoping to hear some good news."

"Maybe he was running late today," I said, trying to stay positive.

"Are you making excuses for him, Mom?"

"You know I wouldn't do that, Gerry. What else is new today?"

"Well, I fed myself again at lunchtime," he stated proudly.

"That's terrific," I said giving him a hug. "Each day will bring new accomplishments, but we all have to be a little more patient."

"I realize that, Mom, but at times it's difficult."

"It's difficult for all of us, Gerry. As a family, it's important that we keep a positive attitude and try to help each other through this." Gerry nodded his head.

"Have you had any other problems today?" I asked.

"I've had a headache off and on during the day."

"Have you told anyone?"

"I hate to complain about the little things."

"You shouldn't be afraid to tell someone when your in pain, Gerry, no matter how insignificant it may seem. It could be something more serious."

"I hear you, Mom. I promise it won't happen again."

As I sat with Gerry, I thought about the time he was injured by a dog. He had been at the neighbors playing with some children when, suddenly, a big dog lunged at him from behind and made quite a gash in his ear. Luckily, the man who lived in the house saw what happened and ran outside to see how badly Gerry was hurt. When they both appeared at my back door, I wasn't overly concerned because he had given Gerry a towel to put over his ear and I couldn't see the injury. He told me that I should take him to the emergency room because he was bleeding quite a bit. Ed was at a meeting, so the neighbor offered to come along with me. Not realizing the seriousness of the injury, I declined his offer and headed to the hospital, three miles away.

The doctor removed the towel from Gerry's ear. I couldn't believe what I saw. The dog's claw had almost torn his ear off; it was sort of hanging. I'd never make it through this on my own, so I called my mother. She was there in less than ten minutes. She stayed with Gerry as the doctor sewed his ear back on; I sat outside the door. When he finished, the doctor said Gerry was a real trooper and hadn't made a peep during the entire procedure. I put my arms around Gerry. "You're quite the kid," I whispered.

Gerry was still quite the kid. He said the brightest part of his day was watching his roommate, Marvin, speed around the rehab floor on his scooter. Gerry kept smiling the whole time he was talking about him. I had a feeling Gerry was wishing he, too, was able to ride around on a scooter. I tried to picture the two of them racing around the rehab floor together, but decided that would be too much for the nurses to handle. Having Marvin for a roommate had been very good for Gerry, and provided much needed cheer. Ed and I had also enjoyed Marvin's sense of humor; he managed to keep everyone around him smiling.

Gerry fell asleep before supper. When his food arrived, he didn't eat anything except his pineapple-cottage cheese salad and a cupcake. Later on, he ate half a sandwich and drank some juice. It was a constant worry that he'd lose his appetite and possibly become depressed. According to the doctor, if that happened, it would mean a big concern for all of us. The fact that he wasn't up to visiting with his friends that night also made me nervous. When I explained the situation to the guys, they assured me it wasn't a problem and said they'd be back soon.

June 3rd was the last day of school for the students. However, I planned to continue working until I completed the inventory. I was happy I had a place to go during the day; I couldn't be at the hospital during Gerry's therapy because he was very involved in the sessions. They were keeping him busy and working him hard. He wanted that. He'd do whatever they asked of him, and wouldn't complain. That's Gerry's style.

When I got to the hospital after school, Gerry wasn't in his room. I found him in the lounge sitting in his wheelchair talking with Ed. "How long have you been sitting here?" I asked.

"About an hour," he smiled.

"How has your day been?"

"Pretty good, but I'd feel a lot better if they'd wash underneath my brace every day like they promised. I think it would help stop the itchiness."

"I'll talk to the doctor today," I said, trying not to show my anger. "I will make sure this is taken care of, or someone at this hospital is going to hear about it."

Later that day when the doctor came by to see Gerry, I discussed the problem with him, and insisted that it be taken care of immediately. Out the door he went. Much to my surprise, he returned in a few minutes and stated firmly, "From now on, Gerry will be washed underneath his brace on a daily basis." He also said, "And, someone will clean around the pins that hold the halo on his head." I felt much better because Gerry had to wear the brace and the halo for at least three months. He needed to be as comfortable as possible, and without pain.

It was getting close to supper time. How would Gerry do feeding himself? The menu was turkey casserole and broccoli, which I thought wouldn't be too hard for him to handle. He used a universal band which fit around his hand, and a fork or any utensil could be attached. I was surprised at how well he did. I offered to help, but he said, "I'd rather do it myself, Mom!" Later, he used the same band to hold his toothbrush while he brushed his teeth. He was learning to do simple things all over again. It became a real learning experience for me as well, because I hadn't realized Gerry would have difficulty holding a fork or a toothbrush. We don't give those mundane things much thought.

Much to our amazement, Gerry sat in the electric wheelchair visiting with family and friends for almost two hours that evening. We were so proud of him, not only for sitting that long, but also for operating the electric wheelchair by himself. He wanted to be independent, so we weren't surprised that he'd attempt anything he thought he could do. He ordered grapes for his snack that night so he could practice eating one at a time, using his thumb and index finger. As he ate them, he got a big kick out of watching us watch him. He could see how excited we were over each grape he put in his mouth. I gave him a big hug, telling him what a spectacular grape eater he was. He laughed and said, "I'm a fast learner, Mom."

Another Saturday had arrived, and because Gerry didn't have a busy schedule on the weekends, I went to the hospital early that day. I wanted to see if the doctor's latest orders were being carried out. Gerry told me he had slept well and, overall, had a pretty good night. He had physical therapy that morning, and had fed himself at lunch time. When I asked if anyone had washed underneath his brace, he told me that so far no one had been in to do it. He said he talked to the doctor about it again that morning, and was told that he had written it in his orders and would look into it.

Gerry could see how agitated I was. "I may as well tell you this, too, Mom. Someone is supposed to lift me every half hour while I'm in the wheelchair, and that's not being done either." At that moment, I wanted to scream so everybody on rehab would hear me.

"That's it!" I blurted out. "I promise you, Gerry, that before today is over, I will take care of this." Since it was the weekend, the doctor wouldn't be available, but I did talk to one of the nurses on duty. My voice was quivering the whole time as I listed the things that weren't being done for Gerry. She said she couldn't do anything about the problem then, so with tears running down my face, I asked her to leave a note for the doctor requesting a meeting with him on Monday. She said she would be glad do that for me. I took a deep breath, and went back to Gerry's room to tell him what had taken place.

"I'm beginning to feel that I'm a burden to everyone," he sighed. I put my arms around him and we both cried. I reminded him that he was definitely not a burden to anyone, and that taking care of him was part of their job. It was one of the worst moments I had had since the night of the accident.

Later that afternoon, while sitting with Gerry in the lounge, an activity therapist stopped by to see us. She introduced herself and then asked Gerry questions about things he liked to do before his accident. Not getting much of a response, she then asked, " Is there anything you'd like to do while you're a patient in the hospital?" Being a little on the shy side, Gerry stared out the window and didn't answer.

"Would you like to go to the mall?" she asked. I sat there in shock. I couldn't believe my ears! Gerry was also stunned.

Suddenly, he glanced at me with a strange look on his face mumbling, "I'm going back to my room, Mom."

"I'm coming with you." As I stood, I turned directly to the therapist, "Gerry isn't up to going to the mall, because he recently found out that he's paralyzed." I then excused myself and followed Gerry out of the lounge. As we headed back to his room, I felt totally confused. Why would an eighteen-year old boy who just became paralyzed want to go to the mall? Gerry had been in the hospital about a week, trying to understand all that was going on with his body, and a professionally-trained person comes along and asks him if he'd like to go to the mall. When we got back to his room, Gerry apologized for what he had done, but he said the therapist really upset him. I told him he didn't need to apologize, and what happened was not any fault of his. His day had started out rather unpleasantly, and then to experience that was too much for him to handle. It was for me as well.

Gerry wanted to go back to bed. He and Marvin watched boxing on television for a while and then he ate his supper. I was happy when John, one of Gerry's very good friends, came by to visit that evening. He said he thought Gerry looked good, and told Ed and me that he was talkative during their time together. He said he'd stop by the next day because he was leaving soon for Missouri; he was in the Air Force. Gerry seemed more relaxed after spending time with John; they were the best of friends in high school. The timing of his visit was perfect because it gave Gerry a chance to think about something other than the unfortunate incident with the activity therapist.

It was another Sunday and to quote Gerry, "Sundays are boring!" But, he also said the same thing about Saturdays. He didn't like the weekends because there were no therapy sessions. He would have liked therapy seven days a week, if it were possible. Gerry was quiet that day. He hadn't been up since our 2:00 arrival. He had spent over an hour in the wheelchair that morning, and had enjoyed it. Another patient with a spinal cord injury had returned for an evaluation, which meant they had to share the electric wheelchair; the hospital had only one. Early that evening, Gerry got to use the chair and I couldn't believe how much better it made him feel. It would've been great if they each had their own, so both patients could spend as much time as they wanted riding around the floor. But, we had to be satisfied with whatever was available to us. Hopefully, the hospital wouldn't need more than one electric wheelchair very often.

Many friends came by to visit that evening, and watching Gerry interact with them was exhilarating. His family was important to him at that time, but he needed his friends. His face lit up when they walked into his room. They talked about so many different things that he was interested in. Gerry wanted that special connection, to be a part of their lives.

It had been two weeks since the accident and still Gerry had no feeling or movement in his legs. I was trying to be patient, but I was finding it very tough. We continued to see on television or read in the newspapers how often families were thrust into similar situations. We weren't handpicked by God to experience such a tragedy, and He would guide us as we moved forward with Gerry's recovery process, but more than anything in this world, I wanted my son to walk again. I had to believe that someday it would happen.

It was Monday, the beginning of a new week, and I was hoping for one better than the last one. Joellyn was already visiting with her brother when I walked into his room. Gerry appeared very tired, so we went to the lounge and let him rest a while. I noticed the doctor walking by outside the lounge so I quickly took off. When I caught up with him I mentioned that we had some concerns about our son's care. He suggested we go into one of the conference rooms where we could talk privately.

I began by telling him how the activity therapist had upset Gerry by asking him if he wanted to go to the mall. The doctor immediately became defensive, and said he didn't see anything wrong with that. He said she always asks that question of young patients, and many of them take her up on the offer. I looked him in the eye and asked, "How many of those patients had just been told they were paralyzed and may never walk again?"

He looked down at the floor for a minute or two. "Do you want to transfer him to another hospital?"

"We've discussed that possibility," I answered, "But we haven't made a decision yet. We want to talk with Gerry about it first."

"Let me know if you do decide to move him," he said. "Is there anything else you want to discuss with me today?"

I realized the meeting hadn't gone very well, but I went on to tell him that I wasn't satisfied with the care Gerry was getting on rehab. I informed him that they hadn't been washing underneath his brace every day as ordered, and he wasn't being lifted every half hour while he was in the wheelchair. As I spoke, I could feel the tears on my cheeks. I waited for him to become defensive again, but he surprised me and said he agreed that I had the right to complain if my son wasn't being cared for properly. He assured me that those problems would be taken care of immediately. I thanked him and walked slowly back to Gerry's room. I hadn't ever confronted a medical person in my life before that meeting. I was learning how to be an advocate for Gerry.

Gerry spent four hours in his wheelchair that night visiting with family and friends. He was in a great mood. He laughed and joked with some of the guys and, for a minute, he appeared to be his old self again. I thought to myself, "Oh, what I wouldn't give to have him back the way he was just a week ago." But, that wasn't going to happen, at least not in the near future.

Jim called to say they were all on their way to the hospital, and I quickly realized I had forgotten to order the pizzas I promised for the family. Later, when the pizzas arrived we invited Marvin and the nurses to join us. Gerry seemed to enjoy the party a lot and downed several slices of pizza while visiting with everyone. We all had a fun night and I suggested to Ed that we do it more often.

Gerry was sleeping when I got to his room the next afternoon. The occupational therapist arrived soon afterwards and woke him up so she could begin working with him. I stayed in the room and watched. She used a pin to check for sharp and dull sensations on his hand and arm. After a few minutes, she said there was some improvement in his right arm, and that he had more sensation than he had the previous week when she checked him. She also said he had feeling in the C7 and C8 cervical which, according to her, meant there wasn't a complete break in the C6 cervical. My heart jumped into my throat. I wasn't sure what she was saying, and I was too afraid to ask. I didn't want her telling me that it didn't mean anything as far as Gerry's paralysis was concerned. I wanted to ask her some questions, but I couldn't get the words out of my mouth. Before I knew it, she was out the door.

I told Gerry I was going to the bathroom and hurried down the hall to see if I could catch her, but she was nowhere in sight. I was upset with myself for not talking to her when I had the opportunity to do so. As I was walking back to Gerry's room, I ran into his doctor, but he didn't speak to me. He probably didn't appreciate the things I'd said to him during our meeting the day before. I hoped he wouldn't hold it against me, because we had a long stretch ahead of us if Gerry decided he wanted to stay at that hospital.

Later that day, I received a phone call from Ed telling me our son, Jim, had been admitted to another hospital for an infection in his leg. Ed said it wasn't serious, but Jim would have to stay there for a few days. "When it rains, it pours," I said. I called the hospital to talk with Jim's doctor and he said he'd have a specialist look at his leg that night, but we wouldn't know anything more until sometime the next day. I told Gerry about Jim, although I still hadn't told him about our dog. I was waiting for the right time, if there ever was a right time for that kind of news.

Gerry didn't feel well the following day; he was nauseated at lunch time and didn't eat anything until 4:30 that afternoon. I was still worried about him losing his appetite, but by early evening he was feeling better. Hamburger and fries sounded good. When Ed left to pick up the order, some friends came by to visit. They were the best medicine Gerry needed at that time. They all came in with smiles on their faces. When his food arrived, Gerry ate every bite. Seeing his friends helped solve his loss of appetite.

A psychologist came by to see me that next afternoon. He talked about taking care of myself. "I think it's important to do things for yourself during such difficult times."

"I am scheduled to attend a library conference in Los Angeles this month, but I'm not planning to go."

"I think you should go," he said.

"My heart isn't in it. I don't think I could leave Gerry at this time."

"Think about it before making a final decision," he suggested. "It might be just what you need right now." I didn't have to think about it all. I had already made my decision. I wasn't going! I couldn't enjoy being at a conference in Los Angeles with Gerry in the hospital, not knowing what his future held. End of discussion.

It was about 9:00 P.M. when Gerry finally ate some supper: a beef sandwich and a candy bar. His weak appetite was a constant worry because, as the doctor told us, one thing leads to another. If he didn't eat, he wouldn't have the strength to continue with his therapy, and no therapy could lead to depression! I'd never been around a young person who suffered from depression. Would I have the strength to handle it? I had to make sure that didn't happen to Gerry, even if it meant bringing in his favorite foods, such as steak and lasagna. There was a great Italian restaurant not far from the hospital which I thought might be the answer. I made plans to check it out.

We were invited to our first meeting with Gerry's doctor and several other staff members the next day. The doctor referred to it as a "staffing." They were going to give us an update on Gerry's progress, and let us know what we could expect from him in the next few weeks. I wasn't sure if I was ready to hear what they had to say, especially if the news was bad. I prayed real hard before I went to bed that night, asking God to help me through the meeting.

I didn't have any trouble falling asleep, but I woke up during the night and wanted to get dressed and go to the hospital. I had dreamt that Marvin had lifted Gerry out of his bed and put him on his scooter. Gerry wanted to go for a ride around the rehab floor to visit some of the other patients. As they headed down the hallway, Marvin was speeding and lost control of the scooter, hitting one of the doctors. Gerry went flying through the air and landed on a nurse who was carrying a tray of food. I saw Marvin fall to the floor, but the scooter kept on going, running into several others before coming to a stop. Marvin got up, hopped back on the scooter, and sped down the hallway. I sat up in bed thinking about my "nightmare." When I realized I had been dreaming, I put my head back on the pillow and tried to fall asleep. I wondered how I'd react to Marvin the next day.

Chapter Four

It was the big day! We were meeting with Gerry's rehab doctor, the occupational therapist, the physical therapist, social services, and an LPN. Joellyn, Ed, and I arrived about 12:45, met in Gerry's room, and then all headed for the conference room. I was a total wreck and didn't know if I'd be able to get through the meeting. I wanted to hear all the positive things they might say about Gerry, but I didn't want to be sitting there if they were planning to tell us he'd never walk again. I was even more afraid for him. Joellyn, seeing how jittery I was, told me to close my eyes and count to ten before we went in to the meeting. That's exactly what I did.

Gerry's rehab doctor sat on a chair reading over some papers, perhaps Gerry's medical file. He glanced at me and smiled, which made me feel a little more relaxed, but I also wondered if he was thinking about our recent discussion. I was wishing I hadn't been so vocal, but then I realized I had an obligation to Gerry, and to myself, to let him know what was bothering us. I could not allow him to intimidate me. As soon as everyone arrived and sat down at the conference table, the doctor told us that he was very pleased with Gerry's progress so far. For a minute, I held my breath. Did he mean that Gerry might be able to walk some day, or did he mean just what he said, that he was pleased with his progress?

He continued, "It will take about six weeks for the swelling to go down in Gerry's neck, and then maybe we'll learn more about his injury."

"Do you mean after six weeks or so you'll be able to tell us if he will walk again?" I asked.

"No," he answered, quickly. "I cannot predict what will happen as far as Gerry's legs are concerned. We just have to wait and see." I glanced at Ed and Joellyn, who both had blank looks on their faces. They were probably thinking the same thing I was, that it might be several weeks before we knew anything definite about Gerry's future.

The occupational therapist informed us that Gerry was having more sensation in the seventh and eighth cervical. "The injury to his neck is between the fifth and sixth cervical," she stated.

"What exactly does that mean?" Ed asked.

"Having sensation below the sixth cervical is definitely a good sign for regaining more feeling," she answered.

"That sounds like good news," I said.

The physical therapist brought a model of the spinal column with him and explained Gerry's injury to all of us. "I'm amazed at how much initiative Gerry has taken on his own," he said. "Gerry has moved his thumb, middle finger, and the pinky on his right hand. I'm quite excited about that accomplishment, but remember it's too early to predict what might or might not happen." Gerry listened attentively.

I was beginning to get his message; we weren't going to know anything definite about Gerry's future for quite some time.

The person from social services and the LPN were there to answer our questions if we had any. "I don't have any questions," I said, "but there have been problems with some of the doctor's orders not being carried out."

"I'm sorry to hear that," the LPN said. "I'll look into it for you."

"Thank you," I said glancing at Ed. "We'd appreciate that." After the meeting, I had a good feeling the problems with respect to Gerry's care would improve. I prayed for that to happen. All in all, it was an interesting meeting even though we didn't learn a whole lot about the prognosis.

We went back to Gerry's room after the meeting to talk about our first staffing. He was pleased with what he had learned. "Mom, would you be able to find me some books on spinal cord injury?" Gerry asked.

"I'll be glad to check the library to see what's available." I said.

"I want to read as much as possible on the subject, so I can better understand what's happening to my body."

"I'll stop today on my way home." I promised. I was so very proud of him for wanting to learn more, but I was also afraid he might realize that not many recover from such a devastating injury.

Friends came by that evening, including Rob and his parents. While we visited with his parents, Gerry visited with Rob and a few of their friends. Later, Rob's mother had an interesting story to tell us. "Gerry told one of the guys that he could feel something when they wash his feet, and when they put his shoes on," she said.

"Hmmm, I haven't heard that," I said. "But I will definitely ask him about it later. Gerry has a tendency to keep secrets and then likes to surprise us later." As soon as we were alone, I asked him about it. "What's this I hear about you being able to feel your feet when someone washes them?"

"Who told you that?"

"Rob's mother mentioned it," I said smiling.

"I wasn't keeping anything from you, Mom. A friend asked me if I could feel anything in my feet, so I told him. I don't blab it to the world, but if someone asks me a direct question, I answer them."

"Gerry Donald," I said with a sigh. "I'm not the world. I'm going to ask you more questions from now on." He knew that I always used their middle names when I wanted to get their attention.

He smiled. "Ask away, Mom." I couldn't believe he waited for me to ask before he'd tell me about any new developments.

At the end of the week, before Bertie and I headed out to see Gerry, we went to see Jim at the hospital where he was a patient.

"I have to stay longer than the doctor first thought," Jim said. "The infection is not clearing up, and my temperature was over one hundred degrees last night. But, I want you to go and be with Gerry. I'll be fine!"

"I'll call you later, Jim," I said, giving him a hug.

When I called Jim from Gerry's room he sounded excited. "Hey Mom, the specialist came by and said he doesn't think I have an infection, after all. He's going to try steroids on me and, if I'm not discharged by the weekend, he'll transfer me to the same hospital as Gerry."

"Well, let's hope you're discharged," I said. "But if that doesn't happen, Jim, it'd be easier to have you here."

I guess if he had to be in the hospital, it would be better if both boys were at the same place so we wouldn't have to run between the two. I would have preferred to have Jim dismissed; one son in the hospital was enough. In fact, it was more than enough. Three days later, Jim found out that he had an abscess on his leg. The doctor lanced it and told him to stay off his leg for a couple of days. We were relieved it wasn't anything more serious. Now if only . . .

I picked up a "pasty" for Gerry and his roommate, Marvin. A pasty is a Cornish dish: meat, potatoes, onions, and vegetables all wrapped up in a crust and baked. The iron ore miners in our area took pasties for lunch when they worked underground; a pasty was like a whole meal in one. They were popular; even I grew up eating pasties. Marvin ate his for a mid-afternoon snack; Gerry ate his later because it was good, hot or cold.

Joellyn and her boyfriend, Al, came to spend some time with Gerry that evening, so Ed and I decided to go to the Italian restaurant for dinner. We hadn't eaten anywhere except the hospital cafeteria since the accident. But it was a big mistake! I was uncomfortable the whole time we were there. I felt as though people were staring at us, wondering why we were out for dinner while our son was a patient in the hospital. Everyone seemed to be having a good time talking and laughing and, deep down, I knew that they weren't looking at us, but I was miserable. I realized that I wasn't ready to go out in public yet. I couldn't eat much of my meal, so I suggested that we go back to the hospital. Ed agreed and asked the waitress to bring our check. When we got outside I took a deep breath of fresh air and whispered, "I'm sorry, Ed. Being there just didn't feel right."

"It's okay," he said. "We can try again another time." He took my hand as we walked to our car. I knew, at that moment, I'd never be able to get through such an ordeal without him, and I thanked God for his strength.

Gerry was sound asleep when we returned to the hospital and when he awoke, he didn't want to get out of bed. He had overdone it earlier by sitting in his wheelchair for several hours. I wasn't much company either, still feeling a little blue about the restaurant. Ed tried to make conversation with Gerry, but he wasn't being very responsive. It was time to call it a night. The next day would be better. If his friends came by over the weekend, they'd be able to cheer him up. He needed them, and so did I.

My wish came true. Mike, Lee and Boogie stopped in to see Gerry on Saturday afternoon, and it made him feel a whole lot better. Boogie was on crutches and told us the story of how he broke his foot playing basketball. Gerry chuckled through the whole explanation. I could already see a difference in Gerry's demeanor, and the boys had only been there a short time. The constant chatter was the best medicine anyone could have given Gerry.

The next day, we discovered a new patient in Marvin's bed. We were also disappointed that Marvin was gone because we knew how much we'd miss him. He was exactly what Gerry needed to help brighten and lighten his day.

Gerry's mood was down that evening, as was mine. I tried to make conversation by asking him about the sensation he was having in his feet. He told me he could still feel something when they washed his feet and when they put his shoes on. It sounded good to me, but I didn't really know what it meant. The doctor knew about the sensation Gerry was having in his feet and hadn't made too much of it. I was afraid to get my hopes up. Gerry mentioned that his brace was bothering him again; he said it was pressing on his shoulder blade. I tried to look behind the brace, but it fit tight against his skin. I told him I would speak to the doctor about it again. He closed his eyes, fell asleep, and didn't wake up until visiting hours were over.

We did have one light moment earlier that evening while we were in the lounge with Gerry and his sisters. One of the patients took out his false teeth and put them on the table. We all looked at each other and tried to keep a straight face, but we didn't quite make it. The patient didn't seem to be aware that we were even in the room. Suddenly, he got up from his chair and left the lounge without his teeth. Gerry started to smile, and then his sisters lost control. Just as we were leaving the lounge, a nurse came in and asked if we had seen a set of false teeth anywhere. I grinned and pointed at the table. She picked them up and headed out the door. It felt good to have something funny happen for a change.

It was the beginning of a new week. During Gerry's physical therapy session, he was able to balance himself for a couple of minutes on the edge of a rehab bench. He was so proud of himself. His face lit up with that wonderful smile of his.

Later that day, the doctor came by. "Gerry, show me what you can do with your arms." Gerry moved his arms up and down in different directions. "Nice job. You're progressing well."

"Doctor," said Gerry, "I have a sore spot on my right shoulder blade where the brace is rubbing."

"Can you feel the area where I'm touching you?"

"Yes, I can feel something."

"I think you're mistaken, Gerry. What you're feeling is coming from the neck area, not from where I'm placing the pressure." He left the room.

"He's wrong, Mom," Gerry said matter-of-factly. "I really could feel it when the doctor touched me."

"I believe you, Ger. After all, it's your body."

I felt like running down the hall after the doctor and confronting him, but I knew it wouldn't have mattered. I had gone that route once before. Despite the doctor's comments, Gerry continued to be in a good mood the remainder of the afternoon and evening.

He was very talkative when Ed got there and told him all about the doctor's visit, including the part about the doctor touching him. "I really could feel it, Dad."

"I believe you," Ed answered, "I'm sure you know what you can feel better than he does."

I was disappointed when I arrived the following afternoon to find Gerry asleep. The occupational therapist was in his room and told us that Gerry had been sick in the morning and didn't have his therapy. She was hoping he was feeling a little better so she could work with him. She also said he didn't sleep well the night before because he was running a low-grade temperature. When the nurse came by and told me Gerry didn't want anything for lunch, my stomach started to hurt. This wasn't going to be one of our better days. I was right.

Gerry's rehab doctor walked into the room and began discussing all kinds of things with us, as if he had no hope for his recovery. I became terribly upset and wanted to take off down the hall. I stood there feeling so helpless, not knowing what to say or do. Suddenly, he started making comments of a more personal nature. "As for your sexual functions, Gerry, you probably won't be able to have children."

I couldn't believe my ears; I felt like jumping out the nearest window. Why was he having this discussion with Gerry while I was in the room? It should have been a meeting just between the two of them. Gerry was a very private person. I wanted to tell the rehab doctor how I felt, but I just stood there getting angrier by the minute. If I opened my mouth there would be no way to stop me, and I didn't want to say anything more that would embarrass Gerry. I waited for him to stop.

Finally, the doctor started out the door, but then he came back saying that we needed to think about making our home accessible for Gerry. He mentioned getting a hospital bed and possibly a van if Gerry wanted to learn to drive. I wanted to tell him to leave; I had had enough of his "inspirational" comments. I thought doctors were supposed to show compassion for their patients, especially to those whose futures were so unpredictable. As he was walking out of the room he made one last comment, "Oh, by the way, Gerry," the supplier wants to be paid before he orders a wheelchair for you." That did it! I couldn't hold my tongue any longer. "That is not Gerry's problem! Please don't bother him with those details; Ed and I will handle that."

The doctor stared at me and then walked out of the room. I was visibly upset, and told Gerry not to worry about the things that had been said to him. "Doctors don't know all the answers. Maybe your doctor's having a bad day." My stomach started to hurt a lot and I didn't know what to do. "I'm going to take a walk to the bathroom." When I got there I shut the door and squeezed the roll of toilet paper as hard as I could. I slammed it against the wall trying to get rid of my frustration. I wanted to scream, but someone might hear me and call security. Later, I went back to Gerry's room.

We watched television most of the afternoon, unable to converse. I kept thinking about everything the doctor had said to us and felt terribly upset. Gerry must have been feeling the same way because he was extremely quiet. I was scared just thinking about making some of the decisions the doctor had talked about. I needed Ed. Why hadn't the doctor asked to meet with us first, instead of dumping it on Gerry as he had done?

Later, I took a walk to the cafeteria and bumped into a former classmate of mine. Her husband was dying of a brain tumor and, believe it or not, she was the one who gave me a pep talk. "Remember, Joann, don't ever give up hope for Gerry. It's what keeps us going. I will pray for him." Being with her made me feel a lot better. There's always someone whose problems are worse than your own. When I got back to Gerry's room, Ed and Bertie were there and I was very happy to see them both.

On the way home that night, I told Ed all the details of the doctor's visit. He shook his head in disbelief. "Don't worry about it," he said. "It will all fall into place." He was my rock! I took a few minutes to thank God that Gerry's life had been spared in the accident, and asked Him to continue looking after our son.

Four of Gerry's friends were at the hospital when I arrived the next day. They seemed to be having a very good time and Gerry appeared to be enjoying them a lot. After they left, he told me he had gone to a rehab picnic that day. I knew about the picnic, but I hadn't mentioned it to him because I didn't think he'd be interested in going. Boy, was I wrong! While he was talking about the picnic, he laughed so hard he couldn't even tell me what he was laughing about. Later, Joellyn mentioned that Gerry found one of the rehab patients terribly amusing while they were outside playing volleyball. It had something to do with the way she punched the ball when they threw it to her. I guess you'd have to be there to see why it was so funny. It didn't matter to me what it was that made him laugh; I was glad that he went to the picnic and had a good time.

That evening, several visitors stopped by the hospital. I couldn't believe how many of Gerry's friends, and ours, continued to come to see us. We knew how important it was for Gerry to have family and friends around, and we were finding out that it was just as important for us. It helped so much for me to be able to sit down with someone and talk about all the emotions I was feeling. Even though most of them had no idea how much my insides hurt, it was good therapy just to vent. One afternoon while visiting with a friend in the lounge, I was unaware of the time until she mentioned she had to get home to make supper. I apologized for keeping her, but was surprised at how long we had visited. I did most of the talking and she did the listening. She was a wonderful friend, and I thanked her for being there for me.

As I arrived at the hospital the next day, Gerry was getting ready to go for his physical therapy. A male nurse was in the room with him and told me that Gerry had bumped his head on the bed rail. However, that wasn't the story I got from Gerry. The nurse had let go of his head while trying to transfer him from the bed to the wheelchair, which caused it to hit the rail. I became concerned. "Has anyone checked Gerry's head?" I asked.

"No," he said. "I talked to the doctor on the phone, and was told that it wasn't necessary since the pins in his head weren't loose."

"Have you checked the pins?" I asked.

"Yes, and they are secure." I felt nervous about the entire incident. Gerry should not be blamed for an injury that took place while someone was transferring him from the bed to the wheelchair, or vice versa. I didn't say anything more to the nurse about the matter, but I wasn't comfortable with his explanation.

Gerry went to physical therapy later by himself, even though I thought the male nurse should go along to make sure he got there safely. The nurse assured me that he'd do fine, but I wasn't convinced. I followed at a distance, until he was safely relocated. In the lounge, I visited with a woman whose husband had been transferred to our hospital where he remained for seven months. She said the doctor at the other hospital had read the X-rays incorrectly and her husband became paralyzed. I felt numb, and very concerned for Gerry.

I went back to Gerry's room and waited patiently for him to return from therapy. Finally, he came wheeling in with a big smile. "I'm fine, Mom! You worry too much."

"Oh, really! That's my job, son. What would I do with all my time if I didn't worry?" We both laughed and he began to play Pac-man. He had no idea how anxious I really was after hearing that woman's story in the lounge. I did not tell him about it.

Joellyn came by at supper time with a bag of Chicken McNuggets and fries. Gerry was thrilled. He yelled, "Yippee. No hospital food for me tonight!" He enjoyed every bite and wanted more. Joellyn told him she'd bring him a double order next time. I decided right then and there to keep an eye on his fast food rage. It wasn't the most nutritious diet for Gerry, but he did eat, and that was my biggest concern.

Later, a male nurse walked in and said, "It's shower time." Gerry was supposed to have three showers a week, but that wasn't happening. Sometimes he got just one.

He was all smiles as he headed for the shower and when he came out, he was ecstatic. "Hey, that was invigorating! I wish I could have a shower every day." It didn't seem like a lot to ask. He was entitled to a clean body especially if it made him feel better, and I could see that it definitely did. Ed suggested that I talk to the doctor about it again. I was willing to try, but I had my doubts that it would do any good.

As Ed and I drove home, all I could think about was the look on Gerry's face after his shower. I could feel myself getting angry all over again. Suddenly, a police car sped by us with the siren blaring. Several cars pulled over ahead of us. Farther up the highway were two police cars and an ambulance at the scene. They removed a person from one of the heavily damaged vehicles. All I could think about was another family getting a phone call that night. I couldn't help remembering the call at 3:00 in the morning telling us that Gerry had had an accident. And, here we were a month later, still not knowing what the future held for him. I went right to bed when we got home, but I kept waking up picturing an injured person being carried into an ambulance and hoping that he or she had survived. The next day our local paper reported that a young man had gone through a red light and hit another car, but luckily, both drivers ended up with only cuts and bruises.

I had an opportunity to talk to one of the nurses shortly after I arrived at the hospital the next afternoon. Gerry noticed his halo was loose so Ed went to get the nurse. She checked the bolts but didn't appear to be concerned about the problem, so I asked her if she would let the doctor know about it.

"The doctor won't be in until morning," she said. "Gerry, It's your job to tell the doctor about the loose halo."

I could feel myself getting hotter by the minute. "Would you please make a note about the loose halo, just in case Gerry doesn't get to see the doctor tomorrow?"

"Yes, I will make a note, but Gerry should be the one to tell him."

I felt it was a good time to air other problems that we had encountered, so I mentioned some of the things that weren't being done for Gerry. "They are supposed to clean around the pins in his head every eight hours, and change his liner once a week. The doctor also told us that someone would wash underneath his brace daily, and give him a shower three times a week."

Just as I started to ask her why those things weren't being done, she turned and walked out of the room without any response. Ed, Gerry and I looked at each other rather surprised, but she returned within a few minutes and stated that the night nurse had been cleaning around the pins in Gerry's head.

"No one has cleaned around the pins since the first week he arrived on rehab," I said. "I've written it down each time. Do you want me to check my notes to see when it was done last?"

She left the room without saying another word, and I could tell by the look on her face that she wasn't very happy with me.

"Way to go, Mom," Gerry said smiling. "Now they'll probably kick me out of here."

"I'm not worried about that, Gerry. Someone needs to be made aware of what's going on around here. I don't like what I'm seeing."

"Your mother's right," said Ed. "Patients do have rights, and one of those rights is to be taken care of properly. We need to check on whatever isn't being done with regard to your treatment."

"I was just kidding, Mom," said Gerry. "I know you and Dad are both concerned about me, and I do appreciate what you're doing."

"You bet, we're concerned about you," I stated. "If we don't look out for you, then who will? I know how busy they are here, but you have the right to have the best care possible, and we're here to see that you get it."

Later, Joellyn and Gerry spent some time together alone while Ed and I went to the lounge. I felt they needed to talk with each other as brother and sister, and be able to share things without having us around every minute. It gave us an opportunity to visit with others who had a family member or a friend in the hospital. I thought of it as a form of therapy. Talking with others made me feel better, and it also helped me put things in perspective.

While we were in the lounge, Joellyn came by with a big smile on her face. She was very excited, and was talking so fast that I could hardly understand a word she said. I told her to slow down and start over. She took a deep breath. "I asked Gerry about his legs. He said that he could feel it when someone tickled the bottom of his feet. He also told me that, at first, he couldn't feel his legs at all, but now he definitely knows they're there." We didn't know what it all meant, and we didn't want to spoil Joellyn's enthusiasm, so we didn't say anything that might change her mood. The doctors weren't absolutely sure of the prognosis, so we saw no harm in letting her be excited until we learned something new.

Nothing much happened around the hospital on Saturday or Sunday, but there was a bit of exciting news. Gerry moved his middle finger on his left hand for the first time. It wasn't much, but for us it was important. Eventually, all those little things could add up to something big, and that was what we prayed for. We tried to take one day at a time and be happy with whatever progress there was, no matter how small it seemed to be.

It was about 1:30 Saturday afternoon when my mom and I got to the hospital. Gerry had a young female visitor, so we went to the lounge until she left. When we got back to his room, I wondered why he hadn't gotten out of bed yet. Was this one of the first signs of depression? My mom and I visited with him, but it was difficult making conversation. He seemed a little down. When his grandmother asked him a question, he appeared not to want to answer it. She was clearly worried about him. It was almost 5:00 before he mentioned that he wanted to get up. Gerry did tell us that the doctor had been by to see him that morning, and had tightened the pins on the halo. I was happy to hear that news. At 7:30, he said he wanted to go back to bed.

Father's Day arrived on Sunday, but it was just another day as far as we were concerned. We had two sons in the hospital and we wanted to spend some time with both of them. Everyone had cards for Ed, but there would be no celebration. Usually on Father's Day, we all got together and went out for brunch, or everyone came to our house for dinner and the kids told "Dad" stories. We always had a few good laughs, and a fun time, but Gerry was our number one priority on that day, and every day, until he was back home with us.

Later that afternoon, we met a patient in the lounge who was from a neighboring town, a cop who had shot himself in the leg. He had a good sense of humor. We introduced him to Gerry and they hit it off right away. Gerry enjoyed him because he didn't hesitate to make jokes about himself. He reminded us of Marvin.

Joellyn and Gerry talked a lot that evening while we were visiting with some friends in the lounge. He told her that he often tried to move his legs, and even though it felt like they were moving, he knew they weren't. I tried to imagine what that must be like. Was it the beginning of something more to come? I mentioned it to Ed, but he told me not to get my hopes up yet. He said we had to be patient, but I kept thinking about it all the way home in the car. I kept asking myself the same question over and over again, "Will Gerry ever walk again?" But, I also knew there was only One who truly had the answer to that question, and we had to wait until He was ready to let us know.

Gerry was dozing when I walked into his room the next day, and I let him sleep. I had stopped at the flower shop and picked up a red rose, and then at the Cookie Cutter to get some cookies. I was hoping to brighten his day. The nurse woke him up around 2:00 to shower, and to change the lining on his brace. This procedure was supposed to be done once a week, but–in five weeks, this was the very first time. Gerry had a headache and felt nauseated; he usually got that way after physical therapy. He wasn't able to eat his lunch, but later on a ham salad sandwich sounded good.

"You know I really like your macaroni and tuna salad, Mom," he said.

"I know you do, Ger, and I will make some tomorrow and bring it for lunch."

"Thanks, I'd like that." He smiled as he looked at the red rose and cookies on his table. "Are those just for me?"

"Especially, for you, Ger." I gave him a hug.

He then began to tell me about his nurse, Bonnie. "She truly cares about my progress, Mom, and she always takes the time to talk to me about it."

"I can see that you and Bonnie get along well, Gerry. It's obvious when she's in the room."

"She also talked to me about her brother's car accident when he was only twelve years old. He suffered a broken neck. His injury was between C2 and C5 cervical, and she said that now all he has is a stiff neck at times."

"Wow, that's great!" I wanted Gerry to remain positive about his future.

Many friends stopped by that night, including Rob. I was glad he continued to visit Gerry. I don't know how well I would have handled the situation if the roles had been reversed. It was hard being the parent of a son who was injured, but it must have been extremely hard being the parents of the one who had caused the injury. And for that reason, I will always keep them in my prayers. Because so many came to visit that evening, Ed and I decided to move down the hall to the lounge. When we left around 9:30, some of the guys were still there, and Gerry was in very good spirits.

When I got to the hospital that next afternoon, Gerry got upset with me because I suggested that he might want to go back to bed for an hour or so. He had been in his chair since 10:30 that morning, and when he went to do some lifts in the wheelchair, I told him to take a break and rest. He didn't want to get into bed, but I insisted, and he finally agreed. He was sound asleep in a matter of minutes. I believe that was one of those times when a mother knew best.

While he was sleeping I went to the family lounge and visited with Doug, one of the other patients. He mentioned that Gerry had been eating lunch in the lounge for the past few days. Gerry hadn't said anything, but that didn't surprise me. He liked to keep things from me and then talk about them later. After I thought about it, I realized he was again following in his dad's footsteps.

As I was walking back to Gerry's room, I ran into Harry, the gentleman from social services. He wanted to talk to me about Gerry going back to the University. I knew that was his job, but I wasn't ready to talk about it yet. And when I was ready, I wanted Ed with me.

"I know we have to make some decisions soon, Harry, but we need more time to think about it. It's an important decision for Gerry and he has to take many things into consideration."

"I totally agree with you," he said. "We can talk later." I felt relieved.

Gerry was awake and hungry when I got back to his room. I ordered him a turkey sandwich from the cafeteria, but he ate only half of it. As we were sitting together, I decided to ask him how he felt about resuming classes at NMU.

"Have you had any thoughts about going back to school, Gerry?"

"It's too soon to think about it, Mom."

"I feel the same way. You don't have to make any immediate decisions, Gerry. We can talk about it later."

"I'm not ready."

We were about to begin our second month at the hospital. It was hard to believe that Gerry had been there that long. Did it seem like forever to him? A month was a long time for an eighteen-year old to be in the hospital, especially when he was so looking forward to spending the summer months with his friends. He probably thought a lot about some things he'd already missed out on, like working for his dad, and our trip to Washington, D.C. in June.

When Joellyn and I arrived that next afternoon, Gerry had been in physical therapy, and because he had been up in his wheelchair since 10:00 he decided, on his own, to get some rest. The physical therapists had been working him hard, which was exactly what he wanted. They could push him as far as possible and he wouldn't complain. He wanted to get out of that wheelchair some day; that was his goal.

Ed and I enjoyed watching Gerry eat his supper that evening. He fed himself and he even drank his milk from a plastic glass. Most of the time he used a straw. He also said his appetite was improving, which was a big relief. He needed to eat to build up his strength.

There I was preaching to him about eating, and I had already lost almost ten pounds. I was sure I wouldn't have any problem putting the weight back on once Gerry started to improve. My mom kept after me to eat, but the food just wouldn't go down.

Later that evening when Gerry was lying on his side in bed, I reached over and tickled his butt. He quickly turned around and said, "Get out of there!"

"I just wanted to see if you were awake," I said.

"I'm more than awake," he answered, "And, I'll prove it to you if you do that again."

"I'm sorry," I said, smiling. "Are you threatening your mother?"

"Dad, take her for a walk so she stops bugging me." At that point we all started to laugh. It was great seeing Gerry get feisty with me.

I told him I was surprised that he felt me tickle him, because I had tried to be careful so he wouldn't see me. I then tickled his toes through the hole in his stocking and he felt that, too. We talked about the feeling he had in his feet and legs, and he said the doctor had talked with him recently about his sensation. "He told me that whatever he got back in two months would be all he could expect." The expression on Gerry's face changed as he spoke those words. He looked scared. I wished the doctor could have been more optimistic with him, but he was trying to prepare him for what might be ahead. As Ed and I were leaving, the nurse told Gerry it was time for his shower. That brought a big smile to his face.

Chapter Five

It was June 23rd, and one month since the day we received a phone call telling us about our son's accident. The doctor told Gerry that whatever movement or sensation he had in his legs at the end of two months would be all he could expect to get back. We had thirty more days. I prayed hard each day and hoped for a miracle.

My friend, Judy, came by the hospital to bring some books on spinal cord injury. I had called her earlier and mentioned that Gerry wanted to read about his injury, and she went straight to the library and picked them up.

As I was walking down the hall to Gerry's room, I ran into Bonnie. She took one look at me and gave me a pep talk about taking care of myself. "You look thin and somewhat pale, Mrs. H." At first, I wasn't paying close attention to what she was saying, but then she warned me, "You could get sick and possibly end up in the hospital."

That last remark got to me. She even suggested that I go home early that night and get some rest. I wasn't feeling the best, so I told her I would probably do just that, and continued on my way. When I got to Gerry's room, Ed was already there.

Gerry said he was looking forward to supper because it was steak night, with a baked potato. I wondered if he would be able to cut the steak by himself, or if I should offer to cut it for him. It wasn't very long before I got my answer. When the tray arrived, he suggested that we go to the lounge while he ate his meal. It was his first steak since he had been at the hospital, and he didn't want us watching him cut every bite. As we left his room and walked to the lounge, I whispered,

"He's quite a guy, that son of ours."

Ed smiled. "That's our Gerry; he so wants to be independent."

We waited almost an hour before we went back to the room. He was wiping his mouth with his napkin just as we walked in. "How'd you do, Ger?"

"Just fine, Mom. But, would you please pick up those pieces of meat on the floor?" Ed and I laughed.

"Just like home," Ed joked. "Would you like me to clean up that piece of potato, as well?"

As the nurse walked in to get his tray, she saw Ed pick up a piece of steak from the floor. "Gerry, maybe you'd like some soup tomorrow?"

Gerry grinned at her. "I love soup. Would you make it chicken noodle, please?" He seemed to enjoy us poking a little fun at him, but he also liked dishing it out. He'd always been a good sport and we loved him for it.

I had good intentions of going home early as Bonnie had suggested, but I didn't make it. Gerry had a lot of company and I enjoyed chatting with everyone. It felt good to be there and before I knew it, it was 9:00. I didn't want to run into Bonnie on my way out, but if I did, I was going to promise her that I'd try again the next night.

Gerry wasn't feeling the best when we got to the hospital. After supper, he complained of a headache and an earache. I talked to the nurse and she got some medication for him, suggesting that he rest for a while. I decided to go to the lounge and say a few prayers.

The next day was Saturday; Gerry disliked the weekends, mostly because there was no physical therapy. HBO had been hooked up, so I was hoping he'd be able to watch some good movies.

Gerry sat in his wheelchair for eight hours, but was quiet and appeared totally bored. I was wishing that someone would stop by; his friends always energized him.

That evening I had dinner with a dear friend. It made me realize how important it was to spend time with my own friends. She convinced me that my faith would get me through the tough times, and I knew she was right. I planned to get together with her more often; the dinner was very therapeutic.

I went to church as usual on Sunday morning and managed to get through most of the service without tears until the choir sang "Amazing Grace." Then the tears began to fall. There was a time I had to stand in the back on the church until the mass was over. On that particular Sunday, a woman walked over and put her hand on my shoulder. She said she knew that I was going through some tough times because she had had a similar incident in her family. I didn't know her, but she must have known about Gerry's accident. "God will look after your son and your family," she said. She was a true believer and I was no longer alone.

When I got to the hospital, I looked around at all the visitors and realized how very thankful I was for our large family. Not only did our four children come by that day, but my mom, my sister Sue and her daughter, Amy. Different faces, different things to talk about, and a lot of love from everyone helped finish off the weekend.

On Monday, when I arrived at the hospital with Bertie, we met Gerry's rehab doctor in the hallway and he asked to talk with me. He suggested that we go into one of the small meeting rooms where it would be more private. Something was up. I followed him inside to some chairs where I thought we were going to sit. But, he didn't sit, nor did he invite me to sit. My stomach was churning, but I was ready for him. "Have you been avoiding me?" he asked.

"As a matter of fact, I have."

"Why is that?"

"I don't want you to upset me again."

"What did I say, or do, to upset you?"

"I didn't appreciate it when you invaded Gerry's privacy by commenting about personal things in my presence. That discussion should have taken place with only two people present, yourself and Gerry." He had no response.

I also informed him of a staff member who had given Gerry a book to read without consulting us first. It was a book about living life as a quadriplegic. "It's been about a month since the accident, and I don't think Gerry was ready to accept the fact that he might never walk again. I think that person was rushing things a bit." Once again, he didn't respond.

Finally, I told him about a certain psychologist who often stopped by Gerry's room, asking us how we were all doing. "We haven't requested him and don't want him hanging around us, or Gerry. Sometimes he appears when Gerry's friends are here, and he interrupts their visit. One evening when the psychologist came by, we had to tell him he couldn't see Gerry."

"I will let the psychologist know that neither you nor Gerry want him to stop by."

"Thank you. Early on, you mentioned bringing in a psychologist, and we told you we'd let you know if we, or Gerry, wanted one. And we would like the option of choosing our own if we were to make that decision."

"I have no problem with that. I'll take care of this immediately."

As for my other complaints, he didn't have anything to say about them. We stood there for a minute or so without saying a word to each other, and then suddenly he stated, "There hasn't been much change in Gerry's condition. How are you coping with everything?" He caught me off guard.

"As well as we can, under the circumstances. We've talked with other families who have gone through a similar experience, and we've found them to be very helpful. One of those families has a son who also broke his neck, and is now walking. It gives us a lot of hope when we hear stories like that."

"But, that isn't always the case," he said. "We never know for sure how these things will turn out."

"I realize that," I offered. "But we can't just give up. We must continue to have faith that Gerry will walk again."

"Of course," he said. "I agree with you on that. But you must also be prepared if that doesn't happen."

"You're right," I said, and he left the room. I walked slowly down the hall to Gerry's room thinking about our discussion. I had hoped the doctor could have been a little more compassionate, but maybe he'd witnessed so many family tragedies over the years that he'd reached a point of not allowing himself to get too involved. And, I had to admit, I didn't blame him. Taking care of severely injured patients over the years must sooner or later get to all doctors who handle difficult cases.

Bertie was with Gerry when I got to his room, and he was in good spirits. His sister must have told him something to perk him up; she had a way of doing that. Ed also came by after his Lion's meeting, but none of Gerry's buddies stopped in. I remember the doctor telling us that the friends would stop coming, but I was really hoping they'd prove him wrong!

The next day, Gerry found me reading in the lounge. Something was up because he was all smiles as he wheeled himself toward me. "Mom, I moved the muscle in my left hip. It happened during my occupational therapy session."

The OT therapists worked with Gerry on personal care aspects: brushing his teeth, manipulating eating utensils, using a hairbrush and dressing himself. He had difficulty grasping things so a strap was attached to many of the items.

It had also been an entertaining therapy session that day. Maureen, one of the therapists, gave Gerry a water pistol to use on Debbie, another therapist, because she got him with the pistol first, and he was anxious to get her back. Gerry was laughing the whole time he was telling me about it, so I knew he was looking forward to his next session. If the games they played helped to keep his spirits up, I'd say to those therapists, "Bring them on."

Dean, one of Gerry's close friends, surprised him that night by bringing lasagna and garlic bread for supper. Dean had a big grin on his face when he walked in, but Gerry had a bigger one. Lasagna was one of his most favorite dishes. Rob also came by and stayed until 10:00. How much Gerry looked forward to spending time with his buddies!

Our second staffing had been scheduled for the next day, and I was feeling nervous about what they might tell us.

I didn't sleep well that night. I kept having the same weird dream over and over. I was at the hospital for the meeting, and suddenly Gerry came walking into the room. I'd wake up in a sweat. It was so strange!

Gerry with Debbie, one of his physical therapists.

Finally, I got out of bed and went downstairs to get a glass of warm milk. As I sat at the kitchen table sipping the milk, I remembered something I used to say to Gerry when he was about three years old. I'd whisper, "Gerry, you didn't give me a kiss today."

He'd say, "I didn't? Oh geeee," and then he'd come over and kiss me on the cheek. By the time he went to kindergarten he caught on to my little trick. He'd just grin at me and say, "No, no, Mom, I know what you're up to." When I finally went back upstairs to bed, I fell asleep and didn't wake up until the alarm went off.

Despite my nervousness, the staffing went well that next day. The doctor made some positive statements about Gerry, and both therapists said that he was doing very well. They all agreed that Gerry was a hard worker, but we already knew that. According to the doctor, the halo would be on for two more months. I was sure that Gerry was looking forward to the day he could finally rest his head on the pillow. It would give me pleasure to walk into his room and see him without all those pieces of metal sticking out, even if there were some scars from the halo. That would be reason enough to celebrate.

The doctor suggested that we think about taking Gerry home for a visit. He said it might do him good to see familiar surroundings. If Gerry would like that, we'd do everything possible to make sure he had the opportunity. The doctor then talked about ordering some equipment, such as a wheelchair and a special chair for the bathroom. I was glad that Gerry was present at the staffing, so he could be part of all the decisions that had to be made.

After the meeting, Gerry rested for a bit before he went for physical therapy. Later, he had a steak for supper and did a much better job cutting it. He even allowed Ed and me to stay in the room while he ate. When he finished he said, "See, practice makes perfect."

"You were magnificent," I commented. Many friends stopped by that evening so Ed and I left earlier than usual. Gerry looked tired, but he was definitely enjoying the company.

It was July 1st, Bertie's fifteenth birthday, but we still thought of her as our baby. Joellyn and I took her out to lunch and then we went shopping for presents. She knew we weren't able to celebrate as we had in the past, and she was okay with that. "I'm happy the three of us can go out to lunch," she said. "It's fun just being together, like old times." I told her we'd make it all up to her on her sixteenth birthday. She laughed and said, "I'll remember that, Mom."

When we got to the hospital, Gerry was watching "Rocky III"

with some friends. I suspected he didn't want us hanging out with them, so we went to the lounge to visit until the movie was over. That was fine with the girls because we had a lot to talk about. We hadn't spent much time together recently. There was never a dull moment with them around.

The previous night, before we left for home, Gerry told me that it wasn't necessary for me to come to the hospital as early as I often did. He was thinking about me and all the hours I'd spent there, but I needed to be there. Knowing him, he was probably worrying about me getting sick. He did say that I looked tired. I wasn't eating as well as I should, which might have been part of the reason. I wondered if my being there most of the day was causing problems for him. I decided to wait a bit and then ask him about it. The next day was the Fourth of July.

The whole family spent the holiday with Gerry. I picked up some Italian food for our supper, and we really enjoyed being with each other. The day went by quickly, but before we left for home, Gerry asked me again not to come to the hospital so early. He said he needed more time for himself. I was glad he brought it up the second time because then I knew he was serious. I had no problem with that; I would adjust. He smiled and said, "Now you'll have more time to make macaroni and tuna salad for me."

"I'll make anything you want, Gerry; your wish is my command."

"That's good to know, Mom. You might be sorry you said that."

"I meant every word," I insisted. "Just try me."

I thought about him all the way home. I was feeling a little down because of what he said, but I knew in my heart where he was coming from. He was a young man going through a very difficult time in his life, and for whatever reason, he wanted more time to himself. Any mother should understand that, right? Then, why was I feeling so down?

It was hard staying away the next day, but Gerry did call and ask me to bring his tennis shoes when I came to the hospital. It was the first time he'd used the phone since he had been there. He said he held the phone in his hand and dialed the number by himself. I found it amazing how such a small thing like using the phone could mean so much, but that was what kept us going from one day to the next.

When we arrived at supper time, Gerry was playing the Atari game with one of the other patients. I had a feeling that he enjoyed the competition, but it also helped pass the time for him. As I gave him his tennis shoes, he asked me to get him a new pair, but not leather ones because they made his feet sweat too much. And he said that when his feet sweat, they didn't smell very nice. I told him I'd pick up some new ones the next day.

The next morning, my mom called and said that she wanted to see Gerry. She always has a difficult time looking at the halo screwed in his head. As we were approaching the hospital parking lot, she was all teary-eyed. I told her that it would be all right once she saw how well Gerry was doing. I also mentioned some of the things he had accomplished recently, such as feeding himself and using the phone. She was surprised that he was able to do so much that soon. "You have an amazing grandson, Mom."

"I know."

It was wonderful to see the look on Gerry's face when she walked into his room. He tried, as best he could, to put his arms around her. She began to get a little emotional, but then Gerry said, "How are you doing, Gram?"

She laughed, "Never mind about me, Gerry. How are you doing?"

"I'm doing okay," he said, smiling. Soon the tension was gone. They visited for a while and my mom seemed more relaxed as the time passed.

When I took Gerry's new tennis shoes out of the box, he asked me to put them on him. After I pulled on the first shoe, I could have sworn he put his foot back on the chair. When I mentioned this to him, he said he hadn't. "But I could feel your hands on my feet."

My mom got so excited that I thought she was going to jump out of her chair. "Does that mean he's going to walk again?" she asked.

"We don't know for sure what it means, Mom," I answered. "We're just happy that he can feel us touching him."

With a big smile, Gerry said, "One day at a time."

"That's right, Gerry," she said. "Take one day at a time and who knows what will happen? Remember, God is looking after you."

"I know He is, Gram. And I have faith that He will help me through this."

While we were at the hospital, fifteen family members and friends stopped by to visit. His sisters and brothers had been there almost every day since the accident, so he definitely knew how much he was loved by everyone. I had a very good feeling that they were going to prove the doctor wrong when he said his friends would stop coming.

On the way to the hospital that next afternoon, Ed and I decided to have a discussion with Gerry regarding his therapy, and the feeling that was returning to his legs. We needed to ask him more questions, so we'd know exactly what was taking place during the day. We wanted him to be getting the best treatment possible.

"Gerry, is someone exercising your legs daily?" I asked.

"My therapist is doing different leg exercises with me each day, except on the weekends."

"Are you noticing any changes?"

"Well, I've got some feeling in my back and stomach, and I've been able to move the muscle in my left hip. I've asked the therapist to get me some information on muscle contraction, so I can learn more about it. She said she would try to do that for me."

"It sounds like you're getting involved in the rehab process." Ed said. "That's good, Gerry. The more you learn about this, the better informed you'll be."

"I've also asked her if I could see the X-rays of my neck." I was surprised at how much initiative Gerry had taken to learn more about his injury, but I was especially proud of him for taking control of the situation.

We wanted to talk with Gerry about the importance of having a positive attitude during his recovery, but before we even brought it up, he told us, "I'm determined to fight all the way to the end."

I truly believed he meant every word. Just as we were finishing our talk, a friend stopped by with some grapes for Gerry. We had mentioned that he enjoyed eating grapes with his thumb and index finger, so this friend made a special trip to the hospital to deliver some. Gerry was most appreciative and thanked him with a big smile. It was amazing how people responded to him.

"Pioneer Days" snuck up on us. This celebration, held in our small town the week after July Fourth is a big deal for all the local people with special things planned for each night: "night on the town," a big dance, a parade and, of course, the fireworks. Gerry told his brothers and sisters that he might come home to see the fireworks, but later told them he was just joking. "I'm not ready to do that yet," he laughed.

When we arrived at the hospital, three friends were visiting with Gerry and he was in very good spirits. Later on his brothers and sisters came by, so Ed and I left early so they could have some private time together. The next day we found out they were afraid of being kicked out of the lounge because they were laughing so hard. I wasn't surprised because I knew how silly they could get when they told stories about each other. I was sure of one thing; everyone, including Gerry, had a good time. And, I was hoping the hospital staff wasn't upset with the noise.

On the weekend I talked with another doctor about Gerry's shower problems.

"Gerry was promised three showers a week, but hardly ever gets three. He would love a daily shower, but it appears to be out of the question. His toenails haven't been clipped in seven weeks, and it's beginning to create a problem. I'd appreciate it if you would look into this for us."

The doctor seemed very receptive and said that he would look into our concerns, and see that they were taken care of. I was hoping he'd follow through so I wouldn't have to deal with the problem again.

Ed and I took Gerry outside for a walk that evening, and he really enjoyed the fresh air. It had been five weeks since he breathed something other than the hospital mixture. I got a kick out of him trying to take deep breaths, as if he were storing it up for later. As he was enjoying all the different foliage around the building, he stopped for a minute saying, "I need to come outside more often; it's so refreshing compared to my room." We suggested that possibly someone from the hospital staff could take him outside during the day, and we'd take him in the evening. He thought that was a good idea. Would it make his weekends less boring? It was worth a try.

On Monday, it was very hot and we were surprised to find Gerry already in bed. He seemed a little down, but it may have been the heat. After supper, we played checkers. That was a mistake! He beat me badly both games and enjoyed every minute of it. Before long, friends started popping in: Jody, Mike, Boogie, John, Laurie and her parents, and the minister from church. They were just what Gerry needed.

After everyone left, Gerry told Ed and me that he could flex both muscles in his thighs. He had me feel underneath one of his legs as he flexed, and I could actually feel the muscle move. "The toes on my left foot hurt and, at times, it feels like there is pressure on them and they are moving around." I was getting more excited by the minute, but also a little nervous. We weren't sure what it all meant, but Gerry was enthusiastic.

I felt really good when we left the hospital, and prayed all the way home. Ed asked me why I was so quiet, and when I told him I was praying for Gerry, he smiled and didn't say another word. At home, we talked about the things that were happening to our son, and we reminded ourselves that we had to remain hopeful, yet cautious. We didn't want to set ourselves up for a big let down.

The next day brought good news and bad news. The good news was that Gerry had his toenails clipped for the first time in seven weeks; the bad news was that he didn't get a shower. To me, it seemed like such a small request unless, of course, they were understaffed. I knew Gerry was miserable when he didn't get his shower, so what happened next didn't surprise me.

"I don't feel so good today. I feel sort of light-headed. While I was sitting up, there were spots in front of my eyes. This place is boring!" Those were some of his remarks when I walked into his room. Things were not going to get much better and they didn't. Later some of his friends dropped in. If anyone could cheer him up, they could. I was right! A smile crossed his face and we took the hint. We said good night.

When I got to the hospital the following day, Gerry told me he had taken a shower. On that note, I gave him a high five and handed him the potato salad and strawberry shortcake that I had made. He loved having food from home; it made him feel connected to his family.

Gerry had many visitors again that evening. Our friends, whose son had injured his spinal cord, also came by. We were so glad to see them because it gave us an opportunity to talk about the things that both our sons had gone through. It was great therapy to share our feelings with people who had had a similar crisis in their own family.

Only a week remained before the two-month period was up. Gerry's doctor said that whatever sensation or movement he got back in two months would be all he could expect. I was scared. We talked to Gerry about transferring him to some other hospital, but he said he didn't want to be moved. I think he was afraid that something worse could happen if we had him transferred to another hospital. He'd have to be flown to wherever we decided to take him. I constantly worried whether we made the right decision to keep him at that hospital; it was something we'd never know for sure.

The following afternoon Ed and I had a good discussion with Gerry about his accident, and how tough it had been for everyone, but we assured him that we were coping. We promised him that we'd be at his side every day. He said he knew we would always be there for him, but he also said that he was worried about us. What a kid! He was the one whose life had changed dramatically, and he was concerned about his mom and dad. I put my arms around him and told him that we were doing fine, and not to worry about us. All three of us became emotional for a few minutes.

Later, when we regained our composure, Gerry told us that he had wet the bed while he was sleeping. He said he told Bonnie about it and she said it could be a good sign. I asked him if that was the first time it happened, and he admitted he had also wet the previous day just before the nurse used the catheter. I just reached for his hand and held it in mine.

Two of Gerry's cousins came to the hospital the next day to visit. Steve, my sister's son, lived in Illinois and had been injured in a car accident about two years before. He was paralyzed from the waist down. Greg, my brother's son, lived in Wisconsin and had become a good friend of Gerry's over the years. I was sure that Gerry was glad to see them both, but I worried about him seeing Steve in a wheelchair, thinking that he might end up the same way. Gerry's facial expression gave nothing away. We were closing in on the two-month period that the doctor said would predict his future, and I wondered how Gerry was dealing with it. The boys had a good visit and before leaving, they both wished Gerry the best of luck.

We walked outside with Steve and Greg as they left the hospital. Steve tried to impress us by doing a couple of "wheelies" down the sidewalk. "Stop!" I commanded. I wasn't ready for such a demonstration at that stage of Gerry's recovery. When I thought about it later I realized I was being too emotional about Steve's "wheelies." He had already accepted what had happened to him. I guess I was afraid to admit that Gerry might also have to accept what happened to him.

Back in Gerry's room, the nurse had taken his temperature; it was 102°. She said he had a few bugs in his urinary tract, and they were going to monitor him to make sure the condition didn't get any worse. He hadn't eaten much, so I decided to order a steak, rigatoni, salad, and garlic bread from the Italian restaurant, hoping it would entice his appetite. It worked! He ate most of it.

A few days later, one of the patients told me that she recently had a dream about Gerry, in which he was a walking quadriplegic. That patient also had suffered a spinal cord injury, and she was back in the hospital for some tests. She had been hit by a car just a few blocks from our house while riding her bicycle across the highway. She told me she had a feeling that some day Gerry would walk out of the hospital. I gave her a big hug and wished her the best. I felt so sad when I left her room, and I couldn't help but think of all the young people who have been seriously injured in accidents that could have been prevented. It was such a heartbreaking experience for the families who had to watch their loved ones suffer. Before I left the hospital that night, I asked God to help us through our difficult times. He would give us the strength we needed.

Gerry had an X-ray of his bowels the next day. It turned out okay, but they still put him on a course of antibiotics to bring his temperature down. He said he was keeping his urinal beside him because he continued to feel the urge to go. I wondered if that was good news, or if it meant nothing at all. When we asked his doctor about it, he said Gerry's urge to urinate could be caused by the infection. We remained cautious.

Gerry wasn't feeling very well when Ed and I got to the hospital the following afternoon. He hadn't used his wheelchair at all. We also found out that he had his therapy session in bed. All he had eaten that day was a few grapes and a bowl of chicken gumbo soup. My stomach ached. Things were going downhill fast. A few friends stopped by in the evening and Gerry asked me to tell them he wasn't up to visiting. I fought tears the entire time I was in his room. He didn't want to talk much, so Ed and I walked down to the lounge and sat for about an hour. When we got back to his room, he was asleep. We talked to one of the nurses and she told us that he hadn't had a very good day. She also said that if he didn't start eating soon, he was headed for big trouble. We sat there and waited for Gerry to wake up, but he didn't. We left for home. I was scared to death.

I was sickened the next afternoon when I got to his room and found out that Gerry hadn't eaten one thing that day. He told me he just didn't have an appetite. I immediately asked the nurse to get him some soup from the cafeteria. I told him that he was going to have to eat, or they would have to feed him through a tube. I think I scared him a little because he did eat most of the soup, and an apple. I began to wonder if I should be with him during meal times to make sure he ate. Maybe he just needed a little encouragement from a family member. I was willing to do whatever it took to get him to eat: cooking at home, or getting some of his favorite dishes from the Italian restaurant.

Once again, Gerry wasn't up to having visitors that night. His two brothers, Jim and Mike, came by but they didn't stay long because it was evident that Gerry wasn't feeling well. Ed and I left about 9:00;

Gerry told us that he wanted to go to sleep. I was very worried, and I knew there would be a lot of prayers before I went to bed.

The following day, I made some chicken soup to bring to Gerry for lunch. My mom had told me many times that chicken soup would cure almost anything. After he ate most of the soup, I asked him what else he had eaten that day and he mentioned grapes for breakfast. It wasn't much food over a four-hour period, but better than nothing. He hadn't had his therapy session because he was too sick, and felt weak. No words came out of my mouth. I just stood at the side of his bed, tears flooding my eyes and feeling more scared than ever before. The doctor told us that whatever he got back in two months would be all we could expect. The next day would mark the two-month deadline, and Gerry hadn't regained any movement in his legs. I suddenly wondered if that was the reason he had stopped eating, and subsequently lost his will to go on. Just as I started to fall apart, Ed walked in and immediately realized what was about to happen. He wrapped his arms around me and quietly asked if I would get him some coffee. I left the room and walked down the hallway to the elevators. I don't remember which button I pressed, but it was the wrong one because I didn't make it to the cafeteria floor. I desperately wanted answers, but there weren't any. How was I going to make it through the next several months? Only one answer came to mind . . . God. I would turn to Him for guidance.

Chapter Six

July 22nd came and went. The two-month period was up, but what did that actually mean for Gerry? I didn't believe the doctor could specify that exactly two months from the time of his accident, all recovery would come to a halt. That made no sense to me. I made the decision not to think about it anymore. Doctors couldn't possibly know everything that goes on inside a person's body; and the tests they run aren't always conclusive. I had a lot of faith that Gerry would recover from his injury, and I wasn't going to let some deadline the doctor gave him change that.

For the next several days I monitored Gerry's eating habits. He did all right at breakfast time, usually eating a bowl of cereal and sometimes a sweet roll. He often didn't eat any lunch at all, or maybe just a bowl of soup. He picked at his supper a few nights and when I asked him why he wasn't eating, he said he still didn't have much of an appetite. He complained of a sore throat. How much longer could this last without the development of a serious problem? I asked if he'd like me to bring some more food from home or from his favorite restaurant, and he said he'd let me know when he wanted me to do that. I couldn't force-feed him, so I had to be patient.

When I got to the hospital the next day, Gerry gave us some good news. He had eaten cereal for breakfast, chicken and vegetables for lunch, and steak, potatoes, and broccoli for supper. He said his appetite was slowly coming back and he was starting to feel better. I was thrilled to see him up in his wheelchair. Before we left, he asked me to bring him some fries and a milkshake for lunch the next day.

Joellyn walked into Gerry's room at lunch time with a box of French fries in one hand and a milkshake in the other. As she put the goodies on his tray table, his face said it all: he was smiling from ear to ear. He didn't have a problem putting each fry between his thumb and index finger and into his mouth, then washing them down with a slurp of the milkshake. We enjoyed watching him eat the last French fry in the bag; Joellyn and I kept grinning at each other. The next day he was having an IVP test to see how his kidneys were functioning. That meant a low-residue lunch and a liquid supper. Gerry smiled and asked, "How much fun is that?" I promised I would pick up Italian food the following day, so he would have something special to look forward to. He asked for a salad, an order of rigatoni, and a loaf of garlic bread.

I was becoming well-known at the Italian restaurant. "Is this for Gerry?" they'd ask. I'd nod and they'd ask, "How's he doing?" As I left, I'd hear, "Give him our best." They were very accommodating and we were appreciative the many months we were at the hospital with our son.

Gerry's appetite was better each day. When Joellyn, Bertie, and I arrived at the hospital that afternoon, we were told Gerry had gone to the rehab picnic. I was excited because I knew he wouldn't have gone if he hadn't felt up to it. We went to the lounge to wait, a place I enjoyed because it was always bright and cheerful. I also got to meet and talk with others who had a loved one in the hospital. As we walked in that day, I noticed a woman sitting by herself, staring out the window. She looked very sad so I went over to her and made a comment about the beautiful day.

"There are no more beautiful days," she said. "My son is a patient here."

"Oh, I'm sorry to hear that. I have a son here, too. He was injured while wrestling with a friend."

"Do you ever say to yourself, why me?" she asked.

She caught me off guard, and at first, I didn't know how to react. But, then I said, "No, I try not to ask myself that question."

"I ask myself that question all the time," she quickly responded. "My son was in a car accident because someone was driving under the influence of alcohol, and he's going to have to be here for weeks."

"I'll keep him in my prayers," I whispered, as I touched her hand with mine.

All of a sudden, the tears fell down her face. She was very upset and needed someone to talk to. "Would you like to have lunch some day?" I asked. "Maybe we could share our feelings with each other."

"Yes, I would like that."

"I will look for you in the lounge."

"Thanks, I'll see you soon."

Shortly after, Gerry returned from the rehab picnic. He was in a great mood and said that he had eaten a bratwurst, taco salad, and some watermelon. He also mentioned how much he enjoyed being outside and was looking forward to the next picnic. He was feeling a lot better because his appetite was back. For supper, he had chicken Kiev, a baked potato, and some vegetables; a grand total of 1,700 calories. Later that evening he wanted pizza. As we left to pick it up, he also asked us to try and find him a rubber snake.

"Why the rubber snake?"

He just smiled. I had a feeling it was going to involve one of the therapists. "Oh, well! I can't watch over you every minute, Gerry. You are an adult."

"That's right, Mom," he answered with a grin. "I am in charge while I'm here."

"I can't imagine what you're planning to do with that snake," I said. "But be careful. Some people are deathly afraid of snakes, your mother for one."

"You worry too much," he insisted. "It's all in a day's fun."

Gerry's doctor stopped by the next day and told him he was scheduled for an X-ray the beginning of the twelfth week, because he wanted to check everything out before removing his halo. Once that happened the doctor said we should be able to take him home for a day. I was excited, but a bit nervous as well. I was concerned about Ed being able to handle him. Our son, Mike, was also going to be there to help. Somehow we'd work it all out.

A mirror had been attached to Gerry's wheelchair. Gerry wanted to see who was approaching him from behind while riding the hallways. He was suspicious of the nurses playing tricks on him, and he wanted to make sure no one sneaked up on him. They had been doing all kinds of stuff to each other. He was as guilty as they were, and enjoying it.

Gerry's appetite was still strong; he had cereal for breakfast, pizza for lunch, and rigatoni for supper. He also munched on peanut butter cookies and grapes. I was thrilled when I heard how much he had eaten. And, that wasn't all the good news; the showers were becoming more regular and we were most grateful because we knew how much it meant to our son.

The next day, he skipped breakfast, but ate some stew for lunch. Pork chops and au gratin potatoes were on the menu for supper. When the tray arrived, Gerry ate everything. "It's not as good as your cooking, Dad," he said, "but it's not bad for hospital food."

"I know," Ed answered with a grin, "I'm the best cook in our house." He was waiting for my rebuttal, but I fooled him.

"We all agree on that subject," I said. "You definitely are the best!" Ed loved to cook, and definitely had the knack for it. On Sundays, the kids always asked, "What's on the menu today, Dad?" He wasn't a fancy cook, but he enjoyed making the good old pot roasts surrounded with vegetables, roasted chicken with mashed potatoes, or a baked ham dinner with all the trimmings. When Ed cooked, we couldn't wait to sit down at the table.

Ed and Gerry continued their conversation about the hospital food, so I took a walk down the hall and ran into Bonnie. She told me that Gerry hadn't felt the sensation to urinate lately because he'd been a little dehydrated, but the sensation to urinate was still a good sign. She also said that he had more control of his bladder than he had before.

As we continued, Bonnie told me that Gerry's emotions had been changing. "He's been letting the food sit on his tray for an hour before he begins to eat. We expected that from him early on, but he's suddenly beginning to take charge."

"I'm not sure what you mean by that?"

"I think it's good news because he's starting to take more control of his emotions."

"Has Gerry ever mentioned that he can flex his muscles behind his thighs?"

"Yes, and he even asked me to put my hand underneath his thigh so I could feel it move. I've tickled his feet at times and he could feel that." Gerry really liked Bonnie and felt very comfortable around her. I felt the same way.

She must be one of the angels God had chosen to become a nurse, because she always tried to keep our spirits up. I shared her comments with Ed on the way home that night. How thankful we were that she was working on rehab the day Gerry was transferred there.

The next day at the hospital, we had to wait to see Gerry because he was having a shower. When he came out and saw Ed and me sitting there, he gave us a big smile, "Boy, that sure felt good! I love when that water splashes all over my body."

Ed and I laughed and gave him a high five. "We brought you some supper," I said. "Your dad made Swiss steak, noodles, and carrots for you because we know how much you miss his cooking."

"You have no idea," said Gerry. "Thanks a lot, Dad."

We sat there and watched him enjoy every bite on his plate. And, I thought to myself, "If only everything was this easy."

As we drove into our yard, I noticed a small black poodle sitting by the back steps. I could have sworn it was our dog; it looked exactly like him. He had little white spots on his front paws just like Reecy. I reached down to pick him up and, much to my surprise, he didn't even squeal. He licked my hand so I took him inside and gave him some water. He finished every drop in the bowl. We didn't have any dog food, so Ed gave him a piece of leftover chicken. He ate it quickly and then looked up at him for more. It felt so strange; it was almost like Reecy had come back home. We played with him for about twenty minutes unsure about what more we could do. It was rather late so we decided to wait until morning to see if someone reported a missing poodle. He slept on the floor in our bedroom, and we didn't hear a sound during the night. He must have been exhausted. I knew just how he felt.

The next morning I called the local police and found out someone had reported that a black poodle named Joey was missing. The owner and his ten-year old son came by to pick up the dog and thanked me for taking such good care of him. I told them about our dog, and how much Joey and Reecy looked alike. I was glad he had chosen our house to stop and rest for a while, because it brought back some very happy memories for me. The girls believed Joey's visit was some kind of sign, telling us that we should get another poodle. I told them they were mistaken, at least for the time being.

Bertie and I got to the hospital about 5:00, and when we arrived, Gerry recounted his food intake for that day. He didn't feel too good after he finished eating. "Could it have been the three tacos?" I asked. "Maybe, you shouldn't have eaten that many."

"You're probably right, Mom. But they tasted so good."

"Maybe the hot spice didn't agree with you," I said. "Should I ask the nurse for something to soothe your stomach?"

"No, I'd rather have a piece of chocolate."

"Now, I get it," I teased. "You're just looking for sympathy so she'll find you some chocolate."

"Are you picking on me?" he asked. I was beginning to think Gerry had some of the nurses wrapped around his little finger. But that didn't concern me. I wanted him to have all the tender loving care he could get.

Gerry was having lots of spasms in his legs and feet, but he didn't seem overly concerned about it. It probably happened regularly and he'd just gotten used to it. I asked him if he could still flex the muscles behind his thighs, and he told Bertie and me to watch him do it. I was amazed at his concentration.

We also talked about how important a positive attitude was for his recovery. He assured me that he felt the same way. "Don't worry, Mom. I'm not giving up." I was very happy to hear those words.

Gerry wanted to get into bed to watch "Foxfire" on HBO, so we called for the nurse. After she helped him get comfortable, he asked her if she could find some chocolate for him. She smiled. "I just might be able to do that, Gerry."

"Way to go, Ger," Bertie said as we said good night and headed for the door. We continued to laugh about it all the way to the parking lot. It was true: Gerry had a couple of those nurses around his little finger.

The next morning I called the Spinal Cord Injury National Organization to ask some questions about Gerry. The phone doctor thought the return of some of Gerry's functions was a good sign. He said we had to be patient because it was difficult to diagnose when and if function would return. That was something I'd learned; none of the doctors knew anything for sure. They had said to us time and time again, "We don't know; we have to wait and see."

At the hospital, Gerry was in the hallway laughing with one of the therapists. When I asked her what was so funny, she told me that Gerry had attacked her with his water gun. I made it clear that I wasn't taking any responsibility for the water gun, or his behavior. She laughed, "Don't worry, I will get my turn." Gerry was in a very good mood. It was obvious he was beginning to feel at ease with the staff, and was enjoying the pranks they continued to play on each other.

Gerry had quite a few muscle spasms while I was talking to him, so I asked him about them. He said that was normal for his type of injury, and that the doctor had started him on muscle relaxers to help lessen the frequency of the spasms. He wanted to go back to bed for a while because his neck was a little sore. With all the metal around his head and neck, it was no wonder. I tried to imagine what it must be like, but I couldn't even begin to know. We were all looking forward to the day the halo would be removed. Hopefully, it would rid him of the pain in his head and neck.

The next afternoon I surprised Gerry with one of his favorite desserts, a piece of homemade blueberry pie. His face lit up as I walked into his room. His appetite had been improving daily, and I was joyful when he asked me to get him steak and rigatoni from the Italian restaurant for dinner. For some reason, he seemed to be especially hungry that day and kept craving all kinds of food. That was just what I wanted to hear.

While Gerry was visiting with some friends, I walked to the lounge to relax for a few minutes. The woman whom I had invited to lunch was sitting by herself reading a magazine. I stopped and asked her how she was doing. She said she was doing a little better, but was still having a difficult time with her son's accident. I asked her about meeting for lunch that next day, but she had family coming into town. She thanked me and went back to her magazine. I had an inkling she wasn't ready to share her feelings with someone she had just met, and I was okay with that. I told her I'd be around if she wanted to talk.

The next day was Saturday, and Gerry hadn't had a shower since Wednesday. I washed him up because they hadn't even given him a bed bath. Gerry said he kept asking about a shower, but it didn't do any good. Nobody came to get him. I was upset, but there wasn't a doctor around to talk with because of the weekend. However, I did talk to one of the nurses and she apologized. She told me to talk to the doctor on Monday. Something had to be done soon. Should we offer to give Gerry a shower ourselves? Or should we contact the hospital administrator? I decided to sleep on it.

Early Sunday morning, I called the hospital and suggested that Ed come down to help someone give Gerry a shower. I was told by the head nurse on rehab that it wasn't necessary for Ed to be there, and that they would make sure he got a shower before noon. I couldn't wait to get to the hospital to see if they had done what they had promised.

It was about 1:15 when Ed, Bertie, and I got to Gerry's room. We knew immediately that he had had a shower because he was smiling from ear to ear. "Did they wash you up good, Gerry?" asked Bertie.

"Every inch of my body."

"Did they have to use a scrub brush to get the dirt off?" she joked.

"They had to use some spot remover with an extra firm brush," he said with a smirk on his face.

"I get the picture!" said Bertie.

"All right, you two," I said, "I think we all get the picture. What else is new, Ger?"

"Well, let me see," he said. "I missed breakfast this morning because I was up until 3:00 A.M. watching HBO, but I did eat lunch."

"It must have been a terrific movie," I said, "By the way, what did you eat for lunch?" I wanted to make sure he had eaten to make up for skipping breakfast.

"Chicken casserole, carrots, and some watermelon," he said. "It tasted really good."

"I'm sure it did," I said. "Especially since you weren't around for breakfast."

"Don't worry about me, Mom," he whispered. "You can always pick me up a steak tonight." He knew that I'd drive across town to get him whatever he wanted.

Later, we had a serious discussion with Gerry about the medication he was taking for the spasms in his legs. We were concerned about the side effects, so I asked the RN on duty about the medication. She offered to have one of the doctors call us. When the call came, the doctor said there were some side effects, but he didn't think they were a problem for Gerry. After the phone call we still didn't know what to do, so we decided to wait until we were able to talk to someone from the SCI National Foundation. Gerry was asleep by 7:30.

That next afternoon, an X-ray was taken of Gerry's neck, but the results were not in. The physical therapist had talked with him about trying to move his legs in bed, and she was going to try him on the mat, working his leg muscles to see what he could do. I began to wonder if she thought there was still a chance he might get some movement back. I was surprised when Gerry asked me if I had talked to the physical therapists about what they were doing. When I told him I hadn't, he felt better knowing that they were the ones who had initiated it. In fact, he was excited about it.

I finally talked to someone from SCI about the medication Gerry was taking for his spasms. The person told me he thought Gerry would be better off without the pills, but said that was his own personal opinion, and not a medical one. He was not a medical doctor. I quickly realized that if I was going to contact that organization, I needed to start asking more questions. There was so much to learn.

I was elated when Gerry called the next morning to say that the halo was scheduled to come off on Friday. It was Tuesday, so he had only three more days to wait. He also said he wasn't going to have a collar as he had thought, because the physical therapist had done a muscle evaluation and his muscles were in good shape.

When Ed and I got to the hospital, Gerry wasn't feeling the best;

he was nauseated. He fell asleep and woke up an hour later, feeling a little better. I asked him about his physical therapy session and he told me they stretched his legs, but they hadn't worked his leg muscles in the manner he had hoped. He was disappointed, but didn't question the therapist about it. I wish she hadn't told him about working his leg muscles, instead of getting his hopes up and then not following through. I wanted to talk to her about it, but I knew it would upset Gerry. He liked to handle those things by himself.

Several friends came by to see Gerry that evening, but he wasn't up to company. The recreational therapist also stopped in, but he didn't want to talk with her either. She then asked to talk to me, and we did visit for a short time. I mentioned that SCI had recommended swimming exercises for Gerry once the halo came off and his neck was stabilized. She indicated that he'd be unable to have the exercises more than once a week because he'd have to go to the University. I told her once a week would be better than not at all, but her response suggested that it probably wasn't going to happen.

I was feeling blue that night after we left the hospital. On the way home, Ed asked if there was anything wrong, and I couldn't even answer him. He put his hand on mine and said so calmly, "We're going to get through this, I promise." I looked at him wondering how I would ever have survived this ordeal without him. As we continued the drive home I closed my eyes and started to relax, when suddenly, the car came to a stop. Ed had stopped at our favorite dinner spot. He smiled at me. "How about going inside for a bite to eat? It might be good for both of us." At first, I hesitated, but he was right; it was just what I needed.

The next afternoon there was a big surprise waiting for me when I got to the hospital. I was met in the hallway by the psychologist, who told me that Gerry had had the halo and vest removed. He wasn't supposed to have it taken off until Friday, so I was totally shocked. I couldn't wait to see him. When I entered his room he looked like a different person. Those metal pieces were no longer growing out of his head. His face was bright and cheery. He was happy. I asked him how he'd like to celebrate, and he suggested his usual steak supper. I ordered it right away. I couldn't wait for Ed and the kids to see the new kid in town!

When I returned from the restaurant with Gerry's supper, I met one of the RNs in the hallway. She told me that the X-ray showed his neck hadn't fused as the neurologist first thought it had. Evidently, the doctor had tried to reach me to let me know that he would be performing surgery on Gerry that next week. He would take a piece of bone from Gerry's hip and fuse it in the neck area.

I couldn't believe my ears! Surgery, after all this time. I was scared to death wishing Ed was there with me. I was also worried sick about Gerry. What must he be thinking? I hurried down to his room. He was devastated. He immediately asked me if I had heard the news. I tried to appear upbeat, but I was sure Gerry could tell that I wasn't very happy with what we had just learned. I knew Ed and the kids were going to be thrilled to see Gerry without his halo, but we also had to tell them the news about the surgery. We had another hurdle to get through. Thank God we had each other.

All four kids came by to see Gerry that night, but they were very positive about the surgery. They convinced him that everything would turn out all right. I was so proud of them. For some reason, young people manage to handle a crisis better than adults do; they seem to know just the right things to say. I was so thankful they were all there; he really needed their support with that latest bombshell.

Gerry was worried about the surgery because he thought it might set him back with his therapy. He didn't want anything to disrupt the progress he had made so far. I told him we'd obtain a second opinion. He was all for doing that. I left a message with a doctor in Pittsburgh, who had been recommended by SCI.

Two of Gerry's friends stopped by to see him and before they went into his room, I told them about the surgery. I wished I hadn't. I didn't realize Gerry would be upset; he wanted to be the one to tell them. I felt terrible. Sometimes it was hard being a mother. When Rob came by later that day, I was glad that Gerry got to tell him all about the neck fusion.

While they were visiting, I went to the cafeteria for a sandwich and thought about my son and all that was ahead of him. While I was sitting there, Ed walked in. I was so glad to see him. We talked a little about the upcoming surgery, and then headed back to Gerry's room with a salad and a beef roll, just in case he was hungry. He wasn't.

As soon as I got off the elevator the following day, the nurse at the desk on rehab told me a doctor from Pittsburgh had called for me. I was disappointed that I had missed his call, but she said he was going to call again.

Gerry's supper tray arrived just as I entered his room. He told me to "cover it, I don't want anything to eat." He was depressed about his neck not fusing the way it was supposed to. I kept trying to think of something to say, but the words just wouldn't come. Gerry knew I was on the verge of tears, so he told me that he had to wear a four-poster collar for six to eight weeks after his surgery, which meant until the end of September. That broke the ice, and I was able to ask him some questions about the collar. He answered as much as he could and then turned and looked out the window. I told him I'd let him rest for a while. Later, when I got back to his room, Gerry and his dad were having one of their good old chats. Joellyn and Jim also came by to visit and it was good for Gerry to have some time alone with them. If anyone could get him in a better mood, it was his brothers and sisters. Ed and I said good night and left for home.

According to Joellyn, Gerry's mood did improve after we left. He even ate some of Joellyn's macaroni salad, potato chips, and a pickle. She said it was her salad that did it. I told her I didn't care what it was as long as it worked. She offered to show me how to make the salad her way; she loved to tease.

Shortly after I arrived at the hospital the next day, I got the call from the doctor in Pittsburgh. He thought the neck fusion was the best way to go. I was so happy that he called, and I couldn't wait to tell Gerry. I hurried down to his room and gave him the good news. He seemed to feel much better about the surgery now that he had a second opinion, and so did I.

Walking into Gerry's room and seeing him without the halo was still surprising; it was the image I saw for almost two months. I loved looking at his head even though there were some scars from the screws used to keep the halo in place. It was a much easier picture to see. Gerry was going to have a shower the next day, and he couldn't wait to get his hair washed. He reminded me how he hated greasy hair, and said it'd be a real treat if he could have it washed every day. I offered to wash it right away, but he said he'd hang in there for one more day.

Sunday came and went quickly; Gerry got his shower and enjoyed it very much. When Ed and I got to the hospital, he told us about his dream and how the water kept falling on him, and how it wouldn't stop even when the shower was turned off. He said he had turned the handle to the "off" position, but it just wouldn't work. Finally, he called for the nurse and when she couldn't get it to work, she ran to get help. When they returned, Gerry said he was sitting there laughing hysterically, because he had just had the longest shower of his life, and was loving every minute of it. Ed and I got a big kick out of Gerry's dream.

We asked him what he would do if that actually happened to him. He said he would do just what he did in his dream–laugh.

Gerry was scheduled for his surgery the next morning at 8:00. That night I prayed to God that everything would turn out all right.

Chapter Seven

Gerry's neck fusion was scheduled for 8:00 A.M., but they came for him at 6:45 to prepare him for the surgery. By 11:00 he was in the recovery room, and at 1:30 he was in his new room on the sixth floor. The neurosurgeon said he removed a piece of bone from Gerry's right hip which he used to fuse his neck. His neck was very unstable so he put a four-poster collar on him; he had to wear it for four months. It was obvious that Gerry was in a lot of pain after the surgery.

An interesting incident happened the day before. Ed had already left the hospital when he received a phone call at work saying he had to pay for the collar right away. He was shocked, but he drove back to the hospital and took care of it. We had had no knowledge of the pre-payment, and I wondered what might have happened if a patient wasn't able to come up with the money. Would they have canceled the surgery, or postponed it until it was paid for? I was glad we didn't have to find out.

I had a hard time sleeping that night. I'd doze for about an hour and then I'd wake up thinking about Gerry, especially the pain he had suffered between the first days of his accident to his latest surgery. I didn't want to see him go through anything more. I couldn't stand to see my son hurting, but there wasn't much I could do to make things better. I felt so helpless. I must have finally fallen asleep because when the alarm went off, I nudged Ed telling him to get the phone. He got out of bed pretending to answer the phone and then said it was for me. I took one look at his face and I knew it was time to get up. I couldn't wait to get to the hospital to see if Gerry had any problems through the night.

As I walked into his room, I found Gerry asleep so I decided to journal. (The rehab doctor had suggested that I keep a journal while at the hospital and write in it each day.) But the notebook was nowhere to be found. I kept the notebook on the floor of Gerry's closet, hidden under some of his clothes. When he was transferred from rehab to the sixth floor, someone had moved his belongings, but for some reason, my journal didn't make it. I went back to the rehab floor and looked everywhere. I inquired at the nurses' station, but they hadn't seen it and knew nothing about it. I was very upset because my writings of two and one-half months had just disappeared. Besides, most of the writing was very personal.

The next day I got to the hospital early. Gerry was sleeping so I went back to rehab and talked to a male LPN about my journal. He suggested we take another look in Gerry's room. I was amazed when I saw it lying on top of the desk. I thanked him for helping me out and went back to the sixth floor feeling extremely happy. But how did it get there? Had someone been reading it?

Gerry's nurse told me he'd had a pretty good night, but he did have a shot for pain around 4:00 A.M. He was a little nauseated, so she sat with him, trying to cool him down until he fell back to sleep. I stood there staring at him. How sad he looked. A lump formed in my throat and my eyes filled with tears. I was glad Gerry was sleeping. Once in a while he'd open his eyes and look at me, but then he'd doze off. I wanted to hold him in my arms.

The surgeon came by in the morning and removed the IV. He asked him to drink something because he wanted to see him swallow. He did quite well. Gerry told him that it hurt a lot. The doctor then checked Gerry's back and found a red sore on each side of his hips. He said he wasn't happy about that happening in one day, but the nurse told him he had those sores when he came down from rehab. The doctor wanted him turned every hour instead of every two hours as they had been doing. He also told us that neck fusion surgery was quite common, but it didn't always solve the problem. He said if it didn't work, he would perform a fusion from the back of the neck. I thought, "How much more can he take? Is there no end to this?" As soon as the doctor left, Gerry said he wouldn't even think of having the surgery again; he said he'd learn to live with the pain. He appeared extremely discouraged. "Forget about what the doctor said, Gerry," I whispered.

"We have plenty of time to worry about that later."

There was a bright side that morning. Three of the therapists from rehab came by to see Gerry. One of them even managed to get him to smile at something she said. They seemed to know just the right thing to say to their patient, and Gerry was pleased they stopped by.

When Ed and I got to the hospital the next day, we were surprised to find Gerry back in his old room on rehab. He also had a new roommate, but we couldn't see who it was because the curtain was pulled between the two beds. All of a sudden, I smelled smoke. A cigarette. I walked around the curtain and nicely asked the woman standing there not to smoke in the room. I told her that Gerry shouldn't be inhaling any smoke because he had a sore throat. Gerry was perturbed with me. I tried to explain my concern about him breathing in smoke, and that he had complained of a tickle in his throat. He whispered that he didn't want to upset anyone, or make any enemies while he was in the hospital. I shouldn't have been surprised by his reaction. That was Gerry; he always thought about the other person before himself. Later, I apologized and tried to explain my actions to Gerry's roommate. He told me not to worry about it because the smoke bothered him as well.

His sisters and brothers came by to see him that night, but Gerry wasn't up to much conversation. We all sat and visited with each other while Gerry watched television. Three girls from his graduating class had stopped by. They didn't stay long because he told them he wasn't feeling very well. Since he sent his friends away, I knew he wasn't up to having anyone stick around. We called it a night.

What a difference a day makes! Gerry was in a much better mood when we arrived the following afternoon. He had eaten a good meal: mashed potatoes, applesauce and a milkshake. He had also had a shower, and said that he'd be getting one on a regular basis. I took a chance and tickled his foot while he was on the bed and his toes moved. In fact, they moved a lot. He didn't get upset with me as he had in the past; he just looked at me and smiled.

That evening all the kids came by to see Gerry, so Ed and I went to the lounge to give them some time to spend together. As we walked in, one of the male patients looked straight at us and said, "Hello boys." We responded with a smile and sat down on the couch.

Ed nudged me. "It must be that short haircut you just got," he whispered. He was trying to keep from grinning.

"If you say another word," I murmured, "you're in big trouble! And, wipe that grin off your face."

"I can't wait to tell Gerry and the kids," he said.

"Be my guest," I answered. "They'll love it!" I was actually amused by his comment and the lightness of the moment.

When we got back to Gerry's room, Ed told the kids about the incident in the lounge. They had a good laugh, but assured me that I still looked like a mom to them. I said thank you and told them how much I appreciated their support. I then reminded Ed that he owed me a steak dinner very soon because he had way too much fun at my expense. The girls agreed saying, "Go get him, Mom." Gerry looked my way giving me one of his beautiful smiles, which I hadn't seen in quite some time. That smile made it all worthwhile.

On the way to the hospital, the next day I picked up another red rose for Gerry so he'd have a fresh one on his table at all times. He was watching a football game when I arrived, so I asked him if he'd mind if I went out for dinner with my friend, Ruth, who had just gotten into town. He told me to go ahead because the game would be on for at least another hour. When we got back Gerry suggested that we go to the lounge to visit. Ruth played the piano and he was hoping she might play for the patients and visitors. The lounge had one entire wall of windows looking out over the city. People often come in to stand in front of those panes of glass, staring out; I was one of them. Ruth headed directly toward the piano. Everyone stopped talking immediately and their eyes focused on her. When she started to sing, one patient, who was blind, moved his head and shoulders in time with the music. She entertained with several songs from long ago. After her last song, everyone clapped and told her how much they enjoyed the music. It was probably the most fun they'd had in a long time. If only she lived closer.

When we got back to the room Ed, Jim, and Mike were there, but Gerry wanted to get into bed because he wasn't feeling the best. I asked the nurse to take his temperature: 99.8°. I hoped he didn't have an infection. Shortly afterward, he fell asleep. On the way home, I thought about Ruth and how much the patients enjoyed her music. It was a real eye-opener to see what one person could accomplish by offering her talents.

Gerry's temperature was 102° when we got to the hospital the next day. A urinary tract infection was one more thing to worry about. Evidently, this type of infection was common in spinal cord injuries.

His new roommate had previously broken his back in a logging accident and was paralyzed from the waist down. He was in the hospital for some skin grafting to relieve a pressure point in his body. He was the fourth patient with spinal cord injury since we'd been there. I hadn't realized how common it was, even though our little town had two such injuries before Gerry's.

Later, I talked with one of the nurses about Gerry's infection. She told me he had been weighed that morning and showed a loss of twenty-five pounds since his accident. They were seriously concerned with his loss of appetite. I immediately headed for Gerry's room to talk with him about the weight loss. I asked him what he had eaten so far that day, and he said French toast for breakfast; yogurt, minestrone soup, and pudding for supper. When I asked him about lunch, he said he didn't have anything. I told him that had to change soon or he was headed for big trouble. "Oh, you must have heard that I lost a few pounds."

"Not just a few pounds, Gerry," I insisted. "You've lost twenty-five pounds, and I'm very worried about you." Just then Ed walked in the door.

"Twenty-five pounds!" said Ed. "That's too much, Gerry."

"I just don't have an appetite," Gerry said, softly.

"Well, we are going to do something about that," I answered. "If you are going to gain that weight back, you have to eat!"

"Will you eat if I make some of your favorite foods?" asked Ed.

"Probably. But, I don't want you to have to keep doing that."

"We'll do whatever it takes," I blurted.

"I'll really try hard to eat more," Gerry said, looking at us, sadly. I quickly suggested a pizza, and he said that sounded good. He could only eat three pieces, but at least he ate. Rob stopped by but didn't stay long because Gerry wasn't up to visiting. I wondered what he thought seeing Gerry in such an unhappy state. I could only imagine. I was sure a lot went through his mind as he left the hospital that evening.

It was Monday, August 22nd! Three months had passed since Gerry's accident. When I got to the hospital his temperature was 99.6°, down somewhat from the day before. I was glad I had brought him some homemade chicken soup, because one of the nurses told me that he hadn't eaten any breakfast. I stuck around to see how he'd do at supper time and, much to my surprise, he ate a slice of ham, potato salad, tossed salad and three orange slices. I was overjoyed!

Ed was at a Lion's Club meeting that night so I had time alone with Gerry. I talked to him again about his eating habits, and told him that it played a major role in his recovery. I only hoped that he was paying attention to what I was trying to get across. The nurse came by at 7:30 to take his temperature and it was back up to 101.6°. She suggested putting a cooling blanket on him, but Gerry asked her to try a fan first. It worked. Within thirty minutes, his temperature was down to 100°.

Gerry was depressed in the evening because when a friend stopped by, he asked me to tell him he wasn't feeling good. I was beginning to think we had something else to worry about. Earlier, I talked to one of the physical therapists and she'd had a discussion with Gerry about coming home for a day. She said he thought it might be too hard on us. I told her it wouldn't be a problem because his brothers and sisters would help out. She felt it might be just what he needed, and suggested we talk with him about it.

That evening, I told Gerry about my visit with the therapist. I told him I agreed with her about his coming home for a day. I made sure he knew that it wouldn't be a problem for us and reminded him that he'd get to enjoy some of his Dad's home cooking. He smiled and said he'd like that. As I was getting ready to leave, he asked me to get him a bag of sour cream and onion potato chips. When I got back to his room, he was sleeping like a baby. I put the chips on his tray table and leaned over to kiss him on the forehead. He opened his eyes and thanked me, saying he'd eat them later. I said good night and left for home.

On my way back I stopped at church, a block from our house. I didn't expect to see anyone at that hour, but one other person knelt two rows ahead of me. Even though it was dark, and the church was dimly lit, I could admire the beautiful stained glass windows that lined each side. I'd been a member of that church for fifteen years, but it had never looked as beautiful as it did that night. I felt calm and peaceful.

As I started to say a prayer for Gerry, I felt something move near my leg. It was a little white kitten. I reached down to put my hand on its head, but it disappeared under the pews. I noticed the woman in front of me looking down toward the floor and smiling. The kitten had paid her a visit, too. Before long, a young girl walked down the aisle, stopped and asked me if I had seen a white kitten. I told her the kitten had come by, but had moved on to the woman sitting in front of me. She said she was playing with it outside when it darted across the street and up the steps of the church. When a man opened the door to go inside, she saw the kitten slip past him. While we were looking around to see if we could spot it, it came running up the aisle and into the arms of the young girl. She had a big smile on her face as she walked toward the back of the church. Once again, I began the prayer I had started earlier. Then I went to the front of the church to light a candle for Gerry. As I knelt at the altar, I could feel God's presence all around me. My heart beat faster and I heard, "Have faith in me, and I will guide you." It was a moment I will never forget.

Ed was home when I got there. He didn't think a home visit for Gerry would be a problem. "It will be good for all of us." We also talked about Gerry's depression, and his loss of appetite. Ed reminded me that the doctor had mentioned the probability of depression early on, that it was something that Gerry would have to deal with. I suggested we ask Gerry if he'd be interested in talking with a psychologist, and Ed thought it was a good idea. I went to bed with a lot of "stuff" on my mind, but soon after my head hit the pillow, I was gone.

The beginning of a new school year was only a week away. The summer had zoomed by. In fact, I couldn't remember anything at all about the month of June; it was a total blank. July was different because we had family and friends from out of town come to visit which kept us busy. Now it was already the third week of August, and summer was hardly a memory.

I asked the girls if they'd come and help me at school that morning, because there was a lot to get done if the library was to open on the first day. They agreed, and we spent the entire morning getting ready for students and teachers. They unpacked some new books, typed library cards, and organized the shelves. We had a good time working together and it gave us a chance to talk about their plans for the fall.

After treating them to lunch for all their hard work, we headed straight to the hospital. Gerry had an egg, toast, and fruit for breakfast, and beef barley soup with cherry pie for lunch. He didn't feel like eating the pasty pie. I decided to stick around to see what would happen at supper time. He'd had his physical therapy in bed that morning, because he hadn't felt like going downstairs. That worried me, but I hoped that once his appetite improved, he'd get back to his regular schedule.

Gerry's friends came by to visit so Joellyn, Bertie and I moved to the lounge. As we walked in the door, the patient who had set his false teeth on the table during one of our visits came in, too. As soon as he sat down, out came the man's teeth. He held them up to the window and picked at them with a toothpick. He'd look over at us as if he were waiting for a response. The girls sat there trying to be polite, but I could see little smiles forming on both their faces. I couldn't sit there and watch, so I got up and walked over to the magazine rack to get something to read. Then the man stood up and handed his teeth to another patient. He told the patient he could have the teeth because they didn't fit right. The patient tried to give them back, but the man took off out the door. We all looked at each other and smiled. The new owner of the teeth just sat there staring at his gift. I asked if he'd like me to give them to one of the nurses. He handed me the teeth and I quickly headed for the nurses' station with the girls right behind me.

When we got back to Gerry's room, he was enjoying a word game called "Boggle" with his friend, Bill, and the recreation therapist. We told them about our experience in the lounge. Gerry said that similar incidents had happened before with that patient, and most of the others were used to his actions in the lounge. I told him his sisters and I were somewhat humored by the incident, but we weren't looking forward to a next time.

For supper, Gerry ate two bowls of chicken rice soup, chocolate pudding, and a strawberry shake from McDonald's. I wasn't sure if he had eaten just to please me or if his appetite had really begun to improve, but it didn't matter.

The next day, Gerry had toast and sausages for breakfast, and a bowl of tomato macaroni soup with a beef sandwich for lunch. Two meals down and one to go, I said to myself. I felt good about his food consumption that day, and asked him if there was anything special he'd like for supper.

"Funny you should ask," he said, with a grin. "How about a steak, some rigatoni, garlic bread, and a salad from my favorite restaurant?"

"Your wish is our command," Joellyn stated.

"I wish that worked for me," complained Bertie.

"Well, let's see what we can do for you, Bertie," I offered. "How about if I go pick up Gerry's food and while he's eating, we go to the Italian restaurant and have our dinner?"

"Sounds good to me, Mom," Bertie said, giving me a hug.

"Sounds good to me, too," Joellyn echoed.

"Okay, then it's all set," I answered. "And, Ger, don't forget to tell your dad when he gets here that I was outnumbered."

"You're always outnumbered, Mom," he remarked. "That's part of being a mom." All three of them looked at me and giggled. Gerry seemed to be in much better spirits, now that his temperature was back to normal. He said it had been normal all day.

Later, on my way out to pick up his supper, I stopped at the nurses' station to write a note to the doctor requesting a steak for Gerry once a week. Would he go along with my idea? Two steaks per week would definitely help Gerry gain back some of his weight.

If Gerry ate everything I brought him for supper, his total calories for the day would be approximately 3,000. When the girls and I returned to the hospital after our own meal, we were happy to learn that Gerry had cleaned his plate. I had a good feeling that he was on his way to gaining back the weight he had lost.

The next day, I continued to monitor Gerry's food intake. He was eating lunch as I walked into his room: chicken, potatoes, vegetables, and blueberry cobbler. He mentioned that he had pancakes for breakfast and they were tasty, but "They weren't as good as Dad's."

"Of course, they weren't," I said. "Nobody cooks like your dad." We were both beginning to sound like a broken record.

"What's on the menu for supper?" I asked.

"I ordered a stacked ham sandwich with cottage cheese and pineapple salad," he answered. "But, I can't remember what I'm getting for dessert."

"Just eat it all," I said. "You have twenty-five pounds to gain back and I'm here to see that you do it."

"I'm trying, Mom," he promised.

"I know you are, Ger," I said, "And, I also know it'll take time to regain the weight, but I promise to be patient."

"Patience isn't one of your best virtues," he said, with a chuckle.

"I know," I said. "You have to help me by eating everything on your plate."

That evening when some of Gerry's friends stopped by, Ed and I went to the lounge to see who was around. While we were visiting with a friend, a patient came walking in with his IV in hand and asked for help. He said he had buzzed several times for a nurse, but the buzzer didn't seem to be working. One of the visitors left to get help and discovered that some of the nurses were on a break, but did find someone to take care of the man. I had a funny feeling that something was up because I'd heard talk earlier of a possible strike.

The hospital nurses went on strike at 3:00 P.M. the next afternoon. All of the patients on rehab were moved to orthopedics or sent to other hospitals, and some were even sent home. Gerry was moved out of his room and in with another patient who had been in a boating accident. I was nervous about the care he'd be getting, but there wasn't much we could do about it. We didn't want to transfer him to another hospital, and we knew he definitely wouldn't want to do that. Maybe the strike wouldn't last long.

I was thrilled that Gerry's appetite was finally back, and he was enjoying the meals. We were also happy to hear that the doctor had given his permission for Gerry to have a steak once a week, to be served on Saturdays. With two steaks a week, and pizza whenever he ordered it, I figured he could gain that weight back in no time at all. At least, that was the plan.

Joellyn and her boyfriend, Al, came by that evening and took Gerry for a stroll around the hospital block. I could see by the look on his face when they returned that he'd enjoyed his venture. In his words, "It was awesome!" He mentioned all the flowers he had seen, and the lonely robin that was sitting on one of the bushes. He said he thought the bird was waiting for him, but he flew away as soon as Gerry stopped to take a look at him. Joellyn reminded him that if he hadn't shaken the branch, maybe the robin would have stuck around. Gerry grinned. "The reason I did that was so I could watch the robin fly; it's been a long time since I've played outside."

"Just let us know when you're in a playful mood again," Joellyn replied. Gerry laughed and promised he would. Those three always had a good time together.

Gerry's roommate was gone when Ed and I got to the hospital the next day. He'd lost his arm in a boating accident and had to be flown to the Mayo Clinic in Rochester, Minnesota. The antibiotics weren't working and the infection had gone into his leg. He was told that he could lose his leg, or even die; he was only twenty-two years old. I had a chance to talk briefly to his wife. She told me they hadn't been married very long. Tears filled her eyes so I put my arms around her to comfort her; she broke down and sobbed. She didn't have any family nearby, but her mother was on her way to pick her up. A cup of coffee in the lounge and a long conversation helped us both.

Several days later friends came by to see Gerry before they headed back to college. He was somewhat depressed after they left, knowing he wouldn't be going back to the university that semester. The last time I brought up the subject, he told me it was too early to think about it, and I agreed with him. I was hoping he'd be able to take a class during the winter semester, but it was his decision to make.

While I talked to Gerry about his food intake that day, he pulled out a peanut butter cup from his tray table and said that he wanted one of those every day. I agreed that chocolate and peanut butter were good for him. He chuckled because he knew how much I loved chocolate.

We talked about an interesting article in Sports Illustrated. The football player, Darryl Stingley, had an accident and also ended up with a broken neck. Like Gerry, the halo traction was part of his treatment. We felt somewhat reassured about the halo. But how would it all end?

When we got home that night, I lay in bed thinking about the young man who had lost his arm in a boating accident. I couldn't imagine dealing with that situation at his and his wife's young age. They had their entire lives ahead of them, and suddenly, were given a very big cross to bear. I prayed that they had enough family and friends around to help them get through their trauma.

Before I closed my eyes, I tapped Ed on the shoulder. "Did you know that I go back to school tomorrow?" He must have been sound asleep because he didn't answer. I was nervous about starting back, but a change of pace might be good for me. It would help keep my mind occupied with something different, at least part of the day.

It was Monday, August 29th, the end of summer vacation. It was fun to watch the children as they came into school, chatting with friends and heading for their classrooms. Some were smiling as they said hello to their teachers from the past year, and others looked a little scared. The first day of school was always a worry for the students because they were anxious to find out if any of their friends were in the same room. They were also curious about having a new teacher, wondering what he or she would be like. As a librarian, I looked forward to their first trip to the library, to their excitement over finding a book they might enjoy. It was the best job in the world. The day was over before I knew it. I was anxious to get to the hospital to see what was happening with the nurses' strike.

When I arrived around 4:00, I saw Gerry's nurse, Bonnie, outside picketing. I stopped and told her that we would miss her a lot, but being a teacher, I understood. I had been through a couple of strikes in my career, but it was a difficult time for everyone involved. As I left, she said to say hello to Gerry and to let him know that she was thinking about him. I wished her the best and told her I hoped the strike would be over soon, partially for the nurses, but mostly for Gerry and the other patients who needed their attention.

Gerry appreciated the message from Bonnie. He had his four-poster collar adjusted while I was in the room and the staples removed from his head. I wasn't prepared to watch that, so I looked out the window while the male LPN went about his job. I'd never make it as a nurse.

Gerry didn't go downstairs for his therapy that afternoon because his spasms were too bad. He had gone in the morning, but he didn't volunteer any more information than that. When I asked him about flexing his muscles behind his thighs, he said he didn't lay there doing that everyday. He was quite short with me, but I understood. He wasn't feeling the best because of the way his body was responding.

Just when I was wondering what I should say next, he volunteers that he had eaten 3,000 calories the day before. He also told me that he was looking forward to tacos for supper. I warned him about the last time he ate three tacos and got sick. He agreed.

Gerry had been a bit down early in the day, but later he started to perk up. He asked me get some crossword puzzles for him. The recreational therapist gave him a few "Find-a-Word" puzzles, but he wanted something more challenging. I told him that was one request I could take care of easily, so when Ed and the girls arrived, I headed out to find the puzzles.

His sisters were a breath of fresh air for Gerry. I asked too many questions. He was going through a time when he didn't want anyone, especially his mother, asking about things he didn't want to answer. I made a promise to myself that, instead of questioning him, I'd allow him to tell me the things he wanted to share. It was probably good that I was back in school during the day, occupying my time with students' and teachers' questions.

I remember when he first started dating. I'd ask him who he was going out with, but he wouldn't give me any answers. He'd just smile and say, "When the time's right, I'll tell you, Mom." Gerry was a very private person. He did surprise me on the day of the prom, however, when he wanted us to meet his date. He brought the young lady to our house for a rather short visit, but at least, we got to meet her. I behaved very well; I didn't ask any questions. I just told them how nice they looked and to have a good time. In fact, I didn't even tell Gerry what time to be home. He was seventeen at the time so I could have given him a curfew, but I didn't. It probably would have been a bad move on my part to embarrass him in front of his date. As it turned out, he didn't give me any reason to wish I had set a time for him to be home.

The following day, Gerry went on a picnic with six other patients and twelve staff members. According to him, the highlight of the picnic was a seagull who dropped something on one of the physical therapists. She had been telling Gerry all week that she was hoping one would drop on him, but he was happy the seagull had chosen her. I told him those therapists would do anything to make him happy. I reminded him to be on the lookout; it was his turn next.

We had a pizza party with Gerry's friends that evening. Gerry and his roommate, Gary, had a lot of fun with everyone. Ed and I left for the lounge so the guys could have a chance to be together. About an hour later, we came back to find Gerry laughing so hard he could hardly speak. When I asked him what was so funny, he just pointed to Gary and laughed some more. Gary claimed he was innocent, but the look on his face suggested that he definitely was the guilty one. Not a tidbit was left of the three large pizzas. It was wonderful to see Gerry laughing and having such a good time; I realized all over again how important friends are.

Before Ed and I left that night, Gerry told us that Harry from social services had been encouraging him to go back to school. Gerry asked Joellyn to pick up a booklet on the classes being offered and, after reviewing the list, he chose a correspondence course in Greek Mythology. We were somewhat surprised by his decision, but pleased that he was moving on. I felt better about Gerry's future than I had in a long time.

Since we hadn't eaten, I suggested that we stop for a pizza on the way home. As we were enjoying our meal, I whispered to Ed, "Can you believe that August is gone?"

Chapter Eight

We learned the next afternoon that a staffing was planned for the following week on Tuesday, and a family meeting on Thursday. Once again, I was afraid to hear what they were going to say about Gerry's recovery, even though I was aware he had come as far as he could with respect to his mobility. Ed and I hadn't talked about it much, but we had discussed getting a second opinion from a doctor with more experience in spinal cord injury. At the time, we weren't sure who that might be, or where we would go, but we wanted to talk with someone from the National Organization for Spinal Cord Injury soon. We were busy getting ready for Gerry's visit home when we heard a rumor that if a patient went home for a weekend, he couldn't be readmitted to the hospital due to the strike. I was hoping it was just a rumor.

Something humorous happened when Mike came to see Gerry that night. As he was getting off the elevator, an elderly patient in a wheelchair asked him to help her get on the elevator. Her wheelchair was equipped with a high flexible metal piece that prevented access to the elevator. As soon as Mike began to help her, one of the nurses realized what was happening and explained that the device stopped her from leaving the hospital. We chuckled as Mike told us the story, although he was embarrassed about the incident.

"It's the thought that counts, Mike," said Ed.

"That's the problem, Dad," he answered. "I didn't think!"

We found out later that a patient had gotten on the elevator and down to the lobby. Luckily, he was caught before he headed out a door, or the hospital could have ended up with a disaster on their hands.

I talked to Social Services the next day about taking Gerry home for Labor Day. However, there was something I had to do before that holiday; I had to tell Gerry that our dog, Reecy, had died. As I approached the subject, Gerry quickly interrupted and said that he knew about the dog. He said one of his friends mentioned it to him shortly after it happened, thinking we had told him about it. I couldn't believe that he knew all this time and hadn't said anything. When I asked him why he hadn't talked to us about it, he said he was afraid I'd get upset. I guess I shouldn't have been surprised. That's Gerry.

The occupational therapist came by that afternoon and talked to Gerry about making pizza with his roommate. Gerry hinted that Gary might turn the situation into a real blast, because he was a mischief-maker. The therapist laughed and said she'd bring someone else along to make sure he behaved. "Some sort of restraints might be in order," Gerry said.

The therapist told me that Gerry was learning to dress himself and needed some pants, but not jeans or corduroys. They had to be a slippery material so he could get his feet in without any problems. I promised to pick some up the next day.

"Guess what, Mom." Gerry said. I tried a car transfer with one of the physical therapists this afternoon, and it went quite well."

Suddenly, I realized things were moving very quickly for the home visit and I was beginning to feel frightened. I didn't know what to say to Gerry, so I changed the subject.

"What are you having for supper?"

"It's steak night, remember!"

"Oh, my goodness. How could I forget that? Hmmm, maybe I can talk your dad into taking me out for dinner tonight."

"You'll probably have to pay," Gerry said.

"No, I don't think so. He owes me one. Remember the night he gave me a bad time about the patient who said 'Hello Boys' when we walked into the lounge."

Gerry laughed and said, "I think you got him, Mom."

Ed and I did go out for dinner that night, and it was a night I won't soon forget. We decided to try a new place located on the top floor of a local hotel. We had a table by the window with a spectacular view of Lake Superior. Our whitefish dinners were superb, and served with elegance. Before we left the restaurant, I detoured to the ladies room down the hallway. Across from the restroom, by the elevator, a young man was holding the door open with one hand and trying to pull a young girl into the elevator with the other hand. She was crouched down, hanging on to the side of the wall. I asked her if she needed help, and she told me she didn't want to go with him. I told the young man to let her go, but he didn't respond. He kept pulling her and mumbling something I couldn't make out. If I left to get help, he'd pull her on the elevator and she'd be gone. Before I realized it, I began striking him with my purse, screaming for help at the same time. Within seconds, people came out of their hotel rooms to see what was going on. Ed recognized my screams because he, too, came running down the hallway. Someone grabbed the young man and held on to him while another called the police.

"Are you all right?" I asked.

"Yes," she said. "He wanted me to go with him, but I told him no."

"Do you need a ride home?"

"No, I'll call a friend."

As I was leaving, she looked at me with tears in her eyes and said, "I don't know what I would've done if you hadn't come by when you did."

"I'm glad I was able to help out," I whispered.

Ed was shocked by what had taken place, but when I explained the situation and asked, "What if it had been one of our daughters?" he nodded his head in approval. Where had I gotten the courage to do what I did? It was a dangerous situation. Would my children consider me a hero or a fool? Maybe I wouldn't tell them.

When we got back to the hospital there were several visitors in Gerry's room, including Jim. One person from out of town, asked Gerry to sign his wife's autograph book. I could tell Gerry wasn't terribly thrilled about doing that, but he signed it anyway. When the man left, Jim took a piece of paper out of his pocket and also asked for his autograph. It brought a big smile to Gerry's face; that was Jim's intention. He tried to make light of an embarrassing moment for his brother, and it worked.

On Saturday, Bertie and I went shopping for some "slippery" pants for Gerry. We picked out three pair, all different colors, but the same style. When we showed him the pants, he pretended to be very excited and then started to act silly. Bertie and I laughed because it had been a long time since we'd seen him carry on in that way. Gerry's great sense of humor was something we all missed.

On Sunday, the kids brought Gerry a bacon double cheeseburger and fries from Burger King. I was glad his brothers and sisters were looking after his special needs. Despite the fact that burgers and fries were loaded with saturated fat, young people still chose them over other restaurant food. And, at that point, I wasn't going to say anything to discourage Gerry from eating whatever he wanted.

Before we left the hospital that night, we asked if there'd be a problem readmitting Gerry due to the nurses' strike. We were told there wouldn't be. Ed and I went home to prepare for the next day, Gerry's first homecoming.

On Labor Day, September 5th, Ed and Mike left to pick up Gerry at the hospital. I was excited about him coming home, but I was also nervous. I wanted to have everything perfect for him. I kept walking back and forth in the kitchen looking out the window. Joellyn and Bertie sat there watching me, and then Bertie told me to "sit down and try to relax or Joellyn and I are going to tie you to a chair!" I laughed and quickly threw myself on her lap telling her to get some rope. Just then, Joellyn yelled, "They're here, Mom."

Gerry sat in the front seat of the car looking at us, smiling as if to say, "I made it." Mike lifted Gerry out while Ed got his wheelchair from the trunk. I could feel the tears beginning to well up in my eyes. Mike carried Gerry up the steps and into the house. What was going through Gerry's mind? I'm sure he never dreamed he'd be coming home in a wheelchair when he left the house that Saturday in May. Neither did I.

Ed and I kept busy in the kitchen preparing a special dinner for everyone while Gerry spent time with his brothers and sisters in the living room. I joined them off and on just to add my two cents. Gerry kept looking around the room he hadn't seen in over three months. Everything was the same as before his accident, but to him it must have looked brand new. I wanted to put my arms around him, but I knew if I did, the girls and I would most likely be in tears.

It wasn't long before Ed announced that it was time to eat. On the table was barbecued chicken, real mashed potatoes, creamed vegetables, and hot rolls. Gerry's big smile made it obvious that he was looking forward to his dad's cooking. Later, my homemade blueberry pie, one of Gerry's favorites, ended the meal. After dinner, the kids stayed and visited for a few hours, but Gerry was getting tired. When I asked him if he wanted to go back to the hospital, he said he was ready.

It took Ed, Jim, and Mike to lift him into the car because rain had started to come fast and furious. They managed to keep Gerry dry with a raincoat over him, but the guys got drenched. I went back to the hospital with Ed, but soon after Gerry got into bed, he fell asleep. It must have been an exhausting trip for him, but he was very happy to be back home again, even if the time was short. Now that the first visit was under our belt, the next one would be much easier.

There was a room full of friends when I arrived at the hospital the next day, but Gerry wasn't feeling the best so they didn't stay long. After everyone left, he told me the doctor felt that he might have another urinary tract infection. A culture on the weekend set in motion another round of antibiotics. Would urinary tract infections continue to be part of the recovery process?

Gerry informed me that he had learned to catheterize himself using a "clean method" instead of a "sterile method." I decided he could explain that to Ed if he wanted to. I prayed that the medication would take care of the infection so he could move on. But, I also worried that it might affect his appetite again, so I asked him what he had eaten that day. He had cereal and toast for breakfast, but hadn't eaten any lunch. He made up for it at supper time, however, by eating three bowls of chicken rice soup and half an egg salad sandwich. I thought it might be a good night to order a pizza, and I was right; he ate four pieces.

"Did I tell you that Gary and I are making pizza for supper tomorrow night?" Gerry asked.

"Oh, really! If I had known that I wouldn't have gotten you one tonight."

"I know you would get me anything I asked for, Mom, right?" He seemed to get a kick out of telling me about their plans because he had the biggest grin on his face.

"Any thing, Gerry, you name it," I said.

Thursday, the day of our staffing, arrived. Ed, Gerry, Joellyn, and I met with Gerry's rehab doctor, an LPN, a physical therapist, an occupational therapist, the hospital psychologist, and a person from social services. Gerry's doctor gave him a score of A+1 in progress, and then referred to him as "an amazing young man." He said Gerry was doing things that he never thought he'd be able to do. I then told him about Finnish *sisu*. He also told us that he'd be discharging him in about a month, which made my knees knock a little. But we'd manage because we had Jim, Mike and the girls to help us. His brothers and sisters thought the world of Gerry. The following weekend he was coming for an overnight so we'd have an idea of what to expect.

The doctor informed us that when Gerry was discharged from the hospital he would need a hospital bed at home, but suggested renting one for the time being. He said that someone needed to learn how to catheterize Gerry, just in case he got sick and couldn't do it himself. When the idea of a van came up, we were told that Gerry would have to go to Grand Rapids to learn how to drive it. Suddenly, I felt over-whelmed. I didn't want to even think about him behind the wheel of a van at that point. I purposely didn't look at Gerry because I was sure he would want that more than anything else. He had made it clear to us weeks ago that he wanted to be as independent as he possibly could. We all sat there looking at each other without saying a word. Finally, the doctor asked Gerry if he had any questions. Gerry asked him if there was anything they could do about his spasms because they were interfering with his physical therapy. The doctor said he could put him on Valium, but it had to be his decision. Our session lasted about thirty minutes.

After the staffing, we talked with Gerry and made a joint decision to take him to another doctor–a spinal cord injury specialist–for a second opinion and an evaluation of his condition. When we finished our discussion, Ed told Gerry that he'd ordered an electric wheelchair, and it would be arriving in about ten days. Gerry was elated. He was moving on.

My stomach was twirling around at school the next day, but I tried very hard to focus on the students. I was glad I had scheduled third graders for library instruction because it definitely helped me get through the day. The children were wonderfully inquisitive; they wanted to know everything about the library. I was surprised when one of the girls asked if we had any books on how to become president. I heard a couple of sighs from the boys, but I reminded the group that girls, as well as boys, could become president. I also told them they'd probably see a woman become president in their life time. "My dad wouldn't vote for a girl," said one student.

At the hospital, Gerry mentioned that his doctor told him he would need a "pusher" if he was planning to go back to the University that next semester. I must have looked pretty confused because Gerry laughed and explained, "Someone to push me to my classes, Mom."

"Oh," I said smiling. "What about me?"

"What will you do, quit your job?" he asked. "Besides, that would be in January, and you'd never be able to push me through all that snow."

"I know," I said. "But, if you need help, we'll make sure you get someone. That's a few months away, so we have plenty of time to work out those details. Right now, we need to concentrate on your coming home."

"You're right, Mom," he said. "Can you believe it? I'm coming home!"

When Ed arrived he talked to Gerry about taking him for a drive on Saturday, and then suggested that he come home and spend the afternoon with us on Sunday. Gerry hated being at the hospital on the weekends, and said that sounded pretty good to him.

Ed worked on Saturday morning and then left around noon to pick up Gerry. It was a nice sunny day so he took him for a ride around Presque Isle to see the fishing boats. Presque Isle is a beautiful island near Lake Superior where people can picnic, take long walks, bike, or just sit and enjoy the view and the sunset. When our children were younger, we took them to the island for picnics, and we always stopped at the ice cream shop before heading home. Ed would pretend he was going to drive by without stopping, but all five would yell, "Stop, Dad, we want some ice cream!" Ed would put on the brake and try to use the excuse that he didn't see the place, but the kids were aware of his "tricks" because he played them often.

I was at the hospital when Gerry and Ed returned, and they both seemed to be in a good mood. I asked how the ride went and Gerry immediately grinned. He told me that as they were returning to the hospital, Ed wanted to stop at Woolworth's for something, but that he chose to stay in the car. He said he fell asleep twice waiting for his dad to come out. When I glanced at Ed, he told me that he couldn't find what he wanted. Gerry had a different idea; he thought his dad had forgotten he was in the car. Gerry couldn't stop chuckling because, for once, he had one over on his dad.

Shortly after he finished his steak dinner that evening, friends started dropping by. When I stopped counting, there were ten people in his room. It was so crowded that I suggested we all move to the lounge. Gerry was in a great mood and chatted a lot with the guys; it was one of the best nights we had had. When we said good night, he told us he was looking forward to coming home the next day. Things were looking up.

On Sunday, September 11th, the Packers were playing. After lunch, Ed picked up Gerry so he could spend the afternoon with his family. All the kids came by. When the Packers weren't playing, Gerry and Ed watched the Lions, but their first choice was the team from Green Bay. We all sat down to watch the game and cheered loudly for the Packers. We especially wanted them to win for Gerry's sake. And, that's what they did.

Ed was between the kitchen and the living room, preparing dinner and trying to catch part of the action on TV. After the game, Ed served one of Gerry's favorite meals, steak and spaghetti. Of course, it was also a favorite of everyone in the family. I was surprised that Gerry had asked for a steak after having had one the night before, but it really didn't matter. I was so happy his appetite was improving.

Ed and the boys took Gerry back to the hospital about 6:00 because of spasms. Before he left, he told us he had decided to go on Valium. I was a little worried, but according to his doctor, he didn't have any other options for controlling the spasms. They would become a part of his life.

There was a bit of good news when I arrived at the hospital the following afternoon: the nurses' strike was over. Gerry had been moved to rehab and was very happy to see his favorite nurse, Bonnie, back on the job. She was teasing him about something when I walked into his room, and he was enjoying it a lot. She seemed to know just the right things to say to get him going. "You look so cute in your new pants, Gerry."

"Oh, so you like my new pants. Thanks, but I want to know why you took so much time off recently? Did you do it so you wouldn't have to deal with me?"

"You're right about that, Gerry. You were the main reason I went on strike."

It was funny to watch the two of them go at it because I knew how much they admired each other. I don't know if he would have handled everything as well if she hadn't been there. Bonnie was someone very special.

Later that day, Gerry told me he had started on Valium and I knew I had to get moving on a second opinion. I called another doctor who said he would respond as soon as he got a letter from me. However, he did say he wasn't keen on Valium. I told Gerry about our conversation; he was anxious to hear what the doctor's response would be to my letter. I wondered what we would do if one doctor prescribed Valium and the other was against it. Gerry's spasms were hard on him; something had to be done to control them. We decided to wait until I received an answer to my letter.

Ed had a Lion's meeting that night, so I stayed with Gerry until Jim and Mike arrived. As I was saying good night to him, Joellyn and Bertie walked in with huge peanut butter and chocolate chip cookies from the Cookie Cutter. Gerry grinned from ear to ear. I stood in the doorway and watched the five of them chomping on monster size cookies. I laughed out loud as I waved goodbye. Getting on the elevator, I thought about our large family, and how thankful I was that we had five children. Gerry must have felt the same way. They hardly missed a day coming to the hospital to spend time with him.

As I was leaving the hospital parking lot, I began to think about the night we got the call from Gerry's friend, Hank. I couldn't get it out of my mind. Should I have stopped him from going to Hank's camp that night? If I had, would he have questioned my reasoning? After all, he was eighteen years old. As I continued driving, the tears began rolling down my face. Suddenly, I was crying out loud, unable to stop. I pulled over to the side of the road, put my face in my hands and cried until there were no tears left. Many minutes later, I walked in the door. Ed took one look at me, somehow sensed that I needed his arms around me, and held me tightly, neither one of us saying a word.

That night I had no trouble falling asleep and woke up only once to the sound of rain hitting our bedroom window. I actually slept better when it rained. Ed was still in bed when I awoke the next morning, so I snuck downstairs to make some coffee. I wanted to thank him for being my rock, and to tell him I'd never make it without him. When he walked into the kitchen, he asked, "How are you feeling this morning?"

"Much better, thanks to you."

"How was your night?"

"Great!" I said. "I didn't wake up until I heard the rain."

"Didn't you hear the thunder and lightning?"

"No. What time was that?"

"Around midnight. I got up and looked out the window, but the rain had stopped. I got back into bed and the noise started again, only this time it was right in our bedroom."

"I'm surprised I didn't hear it if it was so loud."

Ed smiled. "I know why you didn't hear it."

"Why?"

"Because the noise was coming from the bed. You were snoring!"

"I don't snore," I said, defending myself.

"Then I wonder who that was in my bed last night," he teased. We both laughed as we sat and drank our coffee.

It was then that I realized just how important those brief moments together really were. Ed left for work and I dashed upstairs to get into the shower. I was running late, with a forty-minute drive to school on a very foggy morning to look forward to.

The day went by quickly with students and teachers in and out of the library. I was fortunate to have a job that I loved, and a place where students enjoyed spending time. It was fun watching them smile as they discovered the book they were searching for. One student asked if he could check out all the books on cooking because he wanted to be a famous chef some day. Another student wanted a book on trout fishing so she could catch fish like the famous author, John Voelker, whose pen name was Robert Traver. Mr. Voelker lived in our area so the following year I invited him to visit our library and talk with students about writing. He delighted us all by accepting. Most of the children's questions, however, were about fishing.

When I arrived at the hospital that afternoon, Gerry appeared tired. As soon as he ate his supper, he fell asleep. When he woke up, he said he was feeling a little better. But he didn't seem to be interested in what was on TV or in talking to me, and he kept staring out the window. Was he again beginning to show some signs of depression? I was relieved when Joellyn and Al walked into the room; he would talk to them. When they sat down, Gerry talked about a new patient in the hospital, a young man who had been in a three-wheeler accident and had to have his leg amputated. I knew at that moment I'd never be able to work in a hospital and be a witness to such tragedies. I said to the others, "God bless those people who are the servants of our health. They deserve our thanks and our prayers." I was beginning to understand why some hospital care workers lose their patience. They dealt with difficult problems on a daily basis.

The letter from the doctor arrived the following morning. It was what I had expected; he didn't think Gerry should take Valium for his spasms because of the many side effects: rage, irritability, confusion, hallucinations, difficulty breathing and addiction. He suggested that we talk with the doctor about other options. I shared the letter with Gerry. Gerry's cousin Steve had mentioned that he was taking Baclofen, an anti spastic analgesic used to help relax certain muscles. After discussing the drug with his doctor, Gerry decided to switch from Valium to Baclofen.

The next couple of days were uneventful. Bonnie showed Ed how to catheterize Gerry because he was coming home again for the weekend. She also gave us her phone number in case we needed to call for advice. We hadn't been able to purchase a hospital bed for Gerry, so Ed and I talked to one of the social workers about it. Basically, we wouldn't be able to have Gerry overnight if we didn't have a bed. The doctor said we should try to rent one instead of buying one, but we had no luck. As it turned out, we made plans to take him home on Saturday, but not for overnight.

Ed picked up Gerry around 2:00 in the afternoon and he spent most of the day visiting with his brothers and sisters. We ordered pizzas for supper which was always a hit with the kids. As we sat there eating one pizza after another, I noticed Jim staring at Gerry. Was he trying to figure out how such a tragedy could have happened to his youngest brother? Mike and the girls had wondered the same thing at one time or another, just as Ed and I had. Even though it had been almost four months since the accident, I still had days when I asked myself what I could have done to prevent it. I always came up with the same answer . . . nothing. When we took Gerry back to the hospital that evening, he said he wanted to come home again on Sunday. I was glad to hear that.

On Sunday morning, Bertie and I went to get Gerry because Mike and Jim were busy helping Ed build a ramp up to the front door. It started at the end of our driveway and curved along the side of the house, onto the front porch where Gerry could easily enter. The rooms downstairs were spacious, allowing him to go into any room including the bathroom, without a problem. I don't know what we'd have done if we had been living in a small house. We probably would have had to move into a bigger house to accommodate Gerry's needs. I was especially glad that we had a large kitchen because it was easy for Gerry to get around in, and the family spent a lot of time there.

I was nervous having Gerry in the car, so I drove forty-five miles an hour all the way home. When we arrived, Ed and Mike met us in the driveway and they lifted Gerry out of the car. As they were carrying him up the steps, he looked at his Dad and asked, "Where did Mom ever learn to drive like that?"

"Oh, oh, was she speeding again?" Ed asked.

"No. We were moving like a snail."

"Careful, Gerry," I commented. "I may be driving you back to the hospital tonight, and I like snails."

"Sorry, Mom. But, would you mind if Dad and Mike drove me back? We have some things to talk about."

"I'm sure you do. But you know I'll find out what you talked about, so don't be critical of your mother."

"I won't," Gerry promised.

We looked forward to the Packers vs. Dallas football game in the afternoon. Gerry was hoping for another Packer win, and that was exactly what happened. Ed could hear us cheering loudly as he was in the kitchen preparing a delicious dinner. He made pork chops, mashed potatoes, buttered carrots, zucchini casserole and applesauce. My sister, Sue, surprised us with a pan of her heavenly chocolate turtle bars. Gerry ate everything on his plate, including seconds. I reminded him that it wouldn't be long before he'd be enjoying home-cooked meals on a regular basis.

Gerry told us that, while in occupational therapy, he had typed a letter to his doctor regarding the $16.00 per day rental fee for the floating pad on his wheelchair. Ed had discussed it with him previously and suggested that he ask the doctor about the possibility of buying the pad. The doctor advised him to write a letter to him, with a copy to the hospital administrator. In the letter, Gerry explained that after several months, the daily rental fee would eventually end up costing more than the purchase price of the pad.

About 9:00 we took Gerry back to the hospital. All in all, it was a good day. I was feeling more at ease about his coming home for good.

Girls' basketball began that next week, and Bertie had a game scheduled for Tuesday night. Joellyn had also played during her four years in high school. When we went to her first game we discovered that she was one of the most competitive basketball players we'd ever seen. She looked forward to Tuesday and Thursday, the two nights her team played. Bertie enjoyed the game, but it wasn't her only interest.

On Tuesday, I picked up Ed at 6:30 for Bertie's game. Her team lost by one point. For some reason, I was feeling down even before the game was over. Maybe reality was beginning to set in. Whatever it was, I didn't want to face it. I went straight to bed and pulled the blanket up over my head. I just wanted to go to sleep and not think about anything.

When Ed came up to bed, he told me he called Gerry to check on his evening. Several friends had stopped by, including the policeman from Munising who had been a patient there. Gerry said he enjoyed talking with everyone, especially the policeman, who was quite humorous. I remembered some of the funny things he said about himself when he was a patient at the hospital; he always managed to get a smile out of Gerry.

I soon fell asleep, but woke up once during the night after a strange dream. I was driving home from the hospital when suddenly I saw a car behind me with flashing lights. I pulled over to the side of the road. When the policeman walked over to my car, I realized it was the cop from Munising. I looked at him and asked why he wasn't at the hospital. He smiled and said that he had been released the week before, and was now back on the job. When I asked him why he stopped me, he said I was driving on the wrong side of the road and didn't have my lights on. I told him I was sorry and pleaded with him not to give me a ticket. He laughed and asked me for my driver's license. He told me my license had expired on my last birthday. As he wrote the ticket, I cried and told him I was going to be in trouble with my husband. He laughed again, putting his hand on my shoulder and shaking me. Suddenly, I heard a voice whispering, "What's the matter? Are you okay?" It was Ed trying to wake me.

"Yes," I answered. "I was dreaming." It took me awhile before I was able to go back to sleep. I kept thinking about the cop. It was so strange. I was hoping I'd run into him again sometime so I could share my dream, or my "nightmare" with him.

Gerry was in occupational therapy when I got to the hospital the next day. When he got back to his room, he showed me an alarm system they made to awaken him during the night so he could be turned over. It had to be done every three hours in order to prevent bed sores. I had never seen a bed sore, but from what I'd heard, they weren't pretty.

When Ed arrived at the hospital that evening, we again talked with Gerry about a second opinion. We wanted to go where the newest research on spinal cord injury was available. The U of M Hospital had been recommended to us by the National Organization for Spinal Cord Injury. After talking with Gerry's doctors, they agreed with our decision and offered to assist with the transfer.

At 7:00, I left to attend a PTA meeting at school, and Ed stayed at the hospital until I returned around 9:00. Gerry told me I looked tired, so we decided to call it a day and head for home. He was right; my body was moving, but I was feeling numb.

After I left for school the next morning, Ed went to look at a hospital bed that was for sale, but it wasn't in very good condition. He

Gerry with his step-grandfather, Frank Sarvello, on his
ramp at home.

spent the afternoon getting the new ramp ready. As the day grew closer
for Gerry's homecoming, I was feeling more frightened at the responsibility. We needed to care for Gerry properly, and that included a
reliable bed.

After school, I headed straight to the hospital, where one of the
hospital administrators came by to see me. He caught me off guard
when he suddenly asked if we were interested in buying Gerry's hospital bed. I told him I'd talk with Ed about it. He also wanted to
discuss other things, and suggested we go into one of the conference
rooms where it was more private. I began to wonder if he had heard
about some of the problems we had encountered over the past four
months. I told him about the time Ed had just come home from seeing
our son when he got a phone call, telling him he had to come back to
pay for the four poster collar before they'd put it on Gerry. He admitted
the hospital should have taken responsibility to advise us about the pre-
payment of the collar. He said he understood our frustration with that
situation, and with some of the other problems we had had. We visited

for over an hour while Gerry was in therapy. I felt much better afterwards. I truly believed he wanted to make things right by us.

Gerry returned from his therapy session, and I left to get his favorite meal from the Italian restaurant. After he finished eating, we talked about coming home the next day for an overnight, and he convinced me I had nothing to worry about. He was going to sleep in one of the upstairs bedrooms, and he teased me about coming down the steps on his butt, one step at a time. He used to do that when he was a toddler, but I made him promise he wouldn't try it that weekend.

Gerry was getting awfully bored with his present quarters, and he seemed especially anxious to come home. He was probably worried about sleeping in his own bed, but I assured him we'd give him the best of care. I told him I'd be willing to sit in a chair by his bed all night. He smiled, saying he doubted he would sleep a wink if I were to do that. I got the message.

Chapter Nine

The day finally arrived; it was September 24th. Gerry was about to spend his first overnight at home since his accident. I could count on Ed and Mike to be there for Gerry and to help out with whatever he needed. They both would be available day and night, and that made me feel much more relaxed.

Ed left around noon to get Gerry from the hospital. He seemed as calm as an evening breeze and gave me a big smile as he went out the door. "Everything will be fine," he said shutting the kitchen door behind him. I knew he was right, but I couldn't stop those jittery feelings in my stomach. I kept telling myself that once he got home and his brothers and sisters were all around him, I'd be able to relax. It wasn't long before Jim was coming in to tell me that Ed and Gerry had arrived. I ran into the kitchen, and we all hugged Gerry at the same time. After we settled down, Gerry wanted the television turned on because Northern Michigan University and Michigan Tech were playing football. The game took up most of the afternoon, and everyone watched, cheering loudly for NMU, the big winners that day.

As soon as the game was over, Ed announced that dinner was ready. There on the table sat a beautiful ham, mashed potatoes, creamed carrots, cole slaw and hot rolls. I had made an apple pie for dessert. Gerry ate everything and even had seconds. As he was cleaning his plate, he said, "You are the best, Dad. I've really missed your cooking."

"You won't have to worry about that too much longer, Ger," Ed replied. "You'll be back home soon."

"I can't wait," Gerry added. "It's been too long."

Everyone stayed after dinner and visited with Gerry until almost 10:00. His brother, Jim, told a few funny stories, and it was good to hear the sound of laughter back in our house again. It was obvious that Gerry was getting tired because whenever I looked his way, he was yawning. He was ready to call it a night. I suggested that Mike and Ed take him upstairs and get him ready for bed. Shortly thereafter, Jim left for home and the girls and I headed for bed. I tried to fall asleep, but no such luck. I nudged Ed to see if he was still awake, but he didn't respond. I waited another half hour, just staring at the clock on the bedside table.

I finally realized I was not going to fall asleep until I went to Gerry's room to make sure that he was all right. I quietly snuck out of bed, slipped on my bathrobe and headed down the hallway. Funny noises were coming from his bedroom, so I tip-toed in. Gerry was snoring, sleeping like a baby. I went back to bed and didn't wake up until I heard Ed running the water in the bathroom. It was 7:00 A.M. Ed had catheterized Gerry at 2:00 and 6:00, and Mike turned him at 5:00 to make sure he didn't get any bed sores. Amazingly, I had slept through it all.

That Sunday morning, Gerry slept until 9:30. I went upstairs to help him bathe and get dressed; I was surprised at how much he could do for himself. I accidentally put his sweat pants on backwards, and he made me take them off and put them on the right way. We had a good laugh about it, but he told me not to try anything like that again because he wouldn't stand for it. His wonderful sense of humor was still intact.

The remainder of the day went without a hitch. We watched football again for most of the afternoon, and Ed cooked everyone's favorite for dinner that evening, Italian spaghetti, salad and garlic bread. By 8:30, Gerry was all tuckered out and decided it was time to go back to the other hotel. Ed and I drove him to the hospital, and as soon as he got in his room, he said he was ready to "hit the hay." He thanked us both for a fun weekend and said he was looking forward to another overnight.

Everything had gone well, and I knew I wouldn't be afraid the next time. I had prayed to God for guidance the night before Gerry came home, and I didn't forget to thank Him before I went to bed that night.

The next day, I called Ray at social services to get a list of LPNs and RNs who were interested in doing home health care. I also asked him about Gerry's transfer to the University of Minnesota Hospital in Minneapolis. Ray said it wouldn't be a problem, and mentioned he had already talked to the doctor about it. Later that day, Gerry's doctor came by and told him he could be released the following weekend, or whenever we were ready for him to come home. We weren't quite ready because we were still searching for a hospital bed, our number one priority. We had to make sure he'd be comfortable when he did come home. A downstairs family room would be Gerry's new bedroom. An attached bathroom was large enough for Gerry to get in and out of without a problem. A few changes needed to be made, such as removing the doors on the sink vanity so Gerry could get his wheelchair in close enough to brush his teeth, etc. I wasn't too concerned about the minor details because I knew Ed would take care of whatever needed to be done.

When I arrived at the hospital the following day, I was surprised to receive a phone call from the hospital administrator. He asked me to meet with him in one of the conference rooms. Though I wasn't sure what he wanted, I agreed to see him. This administrator knew we were unhappy about some of the things that had happened during Gerry's stay, and I was hoping he wanted to make them right.

"Have you found a hospital bed yet?" he asked.

"No, we haven't."

"Would you prefer to purchase a new bed or buy a demo?"

"We'd like to buy a demo."

"I also want to tell you that the flotation pad on Gerry's wheelchair is his when he leaves the hospital."

"Thank you. Gerry will appreciate that." Gerry's letter complaining about the charge had gotten someone's attention.

When I got back to Gerry's room, his roommate was in the middle of a conversation with his wife. He was saying how much it hurt when the nurse removed the staples from his incision so he told the nurse, "Now that you have my attention, you can cut it out."

I started to laugh, but quickly realized that no one else was laughing. Gerry took one look at me and made a quick exit out of the room. I followed him to the lounge. I was afraid he was upset with me, but as soon as we got inside, he looked at me with a big grin on his face. "You goofed, Mom."

"What else is new? I thought he was pretty funny."

"So did I," Gerry said, "but I always wait to see if the other person laughs before I do. That way, I'm not embarrassed."

"Oh, really! Did I embarrass you?"

"I guess you could say that." We stared at each other and then laughed out loud. He had been "pulling my leg" the whole time. Just then Ed and Joellyn walked into the lounge wondering what we were laughing about. Gerry didn't waste any time telling them about my bad behavior.

After we settled down, Gerry told us about the doctor's visit. The doctor had caught him off guard by asking him why he wanted to transfer to another hospital. Gerry told him he wanted to be checked out completely; in other words, he wanted a second opinion. I was proud of him for being up front with his doctor. Ed and I had already made that clear to the doctor when we spoke earlier, but I was happy Gerry, too, had the courage to speak his mind. The doctor also told him that Ray from social services would make all the necessary arrangements. I felt good when we left that evening because it appeared the transfer to the hospital in Minnesota, which was about 350 miles from home, was moving right along.

The next day I headed straight to the hospital after school because I had a reading council meeting scheduled for 5:00. I didn't want to miss it. It was a group of people I really enjoyed being with, but it also kept my mind occupied with a topic that was fun and exciting . . . reading. The council consisted of teachers, librarians, and volunteers who were involved in planning a variety of reading events for area teachers, parents, and children, such as "Reading Day at the Mall."

Gerry was excited to tell me some good news when I got to his room. He had talked with his doctor about the tingling in his feet; he said it had happened three or four times whenever he leaned over. I felt a twinge in my stomach. Was there still a chance he could regain some movement? The doctor told Gerry he would talk to the neurologist about it. I knew he was hanging on to the hope, as we all were, that something could still happen to change the outcome of his injury. I suggested we wait for the neurologist's evaluation before we attempted any conclusions of our own. We were used to waiting; it had been four months since the accident and we continued to keep a positive outlook.

Ray from social services came by and told us the airfare to Minneapolis would be $103, and gave us the information on flight times. He also called the doctor's office for appointment information. I thanked him and told him how much we appreciated all he had done for us. Because of Ray, our life had been a little easier during some very tough times. He was always willing to do whatever possible to make sure we got the assistance needed.

The neurologist stopped in to check on the tingling in his toes, but he was a man of few words. I tried to reassure Gerry, telling him to be patient and to keep having faith. I had to tell myself the same thing. Every time there was any new development, the doctors didn't seem to be very optimistic. Maybe they didn't want Gerry to have any false hopes about his recovery.

Just before I left school, Gerry called asking my permission to go out that evening with his physical therapist, Jill, and his friend, Bob. I was hesitant at first because it was unexpected, but I told him he should make the decision whether he wanted to go or not. Deep down I didn't want him to go, but as I sat there listening to him, I suddenly realized that a night out with friends would probably do him a world of good. I told him so.

When several of his friends came by to visit later, he told them they had to leave by 6:30 because he was going out on the town. Everyone laughed and began telling him how to behave in public. Gerry told them not to worry about his behavior, that they were the ones who needed some advice on that subject. The guys chuckled at Gerry's rebuttal, but I was hearing an "I-can-take-care-of-myself" response, and I liked it. When Bob came to pick him up, I told them to have a good time and headed for home. This was his first public outing. He would be doing more of them very soon. Once he was released from the hospital, Gerry wouldn't be content to sit in the house day and night; that wasn't our son.

I didn't sleep well that night. I lay in bed until after midnight wondering how Gerry might feel if he ran into a friend, and how that person would react to seeing Gerry in a wheelchair. Counting sheep must have worked because when the alarm went off, I had to remain in bed for a few minutes to figure out which day of the week it was. When I realized it was a work day, I quickly jumped into the shower.

That afternoon, I was surprised to find Gerry already in bed. A bladder infection was causing some leaking problems. His doctor had been in to see him and wanted to watch it for a day or so before he made a decision on what to do. The doctor again told us that bladder infections were very common with spinal cord injuries.

I waited for Gerry to say something about his night out, but that didn't happen. Finally, I asked, "How was your night out, Ger?"

"It was good." I waited for something more, but no such luck.

"Where did you go?" I asked, trying not to appear too nosy.

"The Portside Inn."

"What kind of a place is that?"

"It's a bar and you can get pizza there," he said.

"How was the pizza?"

"It was delicious! You and Dad should try it sometime."

"Well, did you have a good time?"

"Yes, Mom. I had a really, really good time." It was like pulling teeth to get Gerry to share details. I didn't let that stop me, but I just had to work a little harder with him than I did with the other children. He knew I didn't give up easily. I remember once when he said to me, "You don't have to know everything I do, Mom."

"No, not everything, Gerry," I responded. "But just about everything." He made a face at me and then grinned. Because of his sense of humor, I could get away with most anything I said to him. He was one very special kid, and I loved him with all my heart. I was looking forward to his being home again for the weekend. There were no butterflies in my stomach.

Ed picked up Gerry around 1:00 on Saturday. As they arrived in the yard, I went outside to greet him. "It looks like you're happy to be here," I said as I walked over to the car.

"You bet I am. I'm looking forward to some good home cooking and some football."

"Well, you're going to get both," I said as we went into the house. My sister, Sue, was bringing her homemade lasagna for dinner, and the Packers were playing on Sunday. It was going to be a perfect weekend.

When Sue and her family arrived, she also surprised us with a cake for our twenty-fifth wedding anniversary, the following Tuesday. And, it was Jim's birthday so I also had a cake for him. Needless to say, there was no shortage of desserts. We had a wonderful time with everyone. The day went by so fast that before I knew it, the evening was over. Gerry was yawning and giving me the sign. He slept upstairs in his own bed once again, and had a pretty good night.

On Sunday, Gerry was up and ready for Ed's scrambled eggs breakfast by 11:00. Mike was there to assist with his bath and to help him get dressed. He watched football all afternoon (the Packers won!) and after a steak dinner, he was ready to go back to the hospital. Again, I was pleased with how the weekend had gone. We'd be just fine once Gerry was released from the hospital and living back home. I also knew we'd have some difficult days because we still had a lot to learn about Gerry's daily living requirements. One day at a time; that was how I planned to do it.

I stayed home from school the next morning to call Minneapolis for an appointment for Gerry. I didn't get to talk with the doctor, but his secretary set up an October 12th date, which was only nine days away. I was excited about Gerry seeing another doctor, although I wasn't expecting to hear anything different than we had from our doctors. But I wanted the satisfaction of having a second opinion. At least then we'd know we had done everything possible. We didn't ever want to say, "If only . . . "

As soon as I hung up the phone, I made airline reservations for Gerry and myself and then drove straight to the hospital. When I arrived in the lobby, I ran into Ray from social services. I told him Gerry and I would be leaving Wednesday, October 12th, on the early flight, and we needed all of Gerry's records and X-rays to take with us. He said that was no problem and would take care of everything. I was relieved that Ray had been working with us the past several months; he'd been such a big help. I thanked him again for his support and got on the elevator to tell Gerry the good news.

I found him playing the Atari game. I walked in and gave him a big hug.

"What's that for?" he asked.

"Just because I love you so much," I whispered in his ear.

"You seem to be in a very good mood."

"I have some great news. You have a doctor's appointment on October 12th at the University of Minnesota Hospital in Minneapolis."

Gerry's smile was big. "How am I going to get there?"

"Everything is all set," I told him. "I made airline reservations for you and me, but Dad will drive to Minneapolis because he wants a car available while we're there."

"Wow, you move fast, Mom," he said. "Are you going to lift me up the steps so I can get on the plane?"

"No, my dear," I replied. "Someone will meet us and take care of that."

"You've thought of everything, haven't you?"

"We'll soon find out."

One of the nurses came by and said the hospital administrator wanted to meet with me about the hospital bed we were hoping to get for home. I learned we had to go through Northern Home Care for the service, and I was to call them to make the necessary arrangements. I called NHC and left a message for someone to call me. I had a good feeling we were finally going to get the bed we so desperately needed. Once again I was thankful we had a large house with large rooms and wide doorways that were accessible for our son.

The next afternoon I got a call from NHC saying we would be getting the hospital bed. The person on the phone told me the hospital administrator told them to take good care of us, and believe me, they did. I couldn't wait to tell Ed. I left for home around 5:30 to pick him up for Bertie's basketball game. Ed was relieved about the good news of the bed. Bertie's team won, and after the game the three of us went out for pizza. While we were in the restaurant, Bertie handed us a card and said, "Happy Anniversary Mom and Dad."

Ed and I burst out laughing. "Oh my gosh," I said, "I can't believe I forgot our anniversary."

"I remembered," Ed said smiling. "That's why I took you out for pizza."

"Where did the time go?" I asked. "Is it really twenty-five years since we exchanged our vows that beautiful day in October?"

"I can believe it," Ed joked. "Are you sure it's not thirty-five years?"

Bertie let out a chuckle as I gave him a nudge on the shoulder. Our anniversary was the last thing on both our minds; we had more important things to think about. Our youngest son was heading to the University of Minnesota Hospital in Minneapolis for a second opinion on his future. We had a pretty good idea what the doctor was going to tell us. Nevertheless, we were looking forward to the trip. In the back of my mind I kept thinking, "Maybe something more could be done in Minneapolis that they couldn't do at our hospital." I was trying very hard to keep a positive attitude, and I wanted Gerry to do the same.

When we got home that night, I called Gerry and found out his friend, Bill, was still at the hospital. He said, "We've been playing Atari, but now I'm beating Bill at checkers." Bill's family lived across the street from us, and he and Gerry were longtime close friends. I found out the next day that Bill stuck around playing games until 10:30 that evening.

"What a great friend," I thought to myself. "We sometimes take our friends for granted, but it's times like this we find out how much we really appreciate them." Gerry's friends had been great and they continued to come by to see him. Whenever the guys walked into his room, a big smile crossed Gerry's face. There were times when they really had him laughing, but you wouldn't always know Gerry was laughing because he never made a sound. He and his dad were exactly the same in that respect. The kids and I always got a chuckle out of watching Ed laugh, especially when he told one of his boring jokes. His eyes were full of twinkles, but we wouldn't hear a sound coming from his mouth. He thought we were laughing at his joke, but we were really laughing at him because he was so funny.

The next day after school I rushed off for my 3:15 dentist appointment and then to the hospital. Gerry was having physical therapy. I asked if I could go and watch him. She gave me the okay and so I quickly headed for the elevator and then to the PT room. Gerry was lying on a mat and one of the therapists was giving him instructions. I was glad to see Gerry smile when he saw me because I wasn't sure how he'd feel about my walking in on one of his sessions. I was amazed at what he could do and he seemed quite proud of his accomplishments.

Later, in his room, Gerry explained all the different exercises he'd been working on lately. Many of the exercises had to do with balance; transferring from his wheelchair to the mat, scooting around on the mat, and turning over from his back to his stomach. He really looked forward to his therapy sessions and missed having them on the weekends. He again mentioned the "tingle" in his back when he leaned forward, the same "tingle" he felt when they tightened his collar earlier. He was hoping it meant something good was happening. I didn't know what to think, and his doctors didn't seem to be concerned about it.

I wasn't ready for what came next. Gerry turned to me with a very serious look on his face. He started to say something, and then he'd stop and start over again. Finally, he simply smiled and said, "Mom, I want you to start going home from the hospital earlier."

"Why?"

"Because I have things to do."

"What kinds of things?"

"I want to do some reading. I don't have much time to read during the day because of all the interruptions. There's always someone in here doing something to me."

"Oh, I understand, Gerry. I know how busy the daytime hours are in a hospital. I've been there."

"I also want to write letters to a couple of friends who have gone back to college," he said. "I told them I'd keep in touch."

"I think that's a real good idea. I'm glad you're planning to do that."

"And besides, Mom," he said with a big smile, "it won't be long before I'll be back home, and then you'll be able to spend twenty-four hours a day with me."

"You're right, Ger. It'll be you and me, and Dad makes three." We both laughed and continued chatting about his day.

Gerry didn't always let me know about some of the things that took place during the night. But he thought I'd get a kick out of hearing that one of the night nurses put a rectal thermometer in his mouth. He was wrong; I wasn't amused! I told him if it happened again to let me know. He said that wouldn't be necessary because he would take care of it himself. He went on to tell me that someone had forgotten to see that he was catheterized at 3:00 A.M., as the doctor had ordered. He said he woke up at 4:30, feeling all sweaty and had to use his buzzer. I was beginning to feel upset, but he informed me that it had already been taken care of. He wanted to let me know that whatever went wrong, he could handle it, that he was able to take control of his own problems. He was our *sisu* son.

On the brighter side, Gerry's roommate, John, kept us laughing most of the time while I was waiting for Ed. John had had his head shaved before his surgery, and when the nurse walked in he told her he wanted to go to room 817. When she asked him why there, he said he had heard they were doing some fantastic hairstyles in that room. Gerry burst out laughing and suddenly started joking about his own hairstyle. John was good for Gerry; he had a great sense of humor. We could always count on a few laughs when John was around. I was in a good mood when Ed and I left the hospital . . . early enough for Gerry to have time alone.

Less than a week remained before Gerry's appointment at the University of Minnesota Hospital in Minneapolis. I was anxious to get going. I kept thinking about the possibility of the doctor saying there was nothing more that could be done for our son, but I also thought, maybe . . . Ed and I had talked about the prospects of the trip, and we both realized we had no control over the outcome. We would accept whatever the doctor handed us. It had been in God's hands from the beginning, and I had faith He would help us get through that next step.

The next day I headed straight for Physical Therapy when I got to the hospital. As before, I was amazed watching Gerry perform on the mat.

When we got back to his room, Gerry told me Emergency Medical Services would transport him to the airport on Wednesday and I could meet him there. I was happy they agreed to do that because it would be much less complicated than taking him from home. Everything was happening so fast. I was concerned about Gerry. Would he be able to sit on the plane for the two hours it would take to get there? Could I get him on and off the plane? Someone was supposed to meet us on the air strip to take us to the University Hospital. What if no one showed? What would I do then?

Gerry was still having bladder problems and had to miss his occupational therapy that morning. When he talked to the doctor about it, he was told that one muscle in his bladder might be stronger than the other one, causing the wetting. Gerry had hoped it meant something more. Every little thing that transpired gave us hope that he might be in the process of regaining some movement in his legs. It kept us going, and we needed that.

Gerry couldn't come home for the weekend because of the bladder infection. He spent almost forty-five minutes trying to use the urinal Friday evening because he wanted to be able to do this on his own. Knowing him, I was pretty sure he'd accomplish it. Ed and I left early to go to a basketball game and to give Gerry some time with his friends. He called me on Saturday morning and said he didn't remember much after he went to bed. He had taken an antihistamine which really knocked him out. He didn't even remember being catheterized during the night, but said he must have wet because his sweats were on the floor by his bed. He laughed when I asked if he had taken the pants off and tossed them. He answered, "No, but I do plan to do that when I get home, and you know who'll be picking them up."

"Oh, that's very interesting, Gerry Donald," I replied. "There will be a set of rules you'll have to follow when you get home, and if they're broken there will be a penalty."

"And, what might that be?" asked Gerry.

"I'm working on that, but I can tell you this much. There won't be a buzzer to press when you want me to come running. I realize you have some of those nurses under your spell, but your mother knows you better than they do."

Laughter sounded on the other end of the phone. "It won't take me long to convince you the same way I've convinced them," he said. He was right. I knew I'd do everything I could to make him comfortable once he got home. In other words, his wish would be my command. Ed and I, with a little help from his brothers and sisters, were going to make him our number one responsibility.

When Ed and I got to the hospital that evening, I told Gerry that

I had made our hotel reservations in Minneapolis, and in just four days we'd be on our way to get a second opinion. Once we got a second opinion on Gerry's condition, and there were no changes, it would be time for all of us to come to terms with his paralysis. As difficult as that would be, I prayed to God we'd have the strength to accept whatever we were handed. Because of Gerry's strong faith in the Lord, he would await His guidance.

On Sunday, Ed worked on the ramp most of the day trying to get it finished for Gerry's homecoming. I spent my time getting clothes ready for the trip, but I didn't know how much to take because we weren't sure how many days Gerry would be there. I decided to pack enough clothes for one week. If we had to be there longer, I'd find a washer and dryer somewhere. Of course, that was a minor detail. I kept thinking about the new doctor, imagining he was going to tell us that Gerry's paralysis was only temporary. I was even hearing his words, "Don't worry, Gerry," he said, "You'll be up walking very soon." I had to stop. I sat down on the bed trying to figure out why I was putting myself through so much pain. Was I hoping for too much in Minneapolis? Was Gerry going through the same? I needed to relax, so I went downstairs to the kitchen, made a cup of tea, and sat on the front porch for almost an hour watching the dog across the street. He was having a good time chasing after a cat.

That evening, Gerry told us he had a fun afternoon visiting with both his brothers, and his sisters. He mentioned that it was rather difficult getting a word in with Joellyn there. Joellyn was definitely a chatterbox. She could go on for twenty minutes without taking a break. Sometimes I'd ask her to stop so I could take a breath for her, but she'd just laugh and keep right on going. I was happy to see Gerry in such good spirits. He was looking forward to the trip on Wednesday. He reminded me he had only two more days left in the hospital, but after four and one-half months, I didn't have to be reminded of that. I couldn't wait for a change of scenery, and I knew Gerry must be feeling the same way. As we said good night on our way out the door, I asked him if he'd like one more meal from his favorite Italian restaurant. He nodded and I offered to do the same for his roommate. John gave me a big smile saying, "Just get me the same stuff you get for Gerry."

"How about steak and lasagna?"

"That sounds good to me," John replied. Gerry was going to miss John a lot, especially his great sense of humor. We were going to miss him, too.

Gerry and Ed with the belly dancer.

On Monday, while Gerry and John were eating their steak and lasagna, I cleaned out Gerry's hospital closet and drawer. I couldn't believe all the "stuff" he had accumulated in the four and one-half months he had been there: sweats, tee shirts, underwear, socks, and many cards from family and friends. I put most of it in a large plastic bag except for a change of clothes for the next two days. There was a going-away party at 1:00 the next day, and Gerry asked if I would pick up some cards for the nurses on rehab. I told him I'd be glad to do that. I wondered if Gerry would have a hard time saying good bye to certain staff members. He had become close to some of them, especially one. He asked me to get Bonnie a special card and a gift certificate for one of her favorite restaurants. One more day!

I was quite surprised when I got to the hospital the next day and learned that one of the staff members had hired a belly dancer to come and sing to Gerry. Was it the right thing to do? Gerry told me Ed was with him at the time, and they did have a few good laughs. Suddenly, I wondered if Gerry knew about the belly dancer all along, and had invited his dad to come by and join in the fun. Whatever happened, it didn't really matter. I had a good time teasing them both about the unexpected pleasure they had witnessed.

I also learned that Gerry wasn't exactly an innocent bystander at the party. He pulled one last trick on a physical therapist; he had someone sew up the sleeve on her jacket. By the time I arrived, everyone was having a good time eating carrot cake and drinking punch. When it was time for us to leave, there were a lot of hugs and kisses from the staff who had worked with Gerry. The tears flowed every time I saw someone bend over and hug him or give him a kiss on the cheek.

When we got back to his room later, we talked about his party, including the belly dancer. Gerry said he was more embarrassed for his dad than he was for himself. He admitted it was a total surprise and said he noticed Ed's face getting a little red when she first arrived. I told him it probably wasn't embarrassment, but excitement. Gerry grinned from ear to ear. I couldn't get over how much he reminded me of Ed. He was definitely his father's son. I said good night to Gerry and told him I'd see him at the airport early in the morning. He gave me a hug and told me not to worry about the airplane ride; he said he'd do just fine. He must have been reading my mind.

Chapter Ten

The night before the trip I dreamed the doctor in Minneapolis told us not to worry about Gerry's paralysis because it was only temporary. He informed us of three cases he had previously treated, and within six to twelve months, the patients were able to walk. He said he was sure Gerry would have a positive outcome as well. In my dream, Ed and I looked at each other, speechless. Gerry, too, stared at the doctor, unable to speak. And that's when I woke up.

I kept thinking about my dream. What if it was a sign? I knew that wasn't the case, but I wanted to hang on to one small shred of hope. Maybe it was a possibility? I had heard stories about people's dreams coming true on some television show. They probably made up the stories to get on the show. There I was lying in bed doing the same thing. I don't know how long it was before I fell back to sleep.

Joellyn drove me to the airport around 6:15. Emergency Medical Services vehicle arrived minutes later. By then the rain was coming down in buckets. Gerry got quite wet as they transferred him to the plane, where they strapped him in well. The rain didn't seem to bother him; he slept most of the trip. There were no problems. At the Minneapolis airport, a person from Handicapped International was already waiting on the tarmac with a wheelchair for Gerry. The gentleman introduced himself as Ronald and took us directly to "Admitting" at the University Hospital, and then on to Gerry's room. I don't know what I would have done without him; he was terrific! The charge was only $30, but I gave him a tip for his service.

The only tests scheduled for the first day were those that evaluated the amount of sensation Gerry had in his body, especially in his arms and legs. He was scheduled to meet with the doctor the following day. However, he did get to see a group of young interns who worked on the doctor's team. One of them, a fellow named Dave, happened to be from back home. "What a small world," he said, smiling, feeling more relaxed after meeting the team.

Ed arrived later that afternoon after a seven-hour drive. After spending time with Gerry in his room, we took a look around the hospital before heading to our motel. We were amazed at the size of the hospital complex. Even though I didn't know what was ahead for Gerry, my insides were more relaxed than they had been in a long time. The butterflies were finally gone!

I slept like a log that night, not awakening until 8:00. I hurried out of bed and into the shower; we wanted to be at the hospital by 10:00, in case the doctor came by. We were able to park our car and then take a shuttle bus to the area of the hospital where Gerry was a patient. Gerry's room was small, with only one bed; so he wouldn't be getting a roommate.

The doctor and his team had already been in to see Gerry. We were disappointed we had missed him, but were told the doctor wanted to meet with us. At his office, we introduced ourselves to a very tall man in his forties. He was most pleasant and told us about some of the tests Gerry would be having the following morning. He went on to explain that the three-dimensional tests would view the neck at different levels. He also informed us that there could be a decompression of the spinal cord, but said he wouldn't know that until after the tests were completed. He wanted a urologist to run a bladder test on Gerry, and have the results returned by Saturday or Monday. We felt good about Gerry's doctor; it appeared he was looking into all possibilities. We thanked him for meeting with us, and then left to see our son.

Gerry was sitting in his wheelchair eating lunch. We asked him if he was satisfied with what had taken place so far. He said he was very satisfied, and was eager to have the tests that the doctor ordered for him that next morning. He went on talking about it for at least ten minutes, which wasn't like him.

It was almost like a new beginning for the three of us, but we had to be cautious. We couldn't allow ourselves to be too optimistic about something that might never happen. We were well aware of what the doctors had told us back home, and our main purpose for being at the University of Minnesota Hospital was to get another doctor's opinion.

We didn't expect Gerry to leave that hospital without his wheelchair, and we were sure that our son realized that as well. Several months of hospital time made him aware that it was difficult for anyone to make any definite promises about his future.

Ed and I were at the hospital the following morning by 8:30 A.M., but Gerry had already left for some of the tests. One was called a myelogram, which is an X-ray examination performed by a radiologist. A dye is injected into the fluid-filled space around the spinal cord to help the doctor detect any abnormalities of the spine, spinal cord or surrounding structures. He was also scheduled for a tomogram, a selective X-ray that photographs a particular layer of tissue, while blurring out images of other layers. The nurse said he had left about 7:30, before breakfast. Back to his room, Gerry gobbled down his lunch, eating everything on his plate. At 3:30, he was scheduled for a CT Scan and some bladder tests. We hardly saw him except at lunch time, so Ed decided to take Gerry's wheelchair to Abbey Medical to have it checked over. By the time he got back, the urologist had the test results and was in Gerry's room telling him his bladder reflex was normal. He suggested that Gerry use a urinal every two hours by tapping his bladder, and then be catheterized every four hours to see how much urine was left between each session. It was obvious that Gerry was worn out from his very busy day. He later complained of a headache, and the nurse said it was caused from the myelogram. Ed and I left early that evening so he could get some much needed rest.

Ed was rather quiet on the drive back to our motel. I had a feeling we were both thinking the same thing. "How come you're so quiet tonight?"

"Oh, I'm just thinking."

"About what?"

"About everything. I really don't think we're going to find out anything more than we already know about Gerry's condition."

"I've been thinking the same thing, but isn't that why we came here, to get a second opinion?" I asked. "Are you sorry we came?"

"Oh no, not at all," he insisted. "I'm glad we came so that we are able to compare these test results with the test results back home. Otherwise, we would always be wondering if we had done enough."

"I'm glad you feel that way, Ed, because I totally agree with you. I wouldn't feel right if we hadn't taken this extra step."

If we didn't learn anything different than we had from the doctors back home, we would move on and do whatever possible to help make our son's life as "normal" as could be. I especially wanted to make sure that he didn't feel like a burden on us. More than anything, I wanted him to know we loved him very much. I lay in bed wide awake, looking at Ed sleeping next to me. I thanked God he was by my side.

It was Saturday, October 15th. Ed and I decided to go out for breakfast before heading for the hospital, so we stopped at a little family-style restaurant just a block from our motel. As the waitress was setting our eggs and sausage on the table, I noticed a man at another table staring at me. I tried to ignore him, but when I looked up again his eyes were still on me. Suddenly he got up from his chair and walked toward us. I kicked Ed under the table, but it was too late. The man was already standing in front of us with his hand on Ed's shoulder. "Excuse me, sir, but aren't you Andy Griffith?"

Ed smiled, with a red face. "No, I'm not, but you're not the first to ask me that question. I get that a lot."

The man then apologized for staring at me. He said he had to come over and find out for himself if Ed was really Andy. I told him I didn't mind and said that living with a celebrity look-a-like was just something I had to deal with. He smiled and shook Ed's hand before he went back to his table. I looked forward to telling Gerry about his "famous" father. It had happened many times amongst our family and with friends, but that had been the first time a stranger picked up on it. I kidded Ed that maybe he could work as Andy's double in a movie sometime. He said it depended on how much they'd be willing to pay him.

One of the doctors on the team stopped by Gerry's room to say that the tests showed no decompression of the spinal cord, at least in his opinion. However, he said he would leave the final say to Gerry's doctor, the expert. After he left Gerry was quiet and appeared to be a bit down about the news. He slept most of the afternoon. Even though we hadn't expected any miracles, I had hoped they might find something new that could change the prognosis.

There was a bright spot that day. One of Gerry's best friends from back home, along with his girlfriend, were in Minneapolis and stopped by to see him. I know Gerry was wishing he had some good news to tell Bill and Amy, but he was very happy to see them. What was there about friends that always managed to bring a smile? Ed and I left for a cup of coffee to give them a chance to visit. When we got back, we asked Gerry if he'd like to come to our motel on Sunday to watch the Vikings football game. Ed had checked on tickets, but there weren't any available. It would have been great for Gerry if we could have been at the game instead of watching it on television. We left for the motel around 8:00 that evening because Gerry wanted some time to himself.

I was anxious to get through Sunday and on to Monday so we could meet with the doctors and hear what they had to say. We picked up Gerry around 11:00 A.M. and decided to take a ride. We drove around the area for a while, but Gerry didn't seem interested so we went back to the motel to watch the football game. While watching the game, he fell asleep on the bed, so I made a quick trip to the mall to look for a U of M shirt.

He was awake when I got back, and when I showed him the shirt, he gave me only half a grin. I guess he wasn't in the mood for souvenir shirts. After some pizza, we drove Gerry back to the hospital. He was very quiet in the car, and mentioned he was anxious to get home. I think he was hoping for more than he got from the doctor, and was feeling a little sad.

Ed and I were feeling it also, but we had to quickly change our mood because we had our son's future to think about.

By our arrival time on Monday morning, Gerry had already talked with the team rehab doctor and was told he would be released. The doctor said he had had a conversation with Gerry's doctor back home and found out they were doing the same things in rehab that were being done at the University Hospital. I think it was both a happy and a sad time for all of us–happy because we were going back home, and sad because the news was rather anticlimactic. We wanted, and had hoped for, a different outcome. We didn't get one; therefore, we had to face it and move on.

I went straight to bed when Ed and I arrived at the motel that evening. I was mentally exhausted and needed a good night's sleep. Tuesday was going to be a very long day. We had to be at the hospital by 8:00 A.M. Once we talked with Gerry's doctors and his dismissal was taken care of, Ed would leave to drive back home. As before, Gerry and I would fly home. I kept thinking about all that was going to take place the following day, and I felt even more exhausted than when I first went to bed. I was wishing I could've had the time with Ed in the car so we could talk about the plans for Gerry's future. But, we had to put that off for a few more days. I must have finally dozed off because the next thing I remembered was Ed tapping me on the shoulder telling me it was time to get up.

The doctor met with us at noon to discuss Gerry's rehab and to answer any questions. When he walked in the door I was still hoping to hear something new, but that wasn't the case. Since the tests showed no decompression of the spinal cord, the diagnosis remained the same. Physically, Gerry was able to move his arms and hands, had limited finger manipulation, but could not move his legs or feet. He did have some sensation throughout his body. The spasms would be a part of Gerry's life, but could be controlled somewhat with medication. The doctor did put into place a bladder management program which included different medications and an external catheter. "As for rehabilitation, Gerry, I'd like you to continue with the program you're involved in back home. They're doing many of the same things we do here."

"I am planning to do that."

"It's also important that you keep a positive outlook for your future. There's research being done on spinal cord injury, and it's important that you continue with whatever plans you had made prior to your accident. Don't wait around for things to change, Gerry; make the decision now to do the best with what you have."

"I had one year of college in before my accident, and I recently decided to take a correspondence course in Greek Mythology."

"Why Greek Mythology?" the doctor asked.

"It was one of a group of classes I had to choose from," said Gerry, "I decided to get it over with as soon as possible."

"Oh, I remember those," the doctor said with a chuckle. "We tried to pick the one we thought would be the least amount of work."

"It didn't work for me," Gerry said, humorously.

The doctor seemed pleased that Gerry had made the decision to continue with his education and wished him the best. He shook Gerry's hand and told us to give him a call if we had any questions. As soon as the doctor left, Ed said goodbye to Gerry and me and headed out the door for his long drive home. I called Handicapped International and asked if Ronald, the same gentleman who picked us up at the airport, would be able to take us for our 6:45 P.M. flight home. I was pleased when they said he was available and would be there by 6:00. According to plan, we would arrive home shortly after 9:00 that evening.

Ronald was at the hospital and in Gerry's room by 6:00 sharp; he had a big smile on his face. He treated Gerry as if he were the most important person in the world, and he kept asking me if there was anything he could do for me. I thanked him for being so wonderful and told him he was exactly the kind of person needed for that job. He smiled and said, "Well, Ma'am, you just made my day! Thank you from the bottom of my heart."

As I slipped a tip into his hand, I said, "You're most welcome, Ronald, and good luck to you, sir." As I reached the top step of the plane, I turned around to wave and he was standing there holding his cap in his hand waving back. Gerry was already strapped in his seat. Within minutes we were on our way home. Gerry slept most of the flight, but as soon as the plane started to descend, he opened his eyes. "Are we home, Mom?" he whispered.

"Yes, Gerry. We're home and I hope Mike's here to pick us up." A young man assisted Gerry off the plane and into his wheelchair, and as soon as we got into the airport, Ed and Mike were standing by the door. Ed had gotten home about 8:00 so he came along with Mike. Mike walked over with a smile. "I'm here to take my mom and my brother home."

"And home is where we want to go, Mike. Isn't that right, Ger?"

"More than anything in this world," he said quietly. Ed helped Mike get Gerry into the car and we headed for our big old house on Main Street, only ten minutes from the airport.

"What now?" I said to myself. "Where do we go from here? What should we be doing next? Are we prepared?"

Chapter Eleven

It felt great to sleep in my own bed once again, and sleep I did. Before Ed and I went upstairs that night, Mike told us not to worry about anything as far as Gerry was concerned. He said he would set his alarm and get up to turn Gerry every three hours to prevent any bed sores. I gave Mike a hug and told him we appreciated what he was doing, but I already knew how much he wanted to be there for his brother. If Mike hadn't been living at home at the time, Ed would have gotten up during the night without giving it a second thought.

I was glad I hadn't planned to go back to work the next day because I wasn't very energetic. In fact, I was feeling somewhat depressed. I had to get myself into the shower because a home health care worker was coming by to meet with Gerry and discuss a daily schedule. I immediately went downstairs to Gerry's bedroom, but Mike had beat me to it. He took one look at me and said, "You'd better get into the shower, Mom."

"Thanks, Mike," I whispered. "You're the best!" I followed his orders. The home health care nurse arrived soon after. I met up with her in Gerry's room.

"Hi," she said. "My name is Kate. Starting tomorrow, I'll be here every day at 9:00 A.M. to help Gerry bathe and get dressed."

"That sounds good to me." I said. "If there's anything you need, Kate, just let me know."

"Thanks. I'll see you tomorrow morning, Gerry."

"I'll make sure he's awake and ready for you," I said smiling.

"Don't worry about me." Gerry said. "I'm an early riser."

After she left, I helped him bathe and get dressed, and then I made bacon and eggs for his breakfast. He was hungry as a horse, eating every tidbit on his plate, and even asked for another slice of toast. I told him it was probably my home-cookin' that stirred up his appetite. He agreed, and said I had a knack for cooking eggs just the way he liked them. It was one of the few things in the cooking department that I did better than Ed; I liked basting the eggs instead of turning them over because I didn't want the yoke to break. Ed usually broke the yoke and then blamed it on the egg.

After I cleaned up the dishes, I sat with Gerry at the kitchen table and asked if he wanted to talk about anything the doctor discussed with us at the University of Minnesota Hospital. "What's there to talk about?" he asked.

I hesitated. "I'm not sure."

"Don't worry about me, Mom. I'm okay."

"I know you are, but I think we need to talk about some of the things that are on your mind and mine. You'll feel better afterward, and so will I."

"Like what?" asked Gerry.

"Well, for starters, is there anything Dad and I can do to make your life easier at home?"

"I'll need some time before I can answer that." A little smirk appeared on his face. "As long as you and Dad make all of my favorite meals, I won't complain."

"Hey, that sounds pretty easy," I said with a chuckle. "Dad and I will do our best to please you. And, by the way, what would you like for supper tonight?"

"How about a steak?" he suggested. "A side of spaghetti and garlic bread would taste pretty good, too."

"I'll see what I can do, Ger. We aim to please."

With that, the biggest grin came over Gerry's face and I knew then that our talks would continue. I was going to rely on Gerry's humor to get us through the tough times.

Gerry spent most of the morning getting caught up on the local newspapers, and when Ed came by for lunch, the conversation quickly turned to some of the more important things that had to be tended to, such as wheelchair repairs and the stock market. I enjoyed listening to them because they discussed subjects that I didn't think about and didn't have to deal with. I thanked God every day for having Ed in my life, and as Gerry requested, Ed made steak, spaghetti, and garlic bread for supper that night.

During the next several weeks, Gerry continued with his correspondence course in Greek Mythology, and I was thrilled that he was talking about taking another class the following semester. I was back at school, but among Ed, Gerry's nurse, and others in the family, someone was with Gerry most of the time. Ed's business was only a block from our house, so he could be home in minutes if Gerry needed him. Everything was working out quite well with home health care, and I was taking over the responsibilities on the weekends. I helped Gerry with his bath, his daily attire, and his schedule of medications. I knew at times he was bored, so I suggested he invite some of his friends to stop by during the day or evening. I even mentioned that Ed and I would go for a drive or visit family and friends so they could have the time to catch up. Several of the guys were away at school, but some were still working around the area or attending NMU. Just as we were having that conversation, the phone rang; it was one of Gerry's friends asking if he'd like some company.

Gerry hung up the phone. "Mom, how about you and Dad taking a ride after supper."

I kidded with him, asking, "How long should we be gone?"

"Oh, at least a couple hours. We have a lot to talk about, and we may want to order a pizza."

"No problem," I said. "That'll give us time to see a movie or go to my sister's house for a visit."

"Remember, Dad doesn't care for movies," Gerry reminded me. "You'd better call your sister to see if they're busy tonight."

"You're right," I said. "Your Dad fell asleep during the last movie." As it turned out, we did visit my sister, Sue, and her husband, George. We hadn't had an opportunity to visit much since before Gerry's accident. Sue and I were as close as sisters could be and had always shared a lot with each other. It meant the world to me to have her in my life. Of my three sisters, she was the only one who lived in the area; we saw the others only a couple times a year. Before the accident, I hadn't realized how important it was to have family around during a crisis.

Gerry and his friend were finishing their pizza when Ed and I walked in the kitchen door. We visited for a few minutes, and then went to the living room to watch television. I wanted Gerry to realize that his friends were always welcome in our home, and we would never intrude on their time together. It wasn't long before we heard the kitchen door close, and then Gerry came into the living room to sit near us.

"How was your evening with Sue and George?"

"We caught up on a lot of things," I answered. "What about you?"

"It was just what I needed," he said. "I can't believe how much I've missed out on these past months. I'm going to have to do this at least once a week."

"How about twice a week?" I offered. "There's nothing like getting together with your buddies to find out what's happening around town."

"Sounds good," Gerry said, "But, I also have studying to do for my class."

"You'll fit it in somewhere," I said jokingly. "I had to do it when I went back to school, and I had five youngsters to care for." How did I ever manage to take classes during those hectic days? And then it came to me. His name was Ed. He would suggest that I stay at the library after class and get my work done while he was home making supper for the children and helping them with their homework. I'd get home around 8:00 in the evening, and then we'd sit down to eat and chat about our day. What a guy!

For the next several weeks, Gerry's friends continued to come by the house, and we were soon settled into a daily routine. Suddenly, Gerry's birthday was just a few days away; he was about to turn nineteen. It had been six months since his accident, and so far there hadn't been any problems we weren't able to handle. I felt good about the way things were going, and Gerry seemed to be doing quite well. Three days before his birthday, I caught him off guard when I mentioned having a party and inviting some friends over. He had this quizzical look on his face.

I sat down next to him. "It's your birthday on Sunday," I repeated. "I was wondering if you'd like to have some friends over for pizza."

"I haven't thought much about it. Doesn't my birthday fall on a Thursday?"

"No." I walked over and got the calendar off the counter. "See, the 27th falls on a Sunday."

Gerry turned the calendar back a page and admitted that he had been looking at the month of October. "See," he muttered, "The 27th was on a Thursday."

"Okay, Ger. Let's get back to the business of the party. Would you like to have some friends over for pizza?"

"Sounds good to me," he said. "And, there's a Packer game on Sunday so I hope you don't mind if we're kind of loud. Do you think you and Dad can handle loud?"

Nancy,

Thanks for lending me the book. What a courageous family! It touched all my emotions!

Chris

Helping Our Heroes

"We'll try," I answered. "You and your buddies can watch the game in the living room, and we'll see it in the kitchen." I was happy he agreed to a party, because I thought it would be good for him to watch the game with his friends as he had done so many times in the past. I suggested that we celebrate his birthday on Saturday with his brothers and sisters, and he was all for that.

Gerry called some of the guys who were still in the area, and invited them over on Sunday to watch the Packers. Ed picked up the pizza, and when they were finished eating, we surprised Gerry with his favorite birthday cake, chocolate cake with chocolate frosting. After seconds on the cake and a lot of laughs in between, the guys left saying their goodbyes and thanking us for the party. As soon as the last one walked out the door, Gerry told us how much he appreciated having his buddies over. I gave him a big hug and reassured him that they were always welcome in our home.

Monday was quite normal. I went off to school and the rest of the family went about their usual routines of either working or attending classes. But by mid-afternoon, the emotions began to build. I didn't know why it was happening or what might have triggered it, but I could feel myself beginning to lose control. At about 2:30, a young boy came into the library and asked if we had any books about cats dying. I remembered a book called *The Tenth Good Thing About Barney* written by Judy Viorst, and I went to the shelf to look for it. As I handed it to the student, he told me his cat had died over the weekend, and he wanted to know if there was a book that might help him plan the funeral. I started to tell him about the book, but he took my hand and asked me to read it to him. At first I suggested his mom or dad might want to read the story to him, but he again asked me to do it. I sat down at the table, opened the book and began to read:

"My cat Barney died last Friday. I was very sad. I cried, and I didn't watch television. I cried, and I didn't eat my chicken or even the chocolate pudding. I went to bed, and I cried."

As I finished the first page, I felt the tears coming in my eyes. I tried to read the next sentence, but the words were stuck in my throat. I closed the book and apologized to the little boy, suggesting that he take the book home and have someone finish reading the story to him. He got up from his chair, put one arm around me and told me that it was all right to cry. He said he cried a lot over the weekend, but was feeling much better now. I told him to think of ten good things about his cat and to write them down on a piece of paper, then come back the next day and tell me what those ten things were.

After supper that evening, I shared my experience at school. I could feel my voice shaking a little during certain parts of the story, but managed to get through it without any tears. But later that night as I went to say good night to Gerry, I really fell apart. I was putting my arms around him when I felt my lips start to quiver. I couldn't pull myself away. I sobbed hysterically for several minutes. When I finally calmed down, I realized that Gerry was crying, too. I sat on the bed and held him tightly, whispering, "It's been a long time coming, Ger. I'm sorry."

"There's nothing to be sorry about, Mom," he said. "I needed that just as much as you did."

"I think we try so hard to hold back our emotions. I'm sure your dad is going through some of the same feelings we are, but he's one who tries to keep everything inside."

"And I know what you're going to say next," Gerry stated, "that I'm just like him."

"You are definitely your father's son," I declared, smiling. "But, I wouldn't have you any other way." I leaned over and kissed him on the cheek before I headed up to bed.

As I walked toward the stairs, Gerry yelled, "How about a game of Trivial Pursuit tomorrow night?"

"I'd like that," I answered, turning around to see his face. "But do you remember who beat you the last time we played that game?"

"I've been practicing," he threatened. "It's my turn."

"If you're game, then so am I."

"You're on, Mom," he promised. We did play Trivial Pursuit the next evening, and Gerry had no trouble beating me; I told him that I must have gotten all the difficult questions. We were both in a much better mood. The emotional release was something that needed to happen so we could move on.

The days and weeks passed quickly without any major problems, and before I knew it, Christmas was only three days away. I was busy cleaning and decorating the house when I decided to move one of the armchairs from the living room into Gerry's bedroom. I thought it would give him extra seating for his friends. He didn't say anything about it at first, but when I went back in to dust the furniture, he complained about the chair being there. He said it made his room look too crowded. I told him I thought the room looked fine. As soon as the words came out of my mouth, I regretted them. The look on Gerry's face indicated that I'd better move that chair, and do it quickly.

I felt terrible. It was our first disagreement since he'd come home. Tears streamed down my face as I walked out of his room, but I wiped my eyes and went back to apologize. "Your room does look a bit crowded with the extra chair."

"I'm sorry, Mom. I'm just having a bad day."

I gave him a hug and a little time to himself. His friend, Bill, stopped by later and Gerry asked me to bring the chair back into his room.

Christmas came and went before we knew it. We tried to make the holiday the happy occasion it had always been in the past, but it was obvious that everyone was a little tense. I made pork pies for Christmas Eve, which was a family tradition on my mom's side. Everyone in the family loved them. We also opened our presents that night, and each of the kids brought Gerry something special. He looked a little embarrassed as he opened their gifts because he could see that he had more gifts than anyone else. Jim broke the ice by telling him he had to buy two presents for each of their birthdays. Everyone laughed, and Gerry seemed a bit more relaxed. We could always

Gerry enjoys Christmas with his grandma, Marie Sarvello
and her husband, Frank Sarvello

count on Jim for some humor.

Ed made the entire Christmas dinner: turkey, mushroom stuffing, mashed potatoes, sweet potatoes, fresh broccoli, and homemade cranberry sauce. I made one of Gerry's favorite desserts, blueberry pie served with a scoop of ice cream. Two hours later some were still complaining about their aching stomachs. The girls and I cleaned up afterward while the guys sat in the living room chatting about business, which was pretty normal since Jim and Mike both worked with their dad. Later, as I was clearing the dishes from the dining room table, I heard someone ask Gerry how his Mythology class was going. Loud laughter. I hadn't heard his comment, but knowing Gerry's sense of humor, he had probably given them some sort of incredulous response. It felt really good to hear them having fun with each other.

Several months had passed and we were all getting accustomed to having Gerry back home. He still had home health care coming by on a daily basis, and everyone else in the family was going on with their normal lives. He had completed his correspondence course and had signed up for a directed study in history the following semester. In the spring, he was hoping to go back to the University campus to work on a degree in Business Management. When Gerry told us of his plans, I knew then he had definitely decided to make education his number one priority. I'd have bet the house he'd do just that because he was one to set goals.

I must admit he took me by surprise, however, the day he announced he was giving his home health care nurse a two-week notice. We were sitting in the kitchen on a Saturday morning, enjoying a cup of coffee together when he sprung it on me. "Oh by the way, Mom. I'm going to tell Kate on Monday that I won't be needing her anymore."

"What do you mean?" I asked. "Do you have someone else in mind?"

"No. I'm going to start taking care of myself."

"Oh." I studied him. "Do you really think you are able to do that?"

"Well, I'm sure going to try," he insisted. "It'll probably take me a little longer at first, but eventually I'll be able to handle it."

"Knowing you, Ger, you'll do it. Remember, I'm here on the weekends if you want some help." I tried not to let on that I was terribly concerned about what he was planning to do.

"Thanks, Mom. Don't worry about me, I'll be just fine. I know what I'm capable of doing, and what I can't do. You know that I'd never attempt something that was impossible."

"Now wait a minute," I laughed. "What about your boxing days?"

"Are you saying that I didn't win any matches?"

"Win or lose," I declared, "Your face always looked the same the morning after."

"Case closed," he insisted. "Kate has just two more weeks to enjoy my company, and then I'm on my own."

"It's your decision, Gerry, and I'm proud for wanting to give it a try."

On Monday Gerry told his nurse about his plans and gave her a two-week notice. When Kate left that day, she commented how much she admired Gerry for his decision, and that she had no doubts that he could do it. I, too, felt he could do it, but being his mother made it a little more worrisome. I was glad I had two weeks to get used to the idea. The time went by fast and before I knew it Gerry was bathing and getting himself dressed on a daily basis; it was taking him longer, but he didn't seem to mind that at all. He was able to move his body from his bed to his wheelchair without any assistance. He talked to his dad about adapting the shower in the bathroom, and Ed took care of that within a day or two. He removed the glass door and replaced it with a plastic curtain that Gerry could easily slide across. He also built a seat that swung out from the stall. That allowed Gerry to move from his wheelchair into the shower, and back on his bed where he got himself dressed. From that point on, he had no problem taking care of his personal needs. When Gerry made up his mind to do something, there was no holding him back.

Gerry seemed happy with his new independence, and in the spring of 1984 he began taking classes at Northern Michigan University. He made all the arrangements for the transit system to pick him up at home and to drop him off on the campus. He also made arrangements for a note taker since he didn't have full use of his fingers. He had to hold a pencil in a different way, but he didn't let that stop him. I was thrilled that he was going back to finish his degree, but I worried about him traveling across campus alone in a wheelchair. What if he got stuck along the way, or wasn't able to open a door to a building, what then? My hope was that someone would be nearby or come along and give him the help he needed. When I mentioned my concerns to Gerry, he just smiled and told me not to be thinking about things like that. "You worry too much, Mom. Nothing is going to happen to me."

"I know, Ger, but I can't help it," I admitted. "I'm the mom."

It was several weeks later before Gerry told me that he had had a problem entering one of the buildings on campus. He was in the process of opening the door so he could get through, not realizing there was a step on the other side. Suddenly, his wheelchair tipped over and down he went. Luckily, there was a student who came along right behind and helped him up. He kept this from me because he knew if he told me I'd be horrified. He was right. He tried to make it sound humorous, but it didn't work. He could see by the look on my face that I was scared to death that something might happen again. I didn't have to wait very long.

The following winter semester, we were hit with a lot of snow one day. Despite the weather, Gerry was picked up for classes and dropped off at the University. He wheeled himself across campus, through the snow to the building where his class was being held. He was greeted by a sign on the door: "Class canceled because of weather." It happened to be the only class Gerry had on that particular day, so he spent several hours in the library while he waited for his ride back home. When he told us about his experience, I became somewhat frantic. I couldn't believe the instructor wasn't able to get to class if Gerry could make it across a snowy campus in a wheelchair. But, I had to admit, I wasn't surprised by what Gerry had done. He had endured several challenges since his accident without ever giving up. It was that *sisu* thing.

For the next two years, Gerry continued with his education at NMU with no major problems. He was still being picked up for his classes, but began talking to Ed about wanting a van for himself. I overheard their conversations, but I tried to put the idea of a van out of my mind. I couldn't imagine Gerry driving a vehicle, and I didn't even want to discuss it with him. It would be just one more thing for me to worry about. As it turned out, nobody asked for my opinion, and I soon realized that it was about to happen.

In the fall of 1986, our son became the proud owner of a light blue Ford van. He and Mike drove to Minneapolis to have it converted so Gerry would be able to drive it. He would be getting special driving lessons, but I suggested to Mike that he should do most of the driving on the way back home. Ed and I both agreed that Gerry shouldn't drive too many miles after just learning how to operate his new vehicle. Besides, we didn't want to worry while we were waiting for them to return.

As the time of their expected arrival drew close, I was pacing back and forth from one window to another. Suddenly, Ed yelled from the kitchen, "They just drove in." We both headed out the door to watch Mike get out of the van and walk around the other side to give Gerry a hand with the lift. Soon Gerry was on the lift being moved down to the ground where he could wheel himself on to the sidewalk. As they came toward us, both had big smiles on their faces.

"What are you two smiling at?" I asked. Gerry kept it up and didn't say a word.

"Gerry did all of the driving on the way home," Mike said with a big grin, "And he's really good at it."

"I hope you weren't going over the speed limit," remarked Ed.

"No, I kept it between fifty and fifty-five," Gerry said, in a more serious tone.

"Well, what are your thoughts about driving?" asked Ed. "Do you think you'll be able to handle it in the snow?"

"I really enjoy it," said Gerry. "And I can't wait to drive myself to school. As for driving in the snow, you'll have to ask me that after I tackle it a couple of times." He told me later that for the first time since his accident, he felt he had reclaimed his independence, and was looking forward to driving himself to school for his final year of classes.

Gerry did exactly what he set out to do. In the spring of 1987 he received his degree in Business Management from NMU. He had set his goals, worked hard, and successfully reached the most important one of all . . . his education. Ed and I were very proud of what our son had accomplished; we began to wonder what his next goal might be.

It wasn't long before we found out.

Chapter Twelve

In August 1988, Gerry went to Butterworth Hospital in Grand Rapids, Michigan for three months of bicycle therapy. We weren't aware of it at the time, but he had called and put his name on a waiting list as soon as he learned of the special program. It must have been popular for many types of rehabilitation, because he had to wait several months before they had an opening. Bicycle therapy, also known as FES (Functional Electrical Stimulation), allows people with spinal cord injuries to "exercise" their leg muscles through the use of an electrical current. Electrodes are attached to the three large muscle groups in the legs and buttocks, then the patient's legs are strapped to a stationary bike. Gerry could actually "peddle" the bike using his own leg muscles. The research that was being done indicated that this therapy could help reduce muscle atrophy and bone deterioration, as well as have cardiovascular benefits.

Once the call came telling him he was next in line for the therapy, he packed his suitcase and headed downstate in his van. I worried about him driving all those miles by himself, but there wasn't anything I could do about it. He was going to make the trip no matter what, despite anyone's concerns. But I was relieved when we got the call saying he had arrived safely. He told us he had an apartment in the hospital's "Hospitality House" which was across the street from the hospital. It was a place for visiting patients and their families. Gerry was very thankful when Steve, his good friend from high school, met him in Grand Rapids to help him move in.

I waited a couple of weeks before asking Gerry if it was all right to come and see his new place. He gave me the okay, so Ed and I packed a suitcase and headed to the big city. It was about a seven-hour drive, which gave me plenty of time to concoct a vision in my head of Gerry's apartment. I pictured three very small rooms: a kitchen, a bedroom, and a bathroom. The kitchen was so narrow that Gerry wasn't able to turn his wheelchair around; he had to back up to get out of the doorway. The bedroom was a dismal room with one small window and no curtains or shades. And, the bathroom was a total disaster; it had a bathtub, but no shower! I was relieved when I heard Ed asking me if I'd like to stop for a bite to eat. "Yes," I answered quickly and then started laughing.

"Where have you been for the past thirty minutes?" he asked.

"You don't want to know. Why do I do this to myself?"

"Do what?"

"I've been sitting here imagining what Gerry's apartment looks like," I said. "And, it wasn't a pretty sight."

"Try not to think about it until we get there," Ed offered. "You'll probably be pleasantly surprised."

"You're right," I laughed. "Let's stop and eat; I'm starving!" We found a nice little restaurant with a sign on the front that said 'Home Cooking' and we ordered the most delicious chicken pot pie I'd ever tasted.

I tried to keep my mind occupied for the remainder of the trip, taking in all the summer sights of August and chatting with Ed about some of the things I'd seen. There were several fresh fruit stands along the side of the road, and when we came upon one with Michigan cherries, I asked Ed to stop.

Two young children, a boy and a girl, took care of the customers while their mom sat watching on the porch. They were very sweet, and even offered to wash the cherries if we wanted to eat some in the car which, of course, we did. They had several containers of fresh water in which they swished the cherries before putting them in clean plastic bags. I told them what a great job they were doing and asked how long they had been in the cherry business. The young boy said they started about 10:00 that morning. I couldn't help but smile and wished them good luck as I got back into the car. By the time we arrived in Grand Rapids, I had managed to save only a few for Gerry.

Ed was right; I was pleasantly surprised when we walked into Gerry's building. It was a large brick complex with security in place. I breathed a deep sigh of relief. We had to tell the gentleman at the desk who we were, and then he gave us directions to Gerry's apartment, which was a short distance down the hallway. As we were about to knock on the door, it opened and there he was with a big smile on his face. When we asked how he knew we were there, he told us that security had called to say we were on our way. Gerry was definitely in a safe environment, and I could feel myself relaxing more and more as he showed us around his living quarters. We walked through the combined living room and kitchen area; it was nothing like I had envisioned. There were only a few pieces of furniture: a couch with a matching chair, a refrigerator, a cabinet for dishes and food storage, and a kitchen table. There was plenty of space for Gerry to move around in, and that's what he needed more than anything else. He seemed proud of his small apartment, but even more proud of the fact that he was living on his own. Gerry was becoming his own man, and loving every minute of his new-found independence. I had to let go; the time had come for our son to make his own decisions.

We walked from Gerry's apartment across the street to Butterworth Hospital to meet some of the people he worked with. Because his bicycle therapy was only three days a week, he volunteered his free time at the hospital. He enjoyed the work and looked forward to spending time with the people he was involved with. After a couple of days, Ed and I became aware of our son's busy schedule and decided to return home. Gerry was doing exactly what he wanted to do and seemed totally immersed in his new life. He continued to amaze us.

It was strange not having Gerry home with us. I missed him terribly. When I got home from school, we used to sit and talk about his day, and then I'd tell him about my day at school. Gerry always got a kick out of some of the interactions I had with students in the library, like the third-grader who informed me that he wouldn't be able to return his book because his pet had eaten it. When I asked him what kind of a pet, he said it was a snake. At that point, I told him he'd have to pay to replace the book, and he took his hand out of his pocket handing me a one dollar bill. I told him it would probably cost between five and ten dollars, and he said he'd be right back. I thought he had gone back to his room to get more money, but when he returned he handed me the book saying, "I love this book, Mrs. H. It's the best book I've ever read in all my life. Could I buy the book from the library? I have more money at home."

"Maybe you could ask your parents to buy it for you at the book store," I suggested.

"We already checked, and they don't have it," he said.

"I could try to order it for you," I offered.

"Oh, would you?" he asked. "That'd be great," he yelled as he left the library. The book was Chris Van Allsburg's *Jumanji*, a favorite of many at our school. I was able to get the book for the student, but we also had to have a talk about truthfulness.

Ed and I called and talked with Gerry often; we wanted to make sure everything was going well with his therapy and his volunteer work. He called one evening and somewhere during the conversation, I mentioned his therapy coming to an end and that he'd be back home soon. There were a few seconds of silence on the other end of the phone and then he said, "I don't know when I'm coming home, Mom."

"What do you mean?" I asked.

"I . . . (hesitation) I like it here," he said. "I love volunteering at the hospital and I've made some new friends."

"I'm happy to hear that, Gerry, but, does this mean you're not planning on being home anytime soon?"

"I just don't know," he stated. "At least for the time being, I want to stay here."

"That's no problem," I said. "It's your decision to make, and I love you no matter where you choose to live. Here's your dad; tell him your news," and I handed the phone to Ed. Later, we both agreed that we would definitely support him all the way; he was making a new life, in a new place. I did have some sad moments that night. I guess I had still been hanging on to him.

It had been approximately six months since Gerry began his volunteer work at Butterworth Hospital. We talked with him on a weekly basis, and he kept us up to date on what was happening in his life, except for the things he didn't want us to know, until weeks later. One time he fell trying to move from his bed to his wheelchair. It turned out all right, thank goodness, because he was able to reach his phone and call security for help. He kind of joked about it, but I didn't think it was very funny, and told him so. "These things sometimes happen, Mom," he simply said.

One night when the phone rang. I was surprised to hear Gerry's voice because we had just talked with him the day before. He sounded very excited. He had trouble getting it out, but I distinctly heard the words, "hired by the hospital."

"Say that again, Gerry."

"Butterworth hired me, Mom," he repeated.

"What exactly will your job be?"

"I'll be an Office Assistant in the Environmental Services Department."

"Wow, that's fantastic! When did you find out?" I asked.

"Just today," he answered. "I'm so excited, Mom. It's what I've been hoping for all along."

"I had a feeling you were wanting that," I replied softly. "I'm so proud of you, Gerry, and I can't wait to tell your dad."

"Oh darn, I was hoping to catch you both at home tonight."

"Well, how about if I keep it a secret and you call him around 9:00 and give him the good news yourself?" I suggested.

"Sounds good," Gerry said. "I'd really like to tell Dad myself."

As expected, Gerry called back at 9:00 and told his dad about being hired. I wish I had taken a picture of Ed's face when he heard the news. He looked over at me with a big smile on his face, and I gave him a thumbs up to let him know I already knew. After he hung up, we hugged each other and talked about how happy we were that Gerry had accomplished what he had been hoping for. We also realized he had reached another one of his goals: a real job. What was next?

It wasn't long before Gerry had to start looking for another apartment because his building was set up for outpatients. We also learned his bicycle therapy was being moved to Grand Valley State University in Allendale. He started checking the newspaper for rental apartments, going by himself to look them over. As soon as he called to tell us that he had found something, we made plans to head south. Once again, his friend Steve helped Gerry move from the Hospitality House to a place called Apple Ridge Apartment Complex. I wasn't as nervous as I had been when we went to see his first apartment, but I was still a little uneasy. The unknown always gave me the jitters. I worried about the area he'd be living in, as well as the location of his apartment in the building. I also thought about the people who lived next door. What if they weren't the understanding and compassionate type? After long miles of silence, Ed inquired, "You're doing it again, aren't you?"

"Doing what?"

"Worrying about Gerry's new place."

"No, I'm not," I lied. "I'm just thinking of an idea for an 'apartment warming' gift."

"Oh, I see," said Ed with a grin on his face. "I'm sure we can find something he can use. A new toaster. Or a set of dishes."

"Or how about a television," I suggested.

"Let's wait until we get there and see what he needs," Ed answered. "Maybe he's already taken care of everything."

"Whatever. Are we there yet?"

"You sound just like the kids when we used to drive to our camp years ago," he laughed. "Do you remember those days?"

"How could I forget?" Those were the good old days. As soon as the camp was in sight, we'd hear them singing, "I see the camp, I see the camp." Ed started to laugh, and for the rest of the trip we talked about the fun we had spending our summer weekends at the lake.

We finally arrived on the outskirts of Grand Rapids and drove to a large complex where several buildings were surrounded by apple trees. "This is it," Ed said, circling the area.

"You're kidding! Wow, this is beautiful!"

"It sure is," Ed said. "Gerry said it was nice, but this is more than nice." Ed continued to drive around until he found the right building. We parked in the driveway. As we were getting out of the car, Gerry came wheeling out his apartment door.

"Hi Ger," I yelled. "This is quite the place. I like it already."

"I kind of thought you would, Mom," he said. "But you'll have to come back in the spring when the apple blossoms are out."

"That must be quite a sight," Ed said as we followed Gerry back into the building. I was relieved when he turned into an apartment on the first floor because I didn't want to think about him getting stuck in the elevator. That was one of my worst fears. I was claustrophobic and I wouldn't get in one unless someone was already there or I had another person with me. I even walked up five flights of stairs once rather than ride in one alone. I remember the time I got in an elevator with another person and she suddenly got off for some reason; I panicked. I managed to stay on until the next floor, and then I quickly made my exit.

Gerry's apartment was very appealing, with plenty of room for a wheelchair to maneuver. Gerry was more than pleased with his new quarters. Ed kept smiling as we went from one room to the next; he was as happy as I was with the apartment. He suggested we celebrate Gerry's new home by going out for dinner that evening, and we all thought it was a great idea. We went to a popular steak house restaurant and enjoyed a fabulous meal while chatting about Gerry's latest ventures. He was beaming as he told us about his new job at the hospital. The next day as we drove home, I felt totally relaxed and comfortable with everything I had seen. Our son had become a very independent man.

We made several trips to Grand Rapids over the next few years. Gerry usually had an interesting story to tell us about something he had encountered since our previous visit. What he called "interesting" however, I called mental anguish. He told us about the morning he headed outside to where his van was parked. It had snowed six inches during the night. The wipers were frozen to the windshield, and as he was getting his keys out, they slipped out of his hand and into the snow. There was no one else around at the time, and Gerry had to wait out in the cold almost twenty minutes before someone came by so he could ask for help to find his keys. He told the story with a bit of laughter, but being his mother, I was not amused. I wished he hadn't told us the story, and I told him so. Gerry's response was, "You always ask me if anything interesting has happened."

"I know, Ger," I said. "But, that was too scary."

"That's life, Mom. Things will happen to me just like any other person, and I have to learn deal with them."

"You're right," I replied trying to put a smile on my face. "But, I don't have to like it, do I?"

"No, but then you'd better think twice about the questions you ask me." His tone was serious. Ed had sat there watching and listening, but hadn't said a word. Finally, he suggested that maybe he and Gerry should get together beforehand and sort out the details of what I should or shouldn't hear. With that ridiculous comment, we all laughed, and I knew I was probably making too much of the incident. I told Gerry it was a "mom" thing, and that I'd get over it sooner or later.

After years of living in the Apple Ridge Apartment Complex, Gerry decided what he really wanted more than anything else was to have a house built, one that would serve his own special needs. He first discussed the matter with his dad, and then I learned from Ed what he was planning to do. At first, I couldn't believe Gerry would even consider venturing out that far, but the more we talked about it, the more sense it made. Gerry was satisfied with apartment living except when he had to go outside and face the harsh winter weather. All I had to do was think about the morning he dropped his keys in the snow, and there was no doubt in my mind that he deserved something better. That was just one experience he shared with us. Gerry had always been one to keep most of his private life to himself.

After Ed and I talked with him about the pros and cons of the project, Gerry made the decision to go ahead with his plans. Ed drove to Grand Rapids to take a look at the lot Gerry was considering, and called me that evening to say the papers had been signed. That was just the beginning. We made several more trips to help Gerry with the house plans, and sometimes Ed went alone. Once the house was up, Ed headed south again and spent a couple days putting a paint primer on the walls of every room and measuring all the windows for shades. We later learned that Gerry had invited his friend Steve, his wife Jody, and some friends from work to come over and paint all the rooms in his house. He bought pizza for everyone and called it his "painting party." By the beginning of 1993, his latest endeavor was completed, and Gerry moved into his beautiful new home.

I'll never forget the day I walked into our son's house for the first time. Ed and I had planned to stay with Gerry because he had an extra bedroom, completely furnished. Actually, the house had three bedrooms, but he was using the smallest one for a home office. We arrived at his home, and I was about to open the door when Gerry appeared looking very happy to see us. "Hey, what took you so long?"

"Traffic was heavy," I said, giving him a big hug.

"And your mom had to stop several times." Ed answered. "You know how often she likes to eat. I suggested packing a lunch but . . ."

Gerry interrupted, "Let's go inside, I have snacks in there if you

Gerry with his mom on the deck of his new home.

want something to eat, Mom." The door led from the attached garage into a small laundry room and on to the kitchen.

"Wow, this is beautiful," I commented. Oak cupboards lined three of the kitchen walls, all built within Gerry's reach. As we continued further, a beautiful oak table and chairs divided the living room from the kitchen. Next to the kitchen was a sliding door that opened to an outside deck with a view of huge elm trees at the far end of the back yard.

"There's more to see, Mom," Gerry said, proudly. "Follow me." He led us down the hallway to his large bedroom, fully equipped with a closet to fit his needs and a bathroom with a roll-in shower.

"This is awesome," I said. "Dad told me it was a very nice house, but I had no idea it would be like this. I think your dad wanted to surprise me, Ger." We moved on to the home office and the extra bathroom before the tour was finished, and then sat on the living room couch and marveled some more. The attached garage, especially, put my mind at ease because I knew Gerry wouldn't ever again be stuck outside in the cold. He was finally living in his own home, one that he had a part in planning. It was built in a newly-developed subdivision with only a few houses under construction at the time. By our next trip, there were three more finished houses with families already moved in.

Gerry came to spend Christmas with us that year. As he was leaving to go back, he promised to call when he arrived home. When the call didn't come, I called him and found out that someone had broken into his house while he was gone. His neighbor was there at the time so Gerry said he'd call back. I began pacing back and forth, talking with Ed about the horror of his situation. He tried to calm me down, telling me that everything was going to be all right, but it didn't work. I wanted to get in the car and head south so Gerry wouldn't have to spend the night alone. Ed didn't go along with my idea; he suggested we wait for the phone call and then decide what to do. When the call finally came, Gerry's voice was sounding pretty shaken. Someone had broken into his house through an outside door to his bedroom, his personal fire exit.

"Did they take anything?" My voice shaking, too.

"Yes," he answered. "My television is gone and some prescription drugs from the medicine cabinet in my bathroom."

"Are you all right, Gerry?" I asked, nervously. "Do you want us to drive down there?"

"No, my neighbor, Tom, is still here."

"Then, how about tomorrow?" I suggested. "We can leave early in the morning."

"No, Mom," Gerry replied. "Tom is fixing the bedroom door and I'm going to call the police as soon as we hang up. Don't worry about me."

"I'm sorry, Ger," I said breaking into tears. "Why don't you ask Tom to spend the night?" When I didn't get a response, I handed the phone to Ed and he talked with Gerry while I tried to pull myself together. I felt so helpless because we couldn't be there when he really needed us. When Ed got off the phone, he tried to reassure me that Gerry would be all right, but I put myself in Gerry's place, and I knew differently. He'd either stay up all night, or if he did go to bed, he wouldn't sleep because he'd be listening for every little sound. I thought about calling him before I went to bed; I wanted to tell him to think about getting a roommate, but I decided to wait until the next day. Once I got into bed, I tossed and turned until midnight. I was afraid to fall asleep for fear I would dream about someone breaking into Gerry's house. I thought warm milk might help me relax. Instead, I felt even more awake. As I sat at the kitchen table holding my face in my hands, I started to sob uncontrollably. I felt Ed's arm around my shoulders and reached up to grab onto him. He held me in his arms for several minutes until I began to calm down, and then walked me back upstairs to our bedroom.

The alarm went off at 7:00 A.M. and, at first, I didn't know where I was. I sat up in bed looking around the room when suddenly the door opened, and I saw Ed standing there.

"Are you planning on going in to work?" he asked.

"I hadn't thought about it, but, I don't think I'm up to it."

"Why don't I call school and tell them you won't be in today?" Ed suggested.

"Yes, thank you." I got out of bed slowly, knowing I wouldn't be of much use to anyone in my condition. And I wanted to call Gerry to get an update on the break-in.

It was about 9:00 when I decided I couldn't wait any longer. Gerry would be up early and probably heading to the hospital soon. I told Ed I wanted him to make the call, but before I knew it, I had dialed his number. Gerry answered the phone and, surprisingly, he sounded pretty good. He had called the police immediately after we hung up the phone, and they came directly to his house to make out a report. The only items found to be missing were the two things Gerry had mentioned on the phone: the television set, and his prescription drugs. I asked him how his night had gone. He made light of it at first, but then admitted he had slept with one eye open. He said the police assumed there had been at least two people involved because one person couldn't have carried out the television alone. That made me even more fearful thinking about what might have happened if Gerry had been home. I handed the phone to Ed so I could take a few deep breaths, and then I asked to talk to him again. I didn't quite know how to approach the idea of a house mate, so I just blurted it out: "Have you thought about sharing your house with another person?"

"What do you mean?" Gerry asked.

"Well, I'm sure there's someone who'd be willing to live in your house with you," I offered. "Maybe you could rent the extra bedroom."

"That's a possibility," he answered. "I have a friend at the hospital who may be interested. I'll check with him." I didn't know if Gerry was being serious, or if he was just trying to make me feel better, but I wanted to take him at his word. I truly believed that it would be good to have another person living with him, but it wasn't my decision to make.

"I hope you look into that, Gerry. Living this far away from you isn't easy for us."

"I realize that, Mom," he answered. "I'll see what I can do, but now I have to leave for work. I'm coming back home later because I have someone coming over to install deadbolt locks on the front and back doors."

"Oh good, I'm so glad to hear that," I said. Before saying our good byes, I asked Gerry to call when he got a chance and give us an update on the situation. I had a feeling we'd be in touch on a daily basis for some time to come.

When Gerry called that evening, he told us the police had stayed a long time at his house dusting for fingerprints, which left quite a mess to clean up. He also said they followed two sets of footprints in the snow, from the back door to an area down the street where a car had been parked. The police reported that they could see marks in the snow where they had set the 31-inch television down before loading it into their vehicle. I was surprised that no one had come along and witnessed what was taking place. They either planned it very well, or had done it in the middle of the night. Gerry hadn't heard from the police about any possible suspects, but they indicated there had been other break-ins in the area. They also told him they'd be in touch if there were any new developments, or if they had more questions.

After we hung up, Ed decided he should make a quick trip to see if there was something he could do to make Gerry feel safer in his house. He left the next day. When he called that evening, he said he had installed motion type lights in both the back and front of the house. They discovered later that the one near the back door lit up every time the neighbor's dog came by, but Gerry laughed and said it kept them more alert. When Ed returned home, he told me about some other things that were missing from Gerry's house, such as CDs, music tapes, a watch, and a pillowcase they must have used to carry things in. Since his stereo was still lying in the middle of the floor, Gerry surmised that something must have happened during the robbery which made them decide to leave it behind.

After two weeks of very little sleep and restlessness during the day, I knew it was time to see for myself how Gerry was coping. We left around noon on a Friday and drove all the way to the Mackinaw Bridge before we stopped for a quick bite to eat. We arrived at Gerry's later that evening. As we turned the corner of his street, I was surprised to see how the area had grown since our last visit. Several new houses were all lit up, which meant families had already moved in. Seeing Gerry's house surrounded by neighbors made me feel more at ease, and a lot less jittery about him living there. When his house was broken into, he had neighbors living on one side of his house, but there was an empty wooded lot on the other side. I wasn't concerned about it then, but thinking back, it may have been one of the reasons his house was thought to be an easy target.

As we pulled into the driveway, the kitchen light went on. Gerry met us at the back door, very happy to see us. All I wanted to do was put my arms around him and keep him close to me. As I was holding him, he whispered, "I'm so glad you're here, Mom. I've missed you and Dad."

"We've missed you, too," I said as my eyes filled with tears. "Are you all right?"

"Yes, I'm fine," Gerry answered. "But, it isn't easy when you know that someone has broken into your house."

"Have you heard anything more from the police?" Ed asked.

"Nothing," Gerry said with a sickened look on his face. "I just hope they catch them before they pull the same stunt again."

"Is there someone you could ask to look after your house the next time you come home?" I asked.

"I think my neighbor, Tom, would do that for me."

"It wouldn't hurt to have more than one person watching out for your house," Ed suggested. "I'm sure many of the neighbors would be willing to keep an eye out considering the number of break-ins in the area."

"You're probably right, Dad," Gerry agreed. "I'll mention it to Tom when I talk to him."

As we sat around the kitchen table hashing over the robbery, I could see a new television set in the living room. "Hey, Ger, that new TV is pretty neat," I commented.

"I know," he said, "I decided as long as I had to get a new one, I might as well get what I wanted."

"Did your insurance cover it?"

"My insurance covered the TV and everything else they stole," Gerry said. "It also took care of the repairs on the bedroom door. They were really great!"

"But it's always traumatic," I said. Do you remember the time someone came into our house and took our toaster along with a set of mixing bowls and some money out of my purse?"

"I do!" Ed answered. "That person didn't have to break in because someone forgot to lock the door after he walked the dog that night."

"It wasn't me," Gerry said. "I never forgot to lock the door when I walked Reecy."

"Speaking of little Reecy," Ed remarked with a chuckle, "He wasn't much of a watch dog; he didn't even bark that night and normally he barked at every little thing."

"That's true," I admitted, "But, remember, he was a poodle and they are not considered watchdogs; noisy dogs, maybe."

As it turned out, the person who robbed our house that night was one of our former babysitters, looking for items he needed for his new apartment. We did get everything back, eventually, because he was caught in the act of robbing another apartment. We continued the conversation about Reecy for some time, remembering all the fun times over the thirteen years he was with us. We chuckled about our trip to Green Bay, and how we managed to sneak him into our hotel room. We talked about the day he died during Gerry's first week in the hospital, and how we attempted to keep it from Gerry until one of his friends unknowingly offered his condolences. Gerry seemed to enjoy reminiscing about our much-loved little poodle, and as the time passed,

I could feel myself becoming more relaxed. This visit was something we all needed, Ed included. Finally, the three of us unanimously agreed to call it a night. We were all exhausted.

There was plenty to do the following day to keep us busy. I ironed clothes for Gerry, something he always suggested whenever I asked. Ed took care of some odd jobs in and around the house, and after lunch we watched a college football game. In the evening, we went out for a delicious dinner at one of Gerry's favorite Italian restaurants. We began to put that frightful incident behind us. It would be a while before I could stop worrying about what happened, but being with Gerry and sharing our feelings was a good start.

On Sunday morning, we had breakfast together before Ed and I left for home. It was difficult saying goodbye. Gerry had friends he could count on if need be, but I was still hoping he'd find someone to move in with him. I mentioned it only once when we were out to dinner that night; I didn't want him to think I was putting any pressure on him. As we were pulling out of the driveway that day, I could feel myself getting all choked up and tried my best to fight back the tears. I didn't want Ed to see me crying so I took my sunglasses off the visor and covered my eyes. I didn't utter a word for the next fifty miles, and neither did he. He finally broke the silence, speaking in a very gentle voice, "He's going to be fine, and so are we. We can't live each day worrying about something that might never happen again. And, I don't think the people who broke into Gerry's house would be foolish enough to try it a second time. They know the police would be on the lookout for them."

"I know," I murmured, "But, it's Gerry I worry about the most. Do you think he'll ever feel comfortable again when he goes to bed at night?"

"In time, he'll work through it," Ed insisted. "But, we have to help by being as positive as we can when we discuss it with him. If you continue to act scared, he's going to sense that, and it may cause him further problems."

"You're right," I promised. "From now on, I will think and act positively if the subject is ever brought up again."

"How about some lunch?"

"Sounds good to me," I said. "Maybe I'll even have some dessert."

Ed pulled into one of our favorite eating places. It's funny how you get into the habit of stopping at certain restaurants when traveling the same route time after time. After our usual bowl of chili and a delicious piece of banana cream pie, we began the last two hundred miles of our trip home. During the first hundred miles or so, I managed to doze a little, and then I took the wheel for the last hundred. As soon as we got into the house, I gave Gerry a call to let him know we had arrived safely. He sounded relieved, and mentioned that he worried about us making that long drive as much as we worried about him. I suggested that maybe we both worried too much about each other. He said he enjoyed our visit and was looking forward to the next one. I made a promise to myself that I would try very hard to remain positive about Gerry's circumstances.

Chapter Thirteen

Several trips to Grand Rapids during the next year made me finally realize that I could let go of my fears about Gerry living alone. However, when he called to say that his friend, Nick, was moving in while he attended physical therapy classes at Grand Valley State University, I have to admit I was thrilled. I didn't want Gerry to know how I felt, so I purposely didn't make a big deal out of it. I said something like, "Oh, that'll be great for Nick to stay at your house while he goes to school."

"You can say it, Mom," Gerry said with a chuckle. "It'll be even nicer for me to have Nick living here, right?"

"If that's how you feel, Ger," I answered in a serious tone.

"I wish I could see your face right now," Gerry went on. "I bet you're grinning from ear to ear."

"Who me? Remember, Gerry, this is your mom you're talking to. Give it up!"

"Okay," he muttered. "But, I had to tease you a little bit about this. You understand, right?"

"A person has to do what a person has to do," I offered, trying to keep from laughing as I changed the subject. Gerry was making funny little laughing sounds on the other end of the phone; he was having a good time. As it turned out, Nick stayed at the house less than a year; he married a girl from the area and moved away. For me, it was good just knowing that Gerry had another person living with him.

During the next several months, Gerry continued working at the hospital and getting on with the independent life style he had created for himself. We usually talked with him on the weekends, so when Gerry phoned one evening I could hear excitement in his voice. He was calling to tell us that he had been chosen MVP (Most Valuable Professional) for the Environmental Services Department where he now worked as a supervisor. He said he would send us the hospital newsletter as soon as it came out, and we could read all about it ourselves. When it finally arrived, I pulled out the sheet showing all the MVPs from the different departments. There was a picture of Gerry. Next to his picture were these words: "Gerry has taught invaluable lessons to those he works with. He is quiet, yet enthusiastic, and an effective leader. He is always positive, with a can-do attitude, and has helped develop effective procedures for the staff and the department." I was very familiar with his "can-do attitude" because I had witnessed it for the past several years, as he went from his hospital bed to a college degree, and from a volunteer to an employee of Butterworth Hospital.

When Ed came home from work that day, I handed him the newsletter. He could hardly contain himself as he sat down at the kitchen table to read it. He kept staring at Gerry's picture and finally said, "Can you believe this son of ours?"

"Oh yes, I can," I commented. "I wonder what's next?"

"What do you mean?" Ed looked at me as if I knew something he didn't.

"Just look back at all he's accomplished since his accident," I said. "I'm sure he has another goal he's working on right now."

"That's good!" Ed insisted. "People need to set goals in life if they're going to be successful. Look what you did."

"What do you mean?" I asked.

"You decided after child number five that you wanted to go back to school, and you did it."

"Yes, but I wouldn't have been able to do it without your support," I said. "You were willing to help out with the kids and the cooking and anything else I needed. I owe it all to you."

"You're probably right," Ed offered, "But, let's not get too emotional. I did it because I knew how much it meant to you."

"And I'm forever grateful." I wrapped my arms around him. "It gave me twenty-two years of working at a job I love." We looked one more time at the newsletter and together we read what had been written about Gerry. One of the criteria for being nominated MVP caught my eye: "To be recognized for both job performance and hospitality that exceeds the managers' and customers' expectations." Whatever job Gerry took on, big or small, I knew he'd do everything in his power to exceed all expectations; that was his nature. We knew how fortunate we were to have a son who had taken a life-changing incident and, with much patience and *sisu*, had turned it into an unbelievable accomplishment. Later, that evening we called Gerry to let him know how proud we were and to congratulate him on being selected for the MVP award. I could still hear the excitement in his voice; the award meant the world to him.

It is rather amazing to see what transpired over the next few years as Gerry continued working for the hospital's Environmental Services Department. Ed and I talked on the phone with him on a weekly basis, and Gerry made the eight-hour trip home whenever he had a long weekend. During our weekly conversations, I began to notice the frequent casual mention of one of his work acquaintances. Her name was Laurie; she worked for a company that sold supplies to Gerry's department. When he first mentioned her, it was in relation to a practical joke he had played on her at work.

"Gerry Donald! How could you have done that to this poor girl?"

"Don't worry, Mom, she will definitely get me back! We do this sort of thing all the time." Gerry explained.

Apparently, he had her boss, Scott, also a friend of Gerry's, ask Laurie to call a customer of theirs, leaving a message for a "Mr. Lion" that his brushes were in. Scott gave her the phone number and she left a message on the answering machine. She later found out that the phone number had been for the local zoo and she vowed to get even.

"Well, Mom," said Gerry a few weeks later. "She really got me this time."

"What are you talking about?"

"You remember the joke I played on my friend, Laurie, a couple weeks ago? Well, she got me back!" he laughed.

"Oh no! What did she do?"

Gerry went on to say that she had sent him a lovely birthday present which consisted of two cans of spray-on hair. He explained that she knew the girls in Gerry's office joked with him about his receding hair line. I was beginning to think that the two of them might be a little more than just friends.

Confirmation came the following week when Gerry told me about a friend's birthday party the previous Friday. This was their first time getting together outside of work-related activities. According to Gerry, they hit it off. After a little push from a female friend at work, he called Laurie and invited her out to dinner. The date went well, so he decided to invite her to his house the following weekend to watch a football game. He sounded so happy as he told me these details and I was secretly starting to get excited about a possible relationship with this girl. At least she was into football. That seemed to be an important prerequisite for a member of our family.

I was just getting used to the fact that Gerry had started "dating" someone when he called to inform us that he wanted us to meet Laurie. He was thinking of bringing her home to meet Ed and me as well as his brothers and sisters. The Easter holiday was not far off, so I suggested he bring her home that weekend. We always spent Easter with the entire family.

"Wow!" I thought to myself. "This could be serious."

I have to admit that when I hung up the phone, I began to feel nervous. I was worried about everything under the sun. What if she didn't like us? What if we didn't like her?" Gerry said she was an only child. How would she react to our large family? On second thought, maybe Easter weekend wasn't a good idea! My mind was going a mile a minute.

Ed walked in the door as I was standing with my hand still on the phone. "Hey, what's up?"

"I'm scared." I sat down at the kitchen table.

"What do you mean you're scared?"

"Gerry just called and said he's bringing Laurie home to meet the family over the Easter weekend."

Ed instantly relaxed. "So why are you so scared?" he asked, smiling.

"I'm not sure. I guess I didn't expect it. I knew he was beginning to date Laurie, but I had no clue it was this serious."

"Well, maybe it's not a serious relationship," Ed offered. "It could be that they're just good friends."

"No," I insisted. "There was something in the tone of his voice that makes me think otherwise."

"What do you mean? What tone?"

"Oh Ed, it was nothing specific," I countered. "Unlike men, women have a way of knowing these things. If they were just friends, I doubt he would be bringing her home to meet the family."

"You could be right, but we won't know for sure until Easter weekend, so try not to worry about it."

"I'm so glad I have you to help me with these moments." I

admitted as I put my arms around him.

Gerry and Laurie both had Good Friday off, so they started out early that morning and made the drive to the Upper Peninsula of Michigan. We often refer to it as God's Country. Gerry had told us that Laurie had never been to the Mackinaw Bridge, a five-mile bridge that connects the lower part of Michigan with the Upper Peninsula, and I was wondering what she would think as she came across it for the first time.

They arrived in town just before dinner time. We had planned to eat out that night just the four of us, and then Saturday night we would have the whole family over to meet her. We thought this would be a little less intimidating for an only child. Of course, I was such a nervous wreck as we arrived at the restaurant to meet them that I forgot to give Gerry a hug when I first saw him. He introduced Laurie as we waited for our table and I liked her immediately. She was very sweet. I could tell by the way she and Gerry acted during dinner that they cared deeply for one another. It became clear to me why our son had decided to bring her home to meet his family.

On Saturday, before the rest of the family came over, we sat in the kitchen talking over coffee. This was our typical activity during visits from Gerry. Each time he came home, we would sit at the table and hear all about his life in Grand Rapids over several cups of good coffee. This Saturday was a little different though because we had an added point of view from Laurie. I was delighted to see that she seemed quite relaxed as we talked that morning. We began discussing some of the practical jokes they had played on each other over the past few months. Gerry and Laurie are both great story-tellers and they had both Ed and me laughing as they recounted some of their hi-jinks.

They really had us rolling as they described the time they first met face-to-face. Gerry explained that he had arrived at Laurie's office early one morning and waited for her in the conference room, posing as a new customer. Laurie's boss, Scott, helped him out of his wheelchair and into a regular chair at the conference table so Laurie wouldn't know who he was (she knew that he was in a wheelchair). When Laurie came in, Scott told her that Gerry was "Rick," a very important customer. He asked her to tell him that Scott would be right with him and to make sure he was comfortable.

"I was a little shocked that Scott had asked me to do that sort of thing because it's not something I usually do," Laurie explained. "I figured this guy was someone really important, so I turned on the charm

and got him coffee and kept him company while he waited for Scott."
According to Laurie, Scott arrived in the conference room and she participated in a bit of small talk before they began their meeting.

"Scott asked me to explain to this "new customer" how I, as an employee of our company, would be able to make his job easier. I began to explain how our customer service works and that we would be there whenever he needed our help. Basically, I just pitched our company to him. I was surprised at the amount of questions 'Rick' had about our company and about my job especially."

As Laurie was about to leave the room so they could begin their meeting, Scott asked 'Rick' if he had any more questions for Laurie before she left.

"Yes, I do," he said. "Are you single?"

"I couldn't believe he asked me that!" Laurie explained as she told us the story. "He seemed like such a nice guy and he'd been a perfect gentleman up to that point. I didn't know what to say. Scott seemed surprised too and so he laughed it off and asked 'Rick' if he had any serious questions for me. His response was 'Are you a real blonde?' It was then that I knew I had been had!"

Gerry explained that he and Scott had been kidding her about her blonde hair and telling her every "dumb blonde" joke they got their hands on. Ed and I couldn't believe that our Gerry had pulled such a stunt!

"That's OK, he and Scott both paid for their little scheme," Laurie stated with a mischievous look on her face.

I was so glad to see that Gerry had such a fun relationship with Laurie. She seemed to instantly fit into our family and that was evident later that day when our children came for dinner. It was a "mad house" as it usually is at these gatherings. Three of our children have children of their own and the house comes alive when they are all here. Laurie got along well with everyone. The rest of the family really liked her; she was just adorable and had a great sense of humor. We had a fun time after dinner with the kids telling stories on each other, including a couple of good ones about Gerry.

I didn't forget to give hugs that night and gave more hugs when they left after breakfast on Sunday. Ed turned to me as we walked back inside the house and asked, "How do you feel now?"

"Great!" I said. "I worried for nothing. I should have known Gerry would choose someone like Laurie."

"I have a feeling he cares for her a lot."

"Oh, you do," I said, chuckling. "Do men have a way of knowing these things?"

"Yes, we certainly do." He started clearing the breakfast dishes off the table.

"Would you like some help with that?" I asked. "After all, you did make their breakfast."

"That's all right," Ed said with a smirk on his face. "We both know who's cooking dinner tonight."

For the next several weeks, I couldn't stop thinking about Gerry. I wanted to tell everyone about his new relationship. At the time, I didn't know how serious he and Laurie were, but I was aware that they were spending a lot of time together. I also found out from Gerry that he had met her parents when he drove Laurie and her dog, Mack, to Ann Arbor. Her mom and dad had agreed to keep Mack because dogs weren't permitted in the apartment where Laurie had recently moved. I tried to be very patient waiting for Gerry to tell us what was ahead for him and Laurie, but I realized that could be a while. We respected his privacy and knew that when he had something important to say, he would pick up the phone and give us a call. I had no idea when that would happen, and I was not about to ask. I tried that when he was a teenager and didn't have much luck.

I still remember that day in October of 1996. I was in the kitchen making an apple pie for my step-dad, Frank; one of his favorite desserts. I was just about to put it in the oven when the phone rang. Gerry's voice was on the other end. He usually never called in the mornings so I had a feeling something was up. "Hi, Mom. Are you sitting down?"

"No," I answered, moving quickly to a chair, "but, I am now."

"Well," Gerry said in a soft voice, "Tomorrow is Sweetest Day and I'm planning to give Laurie an engagement ring."

"Oh, my goodness! That's wonderful! Does she know she's getting it, or are you going to surprise her?"

"It's a surprise."

"Hmmm," I sighed. "Are you sure she feels the same about you as you feel about her?"

"Of course, Mom," he continued. "We've talked about marriage, but we haven't set a date yet."

"I'm sorry," I said, trying not to offend Gerry. "I thought you meant it was going to be a total surprise to Laurie."

"I wouldn't be that foolish," Gerry insisted, in a sweet way. He didn't want to hurt my feelings either.

"I'm so happy for you, Gerry. I can't wait to tell your dad the good news. I wish he were home so you could tell him yourself."

"I'll let you have the fun of surprising him," Gerry mentioned. "I know you'll enjoy that."

"Thanks, Ger," I answered. "I'm looking forward to it. And make sure you call and let us know Laurie's reaction when you give her the ring."

"I will," Gerry promised. "But, if she hands it back to me, what should I do then?"

"That's not going to happen. She'll be just as thrilled as you are." They had been dating for almost a year, and I couldn't see Gerry giving Laurie an engagement ring unless he knew exactly where he stood in the relationship. I truly believed that.

"I'm not worried. I was just kidding about Laurie giving the ring back. I know we're both on the same wave length here."

"Keep us posted," I said. "Good luck with your sweetie on 'Sweetest Day'."

I was so excited when I hung up the phone. Ed wasn't around so I called my mom and my sister, Sue, to tell them about Gerry's surprise. They were both thrilled and said they were looking forward to meeting Laurie. Ed walked in just as I hung up the phone and stood staring at me, probably wondering why I had that big smile on my face. He finally gave in and asked, "What are you so happy about?"

"I'll give you three guesses," I offered, still smiling from ear to ear.

"You're the big winner in some contest?" Ed asked, looking skeptical.

"No. Try again."

"I can't think of anything else," Ed said. "Don't keep me in suspense."

"All right, I'll tell you," I sighed. "Gerry called and said he's going to surprise Laurie with an engagement ring on Sweetest Day, which happens to be tomorrow."

"No kidding," Ed commented, looking very pleased. "Things must be going very well with them."

"He sounded excited on the phone," I said. "And, he also mentioned that they've talked about marriage."

"Any date mentioned?" Ed asked.

"We probably won't hear about that until after she gets the ring. If Laurie doesn't know she's getting the ring, it's unlikely they've discussed a wedding date."

"Oh, is that the way it works?" Ed challenged, trying to act a little ingenuous about the subject.

"That's how it was back when we got married, right?" I answered. "And, I still remember the night you gave me my engagement ring. It was a Thursday night."

"How do you remember that?" Ed asked, turning around to stare at me.

"Because it was my bowling night." I laughed. "Don't you remember?"

"I think you're mixed up about that," Ed insisted.

"Well, I know it wasn't on Sweetest Day, because there was no such day when we were dating."

"How did we get from Gerry's surprise engagement ring to our engagement?"

"It's easy!" I said. "When one of the children get engaged, it's just natural for me to think back to that special time for us. Maybe it's a woman thing."

"Must be," Ed answered, grinning and nudging me with his elbow. "Now let's get back to the 'ring' at hand."

"Well, Gerry said he'll call us after he gives Laurie the ring tomorrow and update us on any new developments," I explained, "But, knowing our son, we'll have to be patient; it could be a while."

I stayed home the entire next day because I didn't want to miss his phone call, but I had to wait until the following evening before we heard. He said that everything had gone well, and Laurie had accepted the ring with as much love and faith in their relationship as he had when he gave it to her. Ed and I told him how happy we were that he had found someone special to share his life with, and we were looking forward to hearing about the wedding plans.

I don't remember exactly when Gerry told us they had set their wedding date, but I recall it wasn't that long after their engagement. He called one Saturday morning and said, "Hi Mom, I'm going for it!"

"Going for what, Ger?"

"I'm giving up my single life," he declared. "Laurie and I have set the date for our wedding."

"Oh, Gerry. I'm so happy for you and Laurie. When is it going to be?"

"August 30," Gerry replied, "And we're hoping that date is all right with you and Dad."

"Of course, it's all right," I answered. "You're more important than anything else in our life right now; we'd change our plans if we had any."

"One more thing before I let you go," Gerry said. "We'd like Jim, Mike, Joellyn, and Bertie to be in our wedding. Do you think they'd want to do that?"

"Are you kidding?" I asked. "I know they would love to be in your wedding, but you should do the honors of asking them yourself." I didn't even have to second guess on that one because Gerry's brothers and sisters would do anything for him; I could guarantee that.

"I'll call and tell them the good news, and I'll ask them if they're willing to be our attendants," he said.

"Sounds good to me," I continued. "Keep us posted on your plans, dear."

"I will, Mom, but please hold off on telling anyone the wedding date just in case we have to change it. I know you're anxious to spread the word back home, but you need to wait until we have everything and everyone confirmed."

"You have my promise, Ger." I said. "My lips are sealed." As soon as I hung up the phone, I started to dial my mother to tell her about Gerry's wedding, but stopped immediately and began to laugh out loud. I couldn't believe what I had just done.

I must admit, I was flying high for several days, patiently holding off telling my family and friends. Gerry did call his brothers and sisters within the next day or two and asked them to be in his wedding, which then gave me permission to talk about it with the children. They were as thrilled for him as I was, and felt so honored that he wanted each of them to be a part of his special day. I couldn't have asked for a better celebration of family than that. Once the date was final, I called other relatives and friends to give them the news so they could mark it on their calendars. It was now definite; we were going to a wedding at the end of the summer.

After months of planning their big day, Laurie and Gerry said their wedding vows on Saturday, August 30, 1997, at St. Mary's Catholic, a quaint little church in Grand Rapids. I have to admit, it was one of the most beautiful weddings I had ever attended, and I'm not just saying that because it was our son. Gerry's two brothers and two sisters stood on the altar with six other friends who were members of the wedding party. It was an unbelievable sight, and as soon as the music began, I turned around to watch the young ladies and Laurie walk down the aisle. I glanced back at Gerry who was sitting in the front of the church, and when I saw the look on his face, tears began to fill my eyes. He appeared to be in awe as he watched and waited for his bride to join him at the altar. Laurie looked like she had just walked out of one of those bridal magazines; absolutely stunning! When the ceremony

The Hakala Family at Gerry and Laurie's wedding.

was over, Gerry and Laurie went up the aisle with their wedding party, but then returned, stopping at every pew to thank each of the guests for coming. The smiles on their faces told the whole story; it was an experience I will always treasure.

A dinner reception was held at the beautiful Crown Plaza Hotel, followed by dancing until midnight. Once the meal was served and everyone was finished eating, people sat around visiting with each other and waiting for the first song when the bride and groom head to the dance floor alone. I was anxious to see what Gerry and Laurie had planned for that traditional event, because neither had mentioned anything ahead of time. As soon as the song began, you could almost hear a pin drop. Everyone had their eyes on the wedding couple. Laurie walked toward Gerry and carefully positioned herself on his lap, pulling the bottom of her dress up off the floor. With Laurie all situated, Gerry slowly began to move his chair, dancing to the song they had chosen, "I Will Be Here," by Steven Curtis Chapman and beautifully sung by their friend, Scott, as he played his guitar. My insides choked up. I

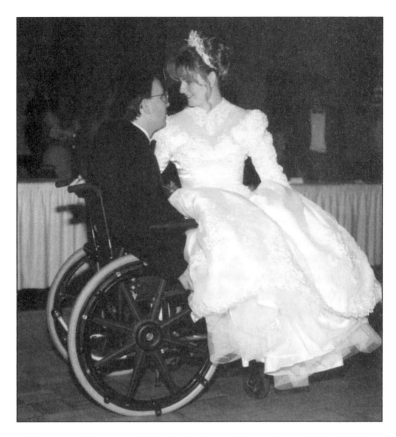

Gerry and Laurie celebrate their wedding, August 30, 1997.

didn't want others to notice so I turned toward some family members who were sitting nearby. I saw one person wiping her eyes, and then another, and another. It was a very special moment that many won't ever forget. When the dance was over, one of my friends unexpectedly walked over to our table and put her arms around me. With tears streaming down her face, she said she had never witnessed anything so beautiful in her entire life. I told her I felt the same way and, as the evening went on, we heard many similar comments from friends and family.

That August weekend will be in my heart forever, and not only because it was Gerry and Laurie's wedding. We were in our hotel room on Sunday morning getting ready to meet with our families for breakfast when I heard the news that Princess Diana had died in a car accident. I sat on the bed in complete shock, staring at the television. How could something so dreadful happen? She was one of the most protected celebrities in the world. What could possibly have gone wrong? As Ed and I headed down the elevator to meet for breakfast, everyone was talking about Princess Diana's death. She was also the main topic of conversation with our family members during breakfast. Because of Gerry and Laurie's wedding that weekend, I will always remember the day she died.

Gerry and Laurie spent their long-awaited honeymoon at Disney World. They had planned it for several months, getting all the information on hotels and shows they were interested in. They left early Monday morning and were going to drive about half way to Orlando. Gerry had asked Ed and me to stop by their house to make sure everything was all right before we left for home that day. We had an early breakfast at the hotel and then went straight to Gerry's. As we walked through the house and into the bedroom, we noticed a large piece of luggage sitting on the bed. Inside the suitcase were some of Gerry's clothes, neatly packed. At first, I was a little concerned, but then decided it must have been left there for a reason. Ed didn't say much about the suitcase, so I didn't think anymore about it. However, when we got back home, Gerry called saying that he and Laurie had gone shopping for some new clothes because one of his suitcases had been left on his bed. I started to say how sorry I was, but Gerry exploded in laughter. "That's just what I wanted to do on the first day of our honeymoon," he said, jokingly, "Shop in those crowded stores in the mall."

"I'm glad you feel that way, Ger. It could have been worse; Laurie's suitcase could have been left behind instead of yours, and that would have taken much longer to replace. I remember when the airline lost my luggage on a trip to Florida once and I had to buy all new clothes. It took a while."

"You always told me not to sweat the small things, Mom," Gerry stated. "I decided I didn't need as many clothes as I had packed, and I finished shopping in no time at all. Laurie was a big help."

"That's great! Now that you have that problem taken care of, the rest of your honeymoon should be terrific. Call us when you get back to Grand Rapids." As I hung up the phone, I thought to myself, "What a guy!" Knowing Gerry's great sense of humor, I wish I could have heard his first comment to Laurie about the missing suitcase. It probably was something like, "No suitcase, hmmm, I really love the clothes

I'm wearing, especially my underwear," or "What size did you say your jeans were?" And, I could hear Laurie saying, "Gerry Donald, we have to go shopping right now!" Two years later, Laurie and Gerry went back to Disney World to celebrate their second wedding anniversary, and this time they remembered to take all their luggage with them.

Chapter Fourteen

After ten years with the Environmental Services Department at Butterworth Hospital, Gerry was promoted in 1999. He took over as Interim Manager for almost a year before he officially became head of his department. He loved his job, but he especially cared for the people he worked with. I will always remember the first time Ed and I visited him in that capacity at the hospital. He asked Karen, an employee, and friend, to meet us downstairs and show us to his department. After she introduced herself, we got on the elevator together and she started talking about Gerry. When I heard the words, "We love him so much," I looked at her for a few seconds, almost speechless, and then said, "I know just how you feel."

At first I was a little embarrassed by my comment, but then she continued saying, "Gerry makes it easy for a person to feel that way."

When the elevator stopped and the door opened, Gerry greeted us with a big smile. As we walked through the area, he introduced Ed and me to several of the hospital employees; he seemed truly happy that we were visiting the place where he spent most of his day. He talked about the hospital and his department many times, but being there with him made it much more meaningful. It was wonderful to watch him in that setting, and to see him so completely at ease. As parents, we were extremely proud of all he had accomplished since his accident. But more excitement was ahead.

Sometime in November of that year, I was talking on the phone with Gerry and asked him about gift suggestions for Christmas. He said he would talk to Laurie and get back to me soon. "Soon" to Gerry didn't necessarily mean a day or two; it could mean weeks. However, three days later he surprised me with a phone call to say he and Laurie had thought of something they both could use. I heard a big sigh and then, "Laurie and I would like a crib for Christmas."

At first I thought I misunderstood him, so I said, "Say that again, Gerry. I couldn't hear you."

He repeated it again, "I said we'd like a crib." At that moment, I almost dropped the phone. Once again I could feel the tears. I tried to speak, but the words wouldn't come out. "Mom, are you still there?"

"Yes," I answered with my voice quivering. "Are you telling me that Laurie is pregnant?"

"We think so," Gerry answered. "Laurie did a home pregnancy test and she said it looks pretty good, but we're going to see the doctor to make sure."

"When will she see the doctor?" I asked, trying not to burst into screams of joy.

"We have an appointment in a couple of days. We'll call and let you know as soon as we get home."

"Oh, please promise me you'll do that," I said. "I'll be praying for both of you."

"Thanks Mom, and don't forget to tell Dad when he comes home."

"Don't you worry about that, Ger. I'll tell him the minute he comes through the door." I tried calling Ed at his office, but he wasn't there so I waited patiently for him to come home for lunch.

As soon as Ed walked in the kitchen that day, I told him about Gerry's phone call. He had a very surprised look on his face and said, "No kidding!" I told him we had to keep it to ourselves for a few days until Gerry and Laurie met with their doctor. He delicately reminded me that it wouldn't be a problem for him, but suggested I stay in the house, and off the phone, until we heard from them. His message was loud and clear, and I didn't breathe a word to anyone, including Gerry's brothers and sisters. It was a long three days!

When the call finally came and I heard his voice, I could feel myself start to quiver. "Hi Mom, what's new up there?"

I wanted to reach through that phone and pinch his cheek, but decided to play along with him, instead.

"Well, let's see." I answered. "Did you hear that NMU won their basketball game last night?"

"Good for them!" Gerry offered, acting rather surprised at my question. "Who did they play?"

"I don't know and I don't really care," I replied, impatiently. "Gerry Donald, tell me what the doctor said."

"Well, Mom, he agreed that we are definitely pregnant." He continued talking, but I was so excited about the pregnancy that I missed what he said about the heartbeat.

"What did you say about the heartbeat?" I asked.

"I said that Laurie and I were able to listen to the heartbeats during the ultrasound." I could hear the excitement in his voice, but I still wasn't sure what he was trying to tell me.

"Did you say heartbeats, Gerry?" I asked, my voice trembling.

"Yes, Mom, the doctor said there are two heartbeats, which means there are two babies," he whispered, softly. "We will need two cribs instead of one."

At first, I thought he was just joking with me and said sharply, "Don't tease me, Gerry."

"I'm not teasing, Mom," he insisted. "The ultrasound showed that we have two babies, one for me, and one for Laurie."

"I can't believe it," I said, "This is so exciting, Gerry. How does Laurie feel about having twins?" I wondered how I would have felt.

"Laurie's just as thrilled as I am," he answered. "Here, I'll let you talk to her."

When I asked Laurie her thoughts on having twins she said, "I've always wanted two children, and now I'll be able to have both on one trip. That's pretty exciting."

As we continued chatting about the pregnancy, Ed walked in the door so I asked Laurie to have Gerry tell his Dad.

I handed the phone to Ed saying, "Gerry has something to tell you."

I watched his sober face turn into a huge smile as he listened to his youngest son tell him the news that would change their lives forever. And, then I heard, "Oh, my goodness. Are you ready for two babies, Gerry?" A bit of laughter, and lots more conversation took place before Ed said good bye and hung up the phone. Afterwards, we sat at the kitchen table staring at each other and smiling. Some of the comments I remember were: "Can you believe it?" "How exciting for Gerry and Laurie!" "I can't wait until we tell the kids." "My mother is going to be ecstatic." "Boy, are they going to be busy!" I felt so joyful when I went to bed that night; I wondered if it was real or if I had had another dream.

It didn't take me long to get on the phone with my mom the next morning. All I remember her saying was, "You're kidding! Is the doctor sure there are two babies?"

"Yes, Mom," I repeated. "Gerry and Laurie are expecting twins in July."

"Oh, that 's wonderful," she said. "Would you ask Gerry to call me? I want to talk to him about this." My mom always wanted the details.

"I'll give him your message," I promised. My mom was thrilled about the news and wanted to let Gerry know how she felt. He was the second grandson who had injured his spinal cord, and she had had a difficult time dealing with the injury. Hearing the news about the twins would make her feel happy after all the sadness she had suffered previously. Gerry's accident was very trying on us as parents, but as a grandparent, it must have been devastating. As we know, the older we are, the more it hurts.

I spent most of the morning calling our kids, and other members of the family. I walked around in a cloud for days telling anyone who would listen, and each time I told the story, I had to pinch myself to make sure I was awake.

Gerry called after each doctor's visit to update us on the pregnancy. I wanted to know every detail: what the ultrasound revealed, the size of the babies, how much weight Laurie gained, and anything else they were willing to share. I remember the day Gerry found out that one of the babies was a boy. He was so funny; he told us the doctor could actually see "it." I could hear the thrill in his voice, and I wished I could have been there to put my arms around him and tell him how happy I was that he was having a son. He said they weren't able to tell the sex of the other baby, although, the doctor said there was a good possibility it was a girl. I had to sit down and think about everything, reminding myself that what I was hearing was real. I tried to imagine what it would be like if it all came to be, Gerry and Laurie, the proud parents of twins, one boy and one girl. "Wow!" My strong faith in God made me realize the twins were a very precious gift, and that someone had been watching over them.

Our next bit of news was due on Good Friday, which was the day Laurie was scheduled for another ultrasound. I really wasn't concerned whether the twins were both boys, or a boy and a girl; I just wanted two healthy babies. Secretly though, I had to admit that one of each would've been exciting. I could see Laurie with a little girl, dressing her up in fancy clothes, and fussing with her hair each morning before school. What mom wouldn't want to do those kind of things? But, Ed and I had talked about the possibilities, and we both knew that having two healthy babies was most important, and that was what we prayed for daily.

I woke up at 6:00 on Good Friday morning and said aloud, "Today is the day!" I wasn't sure the time of Laurie's appointment, but I stayed close to the phone all day so I wouldn't miss the call. Every time the phone rang, I ran quickly to answer it and was disappointed when it wasn't Gerry. By 4:00 in the afternoon, I was getting so restless I wanted to call them, but I held off. I was beginning to worry that maybe something had happened. It was about 5:15 when Ed walked in. He took one look at my face and knew immediately that I hadn't received the call. He tried to comfort me, "They'll call soon," he promised. "Maybe the appointment was later in the day so Gerry didn't have to take time off of work."

"I never thought of that," I answered. "You're probably right." Ed and I sat at the kitchen table like two little kids waiting for the phone to ring. We looked at each other and started to laugh. "Isn't this silly?" I asked.

"Not if it's going to keep you calm," Ed remarked. "A husband has to do what a husband has to do."

"Why is it that these things always touch a chord with women?" I asked. "Men appear to take it all in stride and never let this 'stuff' bother them." Just then, the phone rang. It was Gerry. My heart began to beat a little faster.

"Hi Mom," he said in a cheerful tone.

"Hi Gerry."

"Is Dad home yet?"

"Your dad is right here with me. Did you and Laurie see the doctor today?"

"We sure did."

"Well, don't keep us in suspense," I begged. "It's been a very long day, Ger."

I could hear him chuckling on the other end as my heart pounded, waiting for the news.

"We're going to have a boy and a girl, Mom!" Gerry yelled.

Suddenly, I lost all control. I started laughing and crying at the same time. Ed was staring at me, and then a big smile came over his face as I yelled, "It's a boy, and a girl! I can't believe it! Gerry and Laurie are having a boy and a girl! Did you hear what I said, Ed? Here, talk to your son," and I handed him the phone.

"What did you tell your mother, Gerry?" Ed teased. "She's gone cuckoo." I ignored his comments, jumping up and down a few times while they continued their conversation. Ed was all smiles while he talked with Gerry, and when he hung up he put his arms around me. "According to the ultrasound, the little girl weighs two pounds, three ounces and the little boy two pounds, four ounces." Gerry told Ed that Laurie and both babies were healthy, and for that we were most thankful. Later, before I went to bed, I thanked God for the blessing of joy that had been delivered to our family on a very special "Good Friday."

As the weeks went by, Gerry and Laurie kept us informed on their doctor visits, and everything they learned with each ultrasound. The babies were gaining weight and mom was doing well, except for feeling very tired. She had about ten weeks to go when she made the decision to leave her job and stay at home while she waited for the babies to be born. As Laurie's due date got closer, the doctor said she needed to spend more time resting in preparation for the birth. Around the end of June Gerry called to tell us that the doctor had scheduled a cae-sarean birth for July 13th. We began making our plans for the trip downstate, but a second call came at the end of the week, telling us they had decided to move the birth up a few days. According to the doctor, the babies weighed between five and six pounds each, and he thought it was time for the twins to meet their parents. We left home on Saturday, July 8th, and headed to Grand Rapids for the big event.

Laurie was supposed to check into the hospital at 7:30 Sunday morning, July 9th. As they were getting themselves ready to leave, the phone rang. It was the hospital calling to say they didn't have a room available for Laurie, and to call back at 9:30. When Gerry called back, he was told they still didn't have a room and to try again at 11:30. By then, Gerry and Laurie were beginning to feel overwhelmed. At 11:30, he again made the call and was thrilled when he was told that Laurie could check into the hospital at 12:30 P.M.

We were staying at a nearby motel, but once Gerry made us aware of the schedule, we drove to their house to await the big news. It was one of the longest afternoons I had ever been through. I spent part of the time taking pictures of each grandparent so I could show Gerry and Laurie how impatient we looked as we waited. Laurie's mom kept busy by washing every piece of clothing in the house. I must admit we had a few good laughs when one of the grandpas (I won't mention his name) started imitating Laurie's walk during the last weeks of her preg-nancy. I knew he'd never have gotten away with it had Laurie been there, but nevertheless, it was kind of funny. And, with all of us looking at each other for several hours, we needed something to divert our attention and give us something to laugh about.

It was about 6:00 that evening when Gerry finally called; Laurie's mom answered the phone. I will never forget the look on Barb's face. Laurie was an only child and suddenly Barb was a new grandmother of not one baby, but two. And, to make it even more exciting, she had a boy and a girl. I could only imagine what she was thinking as she listened to Gerry tell her that both babies were born healthy. He went on to say that Andrew John was born at 4:30 P.M., weighing six pounds, seven ounces, and Katelyn Marie at 4:31 P.M., weighing five pounds, five ounces. As Barb passed on the important details to those of us still sitting in our chairs with eyes wide open, we immediately stood up and cheered. And within minutes, all the grandparents were on their way to the hospital to take a long awaited look at two precious babies.

Ed and I were barely out of the driveway when tears of joy began to slide down my face. I couldn't believe the big event had actually taken place; Gerry and Laurie were the proud parents of two healthy babies. I looked at Ed and asked, "Is this really happening? Are we really grandparents of twins?"

"I think that's what Barb said," he answered, happily. "There's a little boy named Andrew John, and a little girl named Katelyn Marie."

"I love those names," I whispered. "I wonder if they'll be called Andy and Katie."

"We'll have to wait and see."

"I remember when Joellyn wanted to name her baby sister Bobbie Sue, so we chose Roberta Sue," I commented. But she ended up with the nickname Bertie, and Berta. I don't recall anyone ever calling her Bobbie Sue, not even Joellyn."

"That's the way it goes sometimes," Ed said, smirking. "Look at me. My birth name was Edwin, but most people call me Ed."

"My sister Fern's nickname was 'Half-a-girl' because she was so tiny. She didn't mind being called that; she usually laughed it off. Now that I think of it, my sister Pauline was called 'Puppy' by some of her friends, but I'm not sure of the connection. My sister Susan was always 'Sue' and I was 'Jo' to some.

When we arrived at the hospital, Gerry met us in the waiting room. I'd never seen him with such a glow on his face. After we gave him some hugs and congratulations, he told us that fifteen babies had been born between 7:00 A.M. and noon that day, which was the reason they had to postpone Laurie's delivery. Those mothers who were having a natural birth couldn't be put off, but with a caesarean birth, delaying it for a few hours wouldn't make much difference. What a fun picture . . . grandparents standing in the hall waiting for the nurse to give us permission to see Laurie and the babies. People from the hospital walked by smiling, and congratulating Gerry. Finally, after several minutes, we were allowed to go into Laurie's room. Once inside, you could hear an abundance of "oohs" and "aahs" as we all stared at Andrew and Katelyn cuddled next to each other in one bassinet. It wasn't long before someone asked, "Who do you think they look like?"

"It's a little hard to tell this early, but I think Andrew looks like Gerry," I offered. "What do you think, Ed?"

"I agree somewhat," Ed said, smiling, "But don't you think he looks more like me?"

"You're right," said Barb, "Andrew looks like his Grandpa Ed. And, who do you think Katelyn looks like?"

"Katelyn is definitely her mother," I insisted. "Just take a look at that face. She looks like an angel."

Because we were busy taking turns holding the babies, and talking to Laurie about her delivery, we weren't aware that we were ignoring Gerry. He must have felt very left out because he suddenly asked, "Hey, what about me? I am the father of these babies, you know!" Everyone laughed, including the nurse who had come into the room to check on Laurie's blood pressure, which had been somewhat high after the delivery. I immediately went to Gerry giving him a hug and congratulating him on the birth of his twins. Ed was right behind me with a big grin on his face. We both knew that Gerry would be the best father in the world to little Katelyn and Andrew. After about an hour of getting to know our newest grandchildren, we all left so Laurie and Gerry could have some time alone with their newborn babies.

After five days in the hospital, Katelyn and Andrew went home with their mom and dad. Gerry took a month off from work, and Barb stayed with them for two weeks to help care for the babies while Laurie recuperated. She was kept busy from morning until night feeding and bathing the twins, changing their diapers, and trying to squeeze in a nap for herself. Laurie was happy and most appreciative that her mom could be there at such an important and busy time. Having five children of my own, I remembered how difficult it was coming home from the hospital with one baby, but I could only imagine what it was like with two babies. Laurie and Gerry took over all duties after her mom left, and Gerry had two more weeks at home before he had to go back to work. Laurie's days were extremely busy. Gerry would hold the babies, help feed them, and change their diapers, the latter being the most difficult due to the limited use of his hands. We were amazed at what he was able to do and how much he wanted to participate in their care. Nothing was going to stop him from doing that.

On our trip home from Grand Rapids, the entire conversation was about the twins and how blessed we were to have been at the hospital soon after their birth. I don't know how many times I looked at Ed and said, "I still can't believe it. Gerry and Laurie are the parents of twins."

"And, we are the grandparents of twins," Ed stated with a bit of sing-song in his voice.

"Who would've ever thought this would be the result when Gerry called last November and suggested that Laurie might be pregnant?" I sighed a happy sigh, as I lay my head against the back of the seat.

"Not me," Ed answered. "It's still hard to believe."

"Maybe it's God's way of answering our prayers," I offered. "He does things in mysterious ways."

"You may be right," Ed acknowledged. "Two healthy babies; what more could we ask for?"

"Nothing." "We have been blessed with eight healthy grandchildren and, for that, I thank God every day."

"How about stopping for some lunch to celebrate the newest additions to our family?"

"I'm all for that!" I cheered. I smiled during our entire lunch, and people in the restaurant smiled back at me. They probably thought, "My, she's a friendly sort."

When we finally arrived back home, we couldn't wait to tell the rest of the family about Katelyn and Andrew. I had taken a few pictures at the hospital so I could share them with the other grandchildren, because I knew the first thing they'd ask was, "Did you take any pictures, Grandma?"

"You bet I did. Can you tell which one is Katelyn and which one is Andrew?"

"This is Katelyn," said Sara, pointing at the photo.

"That's Andrew," said Amanda.

"Why do you think that's Andrew?" I asked.

"Because he's wearing a blue outfit. Baby boys usually wear blue and baby girls wear pink," said Amanda.

"I wear blue sometimes," said Sara.

"When you were a newborn baby, you probably wore pink," I said.

"I can't wait to meet them," said Sara.

"When are they coming to visit?" Amanda asked.

"It won't be soon. Laurie and Gerry are going to be very busy with two babies to take care of. Maybe they'll come for Thanksgiving." I said, sounding hopeful.

It wasn't long before Gerry started sending us weekly pictures over the internet. He also called in the evenings when he had a free moment to tell us about their feeding schedules and sleeping habits. With two babies to take care of, their lives had changed forever and even though it was quite hectic, he wouldn't have it any other way. However, he did say, "Would you and Dad be interested in hiring us a nanny?" He laughed as we continued our conversation about the babies, but I knew he was trying to say; "It's tough!" Laurie joined a club for "Mothers of Twins and Triplets" which she found to be a blessing in so many ways. Andrew had a problem with acid reflux and some of the moms were able to suggest ways to help him and his parents through it. They also had good ideas for getting the twins on feeding and sleeping schedules which Laurie found very helpful. She continues to meet regularly with the group and looks forward to their meetings and activities.

On August 13, 2000, the grandparents returned to Grand Rapids for the christening of Katelyn and Andrew. The service was held at St. John's United Church of Christ, a beautiful, older church with stone walls and stained glass windows. Gerry and Laurie had been attending this church for a few years. Joellyn and Al, who married in August 1984, were asked to be the godparents. Just before the baptismal began, their five-year-old daughter, Sara, who was sitting with us, stood up and inched her way to the front of the church next to her mom. Sara wasn't about to miss out on anything. As the pastor continued with the christening, I could feel tears of joy filling my eyes, and I took that moment to thank God for the special blessing he had given our family. To me, it was the "*Miracle of 2000*." When it was over, we all chuckled watching the pastor holding Andrew in one arm, and Katelyn in the other, walk up the aisle so everyone could see them. I will always remember the smile on his face; it was as if he were saying, "Look at these babies. Have you ever seen anything so precious?" Afterwards, Gerry and Laurie held a reception at their house and we, the grandparents, spent most of the afternoon passing the twins back and forth to each other. What a day we had!

Ed and I left the following day, and on the way home, I kept thinking about the day Andrew and Katelyn were born. Gerry had told us a few things about the birth when we arrived at the hospital but, later on, Laurie filled us in on some of the more specific details. She mentioned that as soon as Andrew was born, someone wrapped him in a blanket and handed him to Gerry. However, when it was Katelyn's turn, she was given to one of the nurses, who put her on a warming table. Laurie's immediate thoughts were that something was wrong. But, before too long, Katelyn was also wrapped in a blanket and Gerry got to hold his little baby girl. Laurie said it was very frightening during those moments, and often thinks about it when she's holding her precious Katie. I couldn't get Laurie's thoughts off my mind, so a few days later I sat down and wrote the following story as a tribute to their arrival:

THE DAY WE MET MOM AND DAD

I remember the day we were born. Yes, I said we because there were two of us: my brother, Andrew, and me, Katelyn. Mom and Dad were up early that morning because Mom had an appointment at the hospital at 7:30 A.M. But, suddenly the phone rang and someone from the hospital was calling to tell us not to come at 7:30 because they didn't have a room for Mom. They told Dad to call back at 9:30, but when he called back they still didn't have a room for Mom. "Call back at 11:30," someone said and when Dad called back, they finally told him to bring Mom to the hospital at 12:30 P.M.

"It's about time," I said to my brother, Andrew. "We've been waiting a long time for this day."

"We sure have," said Andrew. "I was beginning to wonder if we'd ever be born."

"How long have we been in here?" asked Katelyn.

"It's more than eight months," said Andrew, "I've been counting on my fingers, and I'm almost up to number nine."

"Wow!" yelled Katelyn. "That's a very long time."

"Yes, and you've been making so much noise when I've been trying to sleep," said Andrew. "I hope you quiet down after we're born."

"I'll try," said Katelyn, "But, how else will I get Mom's and Dad's attention?"

"We'll have to wait until we're born before we make that decision," replied Andrew.

"Oh, you're so smart, Andrew," said Katelyn. "I guess we can wait until then."

"Go to sleep now," Andrew begged.

"Good night, Andrew," whispered Katelyn.

It wasn't long before Katelyn was awakened by something that sounded like a motor running. She knew that sound because she remembered hearing it whenever Dad took Mom to see the doctor. She woke up her brother and said, "Listen Andrew, it sounds like we're going for a ride. Maybe it's time for us to be born."

Andrew opened his eyes and said that he, too, remembered hearing that sound on the way to the doctor. "It always felt so bumpy," said Andrew. "Sometimes it even made me sick to my stomach."

"Nothing bothers my stomach," insisted Katelyn.

"You're lucky," Andrew said. "It's not fun when your stomach hurts."

"I wish I could do something to help you, Andrew," said Katelyn. "But, you'll have to wait until we're born. Mom and Dad will know what to do to make it better."

"Do you truly think this is it?" asked Katelyn. "Are we really going to be born today?"

"I don't know, but I have a good feeling about this ride we're taking," yelled Andrew.

"I hope you're right," said Katelyn. "I want to meet Mom and Dad."

"Be patient, Katelyn," Andrew said. "It won't be long now." Suddenly, we were getting out of the car, and I couldn't wait to see what was going to happen next.

I could hear Mom talking to someone about us. I listened carefully and a voice said, "I understand you're having twins."

"Yes," answered Mom. "I can't wait to meet our little girl and boy."

"Wow," said Katelyn, "Mom sounds real nice. I wonder what Dad will be like."

"I heard Mom telling someone that Dad once lived in the Upper Peninsula of Michigan," said Andrew. "She said the people up there talk with a funny accent."

"I remember Mom saying that, too," whispered Katelyn. "In fact, she said that people who live in the U.P. sometimes call each other a 'dandy.'

"I wonder what that word 'dandy' means," said Andrew.

"What if Dad calls one of us a dandy?" asked Katelyn.

"If he calls us that silly name, we'll ask him to tell us what it *means,"* said Andrew.

"That's a good idea," said Katelyn. "What would I ever do without you, Andrew?"

"I'll always be here for you, Katie," Andrew said.

Suddenly, a bright light was shining on our faces and when I looked over toward my brother, Andrew, he was gone. I heard a voice say it was 4:30 P.M. I began to squint and tried to open my eyes. I tried to see what was happening and then I heard that same voice say it was 4:31 P.M. It hit me! My brother, Andrew, and I were being born. We were finally going to meet Mom and Dad. I was so excited. When the nurse put me into Mom's arms, I looked up at her and she was smiling down at me. She whispered, "Hi, Katie."

I smiled back and said, "Hi, Mom, it's about time we met." I looked over and saw someone holding Andrew. I knew it must be Dad because he was acting all goo goo over my brother. What would he think of me? Then Mom gave me to Dad, and Dad gave Andrew to Mom.

"Hi, Dad," I whispered. "What do you think of this spectacular event?"

Dad smiled and then held me close to his face, kissing me on the cheek. He told me that Andrew and I were the most beautiful babies he'd ever seen. He seemed very happy.

Dad looked at Mom and said, "I think Katelyn looks like you. She definitely has your blue eyes, and I think she has her mom's cute little nose."

"Do you really think so?" asked Mom.

"Yup!" said Dad. "She's a sweetie pie just like her mom. And, who do you think Andrew looks like?"

"Well," said Mom, "He has your blue eyes for sure, and I think he has your mouth as well. He's a handsome little fellow just like his dad."

Once we were alone together in our crib, I asked, "What do you think of our parents, Andrew?"

"I think we are the luckiest babies in the world, Katie. We have a mom and dad who love us very much."

"But, Andrew," said Katie, "I just heard Dad tell Mom that we sure are a couple of dandies."

"What more could we ask for?" said Andrew.

"I don't know about you, but I'm going to ask Dad what that word means," said Katelyn.

"Good idea!" whispered Andrew, "When are you going to ask him?"

"Right now!" said Katelyn, and she started to scream loudly. Mom came running. She picked me up and then handed me to Dad. I stopped crying immediately. I looked at Dad and popped the question I'd been waiting to ask, "What's a 'dandy'?

Dad laughed and gave me a big hug. "Oh Katie," said Dad. "A 'dandy' is a word people in our area use when they describe someone who is silly, or funny, or even a fancy dresser. Do you think you'll be a fancy dresser, Katie?"

"I think it would be fun to dress up in fancy clothes," Katie said smiling.

"I'd like that," said Dad. "Now go back to sleep, Katie, and try not to wake up Andrew. Good night my little Katie bug."

"Good night, Dad," Katie whispered. Katie couldn't wait for Dad to leave so she could tell her brother what the word 'dandy' meant. But, she was going to have to tell him in the morning because Andrew was fast asleep.

I read the story to Gerry and Laurie on their next trip to the Upper Peninsula. As I came to the end, the looks on their faces told me how much they enjoyed it, but when Laurie asked me for a copy to put in their baby albums, I realized it was more meaningful than I had imagined. I still remember how Gerry smiled as he put his arm around me and said, "Thanks for doing that, Mom." Being a new dad, it had touched Gerry's heart in a very special way.

As I think about that early morning phone call several years ago telling us that Gerry had been hurt, and the unsettling emotions I tried so hard to calm, I have to pinch myself when I realize all that has happened since then. I remember wondering if Gerry would be able to continue his classes at NMU, or if he'd have to face the fact that his college days were pretty much over. What I didn't know was that graduating from college was his number one goal, and not too surprisingly, he accomplished it. His second goal was to find a job, which came about when he was hired by Butterworth Hospital. Being later promoted to head of his department was the frosting on the cake.

As I look back over the past several years of Gerry's life, I must admit that I should have seen the signs. Gerry, like his father, had exactly what he needed to attain the goals he'd set for himself. He had the strength, or *sisu*, to go forward with his life, instead of allowing his injury to hold him back. He was willing to take one day at a time to achieve his objective, and then slowly move on to the finish line. His strong faith in God, along with his goals, have helped get him to where he is today. He has made his family extremely proud and has given others the courage to challenge whatever life may hand them. And, when Andrew and Katelyn are old enough to read this book, they will learn how very special this person is, the one they call Dad, the one we call Gerry.

Gerry, Laurie, Katelyn and Andrew Hakala.

Joann Hakala with her son, Gerry.

Joann Hakala and her husband, Edwin, reside in Negaunee, Michigan and have five grown children, three sons and two daughters. The author is a graduate of Ishpeming High School, and received a Master of Arts and an Education Specialist degree in Elementary Education from Northern Michigan University. She worked for the Marquette Area Public Schools for twenty-two years, as an elementary school librarian and a third grade teacher. In 1997, she spent one more year in education teaching Children's Literature at NMU. *A Matter of Courage* is the author's first book, but she also enjoys writing stories about her grandchildren.

You may contact Joann at joooha@aol.com or write to her at:
Joann Hakala, P.O. Box 328, Negaunee, MI 49866